Praise for

The Lobster Lake Bandits: Mystery at Moosehead

The Lobster Lake Bandits is a real mystery thriller set in the north woods of rural Maine. The story will have you in suspense trying to guess what was happening in the woods surrounding the Parker family hunting camp. Solving the mystery becomes a joint effort between the game warden, the camp owner and his son, Joe, and a stranger who may have ulterior motives. The end results will keep you hooked right up until the end. It indeed is a great read.

John Ford Sr.
Author & Retired Maine Game Warden and County Sheriff

Books by John Ford:
- Suddenly, the Cider Didn't Taste So Good: Adventures of a Game Warden in Maine
- This Cider Still Tastes Funny! Further Adventures of a Game Warden in Maine
- Deer Diaries

"Refreshing and beautiful. Carbone is a natural storyteller in his novel about northern Maine. His descriptions and dialogue make the characters come alive.
I loved the whole book and recommend it highly."
- - The Book Corner
Maine's Journal Tribune

"This book is absolutely a love letter to the north woods of Maine and definitely made me want to visit."
- - The Golden State Media Concepts
Book Review Podcast

"A very compelling read. I raced through the book in a weekend because I had to find out how the book ended!"

- - George Smith
Maine's Bangor Daily News

THE
LOBSTER LAKE
BANDITS

Mystery at Moosehead

Also by

Tommy Carbone

Growing Up Greenpoint

A Kid's Life in 1970s Brooklyn

A Memoir

"This book is a lot of fun. Carbone's stories are funny and full of heart, and he brings his childhood to life in vivid detail."

-- The Golden State Media Concepts Book Review

THE

LOBSTER LAKE

BANDITS

MYSTERY AT MOOSEHEAD

A NOVEL

By

Tommy CARBONE

Burnt Jacket Publishing
Greenville, Maine

20210917AMPB
Library of Congress Control Number: 2020901769
ISBN: 978-1-7321117-3-8
Also available:
       Trade Paperback - 9781732111790
       Hardcover - 9781732111776
       eBook - 9781732111769
       Large Print - 9781732111752
          www.tommycarbone.com

For Marisa – Your love of reading is inspiring.

For Gina – Your love of animals is contagious.

For Meredith – For your love and support.

Acknowledgments

I want to thank John Ford, who is not only a retired Maine Game Warden and Maine author, he was also a source of encouragement during my writing project. I hope I did the profession justice. We are all grateful for those who serve, knowing they are there when we need them. For more on north woods adventures check out John's funny and witty books. He also draws a heck of a moose.

Thank you to my beta readers who went above and beyond with story and editing advice. Special appreciation to Jeanette, Mary Lou, Sarah, Rebecca, and Amy.

I could not have done this without the help of my wife, Meredith, who always reads the painful early drafts and encourages me to paddle on.

Finally, I want to thank all of you who read my books. Your support, emails, and reviews are so appreciated, thank you.

The Lobster Lake Bandits

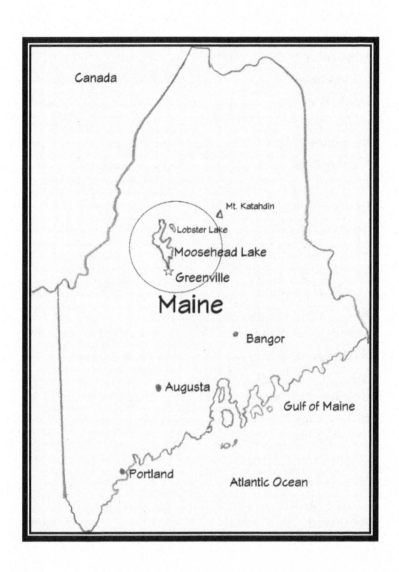

End of the Season

Another Maine camp season in the north woods had come to an end. The last of the oak, maple, and aspen autumn foliage had fallen to the ground, already turned an indistinguishable color of plain brown. A red squirrel, Joe had named Spencer after the mountain that rose to the south of the camp, ran through the crunchy leaves collecting pinecone seeds to bury for the winter. Standing on the slanted camp porch, Joe looked towards the stream and took a deep breath of the air that smelled of evergreen. He was going to miss the sound of the water bubbling over and around the rocks. Unfortunately, the crispness in the late October breeze hinted that a freeze was soon on the way, and he had to be gone before it arrived. As he pulled his coat a little tighter, he realized he had been ending camp seasons, at this same family camp, for fifty years. Of course, his earliest memories were based on family stories and a sparse number of faded black and white photos tacked on the wall behind the worn lime-green sofa.

Fall at camp was Joe's favorite season. The bugs were mostly gone, the days were warm, and the fishing was good. He always had a sad feeling when he finally had to close the camp and head home. The sadness dug a bit deeper over the past three years. Years he had been at camp alone, other than a visiting friend or passing hikers. Camp just hadn't been the same without his dad. Although, he wasn't totally alone, he had his dog R.C., who at the moment was meandering along the trees, saying his own goodbyes.

Spencer scrambled up to the porch, begging for one last handout. Joe reached in the pocket of his wool coat and pitched the last of the Planters peanuts to the ground. The squirrel took off with his cheeks full of treasure to hide away. Keeping an eye on R.C., Joe ran through his own winter preparation checklist one more time.

The birch bark canoe was stored away in the shed. Just last weekend he had smeared a mixture of spruce gum, charcoal, and a little bit of roofing tar on the boat's seams. The canoe would now be ready for the spring fishing season. The fishing gear, poles, nets, and buckets that were in the boat all summer, were cleaned and hung on hooks.

Next to the shed, the aluminum row boat was covered to keep out the pine needles and falling leaves. He followed the same steps his dad would have. First, he tied the brown tarp tightly around the boat and under the trailer. Then he added the blue top, an extra layer against the snow and spring rains. Finally, a few large rocks and odd-sized pine logs were added to hold it down against the winter winds.

The rickety wood boat dock had been pulled out of the pond and tipped up on the shore. All food items that might freeze, or be of interest to critters, were packed in boxes and stowed in the truck to take home. Joe took note of the sagging moss-covered roof on the shed. That would be a project he'd have to tackle in the spring. He couldn't think of anything else that needed to be done, except for getting around to writing down the shut-down list so he didn't have to worry about remembering it every October. He decided to confirm he had taken care of the most critical item one more time. Joe knelt on the ground next to the camp, and reached under the framing for the valves used to drain the pipes. Having a camp with running water was a camp improvement everyone enjoyed and it worked great, as long as the pipes were emptied before Maine's winter freeze.

To get water to the camp, a small gas-powered pump pulled water from Parker Pond to a holding tank set on high ground. From there, through the employment of gravity, water was delivered through copper pipes to the camp for bathing and washing dishes. The drinking water came from a well dug by Grandpa George, who carefully crafted a wall, stone by stone, which circled the inside of the deep pit.

The pipe draining was a yearly routine the Parkers had forgotten only once – the fall Joe's dad, Stan, and his Grandpa George had closed the camp in a rush. Stan wanted to get home to listen to the speech from President Kennedy. Joe would never forget the date – October 22, 1962. Grandpa George, on the other hand, was apprehensive about leaving camp. He told Stan if there were to be a missile launch from Cuba, he would rather take his chances at camp than at home. At least out here in the woods he reasoned they could hunt and fish for food.

Stan, however, wanted to get back to Bangor. First off, that's where Joe, who was working for the local paper, was at the time. Since his wife Louise, Joe's mom, had passed away several years prior, Stan felt it was important to be close to his son. And second, it was also where the rest of their relatives were. If the Russians and Castro were to start trouble, Stan wanted to be close to family. So, he won that argument with Grandpa George, and home they went.

The following spring when they returned, Stan hooked up the pump and pulled the starter rope. The gas engine choked to life. Seconds later, Grandpa and Joe came running from the camp.

"Stan, shut it. Shut the pump!" yelled Grandpa.

By the time Dad heard them over the pump's engine and realized what was happening, mini sprinklers from the cracked pipes had soaked the kitchen and bathroom. They had lost the Parker Camp Cold War. Instead of fishing, the three of them spent the next five days repairing pipes that had burst during the winter freeze. Ever since then, Stan, and now Joe, had been extra careful about draining the water.

Once Joe was sure all the pipes were empty, he looked over the firewood he had stacked on the porch. Stacking the wood was another of the required fall camp routines he had repeated since he was old enough to carry a log. Having a good supply of wood was necessary for the winter trip to the cabin, even if he hadn't continued the annual tradition for ice fishing and back country hiking the past few years. He hadn't had the desire to make the trip without Dad. But he might come back this winter, so he stacked the wood. Better to learn from Spencer the squirrel and be prepared.

Joe whistled. He whistled again. Then he noticed that R.C. was already on the front seat of the pickup truck.

"Good boy. Already said your goodbyes? All right then. Let's head home." Driving down the private unmarked lane, he watched in the rear-view mirror as the camp faded away.

He'd be driving on the bumpy, rutted, dirt logging road for more than an hour before reaching pavement. While sightings of deer or fox were frequent along the roadside, he would likely not see another car or person the entire time. The summer residents and campers had been gone for more than a month. The loggers had Sunday off, an area tradition that Joe was glad had not ended, making Sunday the safest day to travel on these roads. It would be another month or so before hunters might turn up, most not venturing as far as his family's camp. Even if they did, the odds of taking the correct turns on barely noticeable roads, which looked more like deer trails, meant that unknown visitors to their cabin location were rare. When someone unknown did turn up in their dooryard, it usually meant they were lost and needed help.

Joe absentmindedly turned on the truck's radio. It was all static. He laughed to himself. He knew better than to think there would be a signal during this part of the drive. There would be no radio until he reached the small town of Greenville, and after that it would be spotty as he drove over the mountains. He looked at his watch. He was hoping to make the two-and-a-half-hour drive home in time to catch game four of the playoffs between Oakland and Boston. As he drove with just the hum of the engine, he thought about his beloved Red Sox team.

If the Sox didn't pull out a win tonight, it would be the end of their hopes for yet another season. They hadn't won a World Series since winning game six on September 11, 1918. That was the year his dad was born, and Babe Ruth pitched, hit, and played outfield for the Red Sox. That was also the year the baseball season was shortened by several weeks due to World

War I and pressure from the war department. Without the short season, fans always wondered if the Sox would have prevailed even that year.

The yellowing newspaper clipping, exclaiming that historic series win, still hung in a birch twig picture frame on the camp's living room wall, a relic his grandfather had saved. The family, and just about every guest to the cabin, talked about the prospects of a Sox win every year since. Entire evenings around the campfire were often filled with Red Sox stories and second-guessing manager decisions.

Until recently, there were only two ways to keep up with the two most important pieces of information – baseball news and the weather forecast – while staying at camp. The first was on trips to town for church, supplies, and the Sunday paper. Grandpa had stored Red Sox articles from the sports section in those papers away in the camp cabinet. From time to time, Joe would read the old clippings, fantasizing about what it would have been like to be at Fenway back in the 1930s and 40s.

The second way Grandpa kept up with the Red Sox was word of mouth. Stan would say, "If your grandpa would happen upon people out fishing, after saying 'Hello,' his first question was, 'How are the Red Sox doing?' I think he sometimes would go out hiking looking for someone who might know the teams' standings."

It was different now. Joe had listened to most of the baseball season on the radio, something his grandfather never could have imagined. Back then, no signal would have reached their part of the woods, and it wouldn't have mattered if it did, Grandpa had no way to power a radio. Power at camp didn't happen until 1976, the year Stan purchased a small gas generator that provided enough electricity for the new water pump, a few lights, and what Joe thought he'd never see at camp – a radio. The AM radio was housed in a heavy dark walnut wooden case. It had a built-in speaker and heavy-duty dials to adjust the volume and the tuning needle. That summer, he helped his dad rig up a rooftop antenna. If the antenna had been sitting on the ground, it would have been taller than the camp. They were able to get two or three stations, depending on the weather and time of the day, one of which was from Canada and all in French, which neither of them could understand. The signal was always spotty and had a way of giving up to static at the worst times. That old radio was appreciated, and at the same time scorned, two baseball seasons ago during the playoffs. With miles of dirt road in front of him, Joe thought back on that memory.

Joe had stayed at camp that fall to enjoy the fishing. While listening to the playoff games, he worked on his sketches for his job at the Bangor News. For game number six, it was a frosty October night. Through the camp's thin walls, he heard the shrill sounds of a howling pack of coyotes from in the direction of Rum Ridge. The howls even had R.C., who was half asleep on the rug next to the crackling stove, on alert. Joe saw R.C. raise one ear to listen before he let out a low rumble growl, and then went back to snoring.

The sports announcer said with excitement, "Boston is now three outs away from winning their first World Series in seventy years."

Joe warmed a mug of milk on the woodstove and sat on the edge of his seat, the drink doing little to calm his nerves. He yelled at the radio, "Come on boys. Get 'em out!"

R.C. let out a groan and rolled over.

No longer able to sit still in his re-stuffed lumpy chair, Joe stood and paced. From the front wall to the back wall, the cabin was only twenty feet long. Eight paces each way with his long stride.

The woodstove flared, the thin-paned windows rattled, the radio crackled, and then went silent. Joe strode over and fiddled with the antenna wire. He banged on the top of the case. Nothing. It was dead. He couldn't believe his bad luck. Of all times for this to happen. Disappointed, Joe hit the generator off switch and went to bed.

Not able to sleep, he went to the shelf in the living room and brought back a camp journal he hadn't read in years. He opened to the pages he wrote when he was a teenager. It was the year of strange events in the woods near the cabin. He fell asleep reading his story about the beautiful nameless girl with the wavy hair, and the mysterious man in the odd green cap.

Sunday morning, on his walk back from the outhouse he tripped on a wire. Looking up he saw the rusty antenna tower tilting sideways. After his coffee, he climbed up on the roof and spliced the wire back together.

Back inside he turned the dial, past the morning devotions, and past the French station from Canada, until he found the news.

> *"And in baseball last night, the Red Sox lost to the Mets on an error by Bill Buckner in the bottom of the tenth. The World Series is now tied at three games apiece."*

To Joe's, and all of Boston's continued disappointment, the Mets won the '86 World Series in the seventh game, and the Curse of the Bambino continued to vex the Red Sox.

This year, he was taking no chances with the radio. He had purposely finished the camp's winter preparations early and was headed home to not miss any of the playoff games. With no radio signal while traveling on the washboard camp roads, the only sounds were the roughness of the old truck's engine along with the squeaks and rattles of the doors and shocks.

Reaching Abbot, Joe stopped at the bakery. Bobby, the local baker, was behind the counter.

"Afternoon, Uncle Joe," Bobby said.

Joe reached over and shook Bobby's hand.

"How are you, Bobby."

"I'm doing okay, it's been a lot less busy around here the past couple of weeks."

While Bobby wasn't really Joe's nephew, he took his role model responsibility seriously. A Parker family friend, the late Henry Ford, a local game warden, was Bobby's uncle. Over the years Joe had made it a point of being involved in Bobby's life, just as Henry had been for Joe.

Before even being asked, Bobby handed Joe a styrofoam cup of black coffee. "I read the write-up in the Telegram. That reporter wrote a great article about the Fly-In. I was a bit of a celebrity around here since she mentioned your name. What was her name again?"

"Sarah – Sarah Molloy."

"I saved a copy of the paper, it's somewhere under here." With his head rummaging around under the counter, Bobby continued, "Is it true you saved Sarah's life when you were kids, Uncle Joe?" He popped up with a copy of the paper.

"I wouldn't go that far. She was a bit turned around in the woods and I helped her out. In fact, it was your Uncle Henry that drove her back to town that day in his cruiser." Joe looked down at the article. He had already read it a hundred times. He was so proud of the story he had hung a copy on the camp wall, right next to the Red Sox 1918 framed article.

"No kidding? Mom never told me that story about Uncle Henry."

"Your Uncle helped people every week of the year. I'm sure your mom couldn't have kept track of all her brother's game warden activity."

"Are you kidding? The old store log included not only the daily sales, but every bit of gossip she came across."

Joe laughed. "That sounds about right for Bonnie."

"I liked your sketches included with the article. That was cool to see. The story said you and Sarah were going to be working together writing about the Moosehead area. Is that true?"

"Could be a possibility. We'll see. Right now, I'm just planning on getting home to catch the game this afternoon," Joe replied, although he was really hoping to see more of Sarah.

Sunday Telegram	September 18, 1988

Moosehead Lake's 15th Annual Seaplane Fly-In
By Sarah Molloy

The last time I visited the Moosehead Lake area I was only sixteen, and I became lost in the woods. If it wasn't for Joe Parker finding me on the trail, I might not be here to write this story. Thirty-two years later, I would have never guessed that it would again be Joe who would guide me around this beautiful area and make my first Fly-In experience something to remember. (*For the full story and illustrations see page A5*).

Illustrations by Joe Parker, Lobster Lake, Maine

"I'll be closing the store early for the same reason," said Bobby, who was wearing his Red Sox shirt and cap. He already had the radio on the shelf tuned to the pre-game show.

"What else can I get you for the road?"

"I'll have one of your skidder donuts, please." A skidder wasn't the actual size of a logging skidder tire, but it was big.

Bobby handed Joe a brown paper bag. "Will you be coming back up for ice fishing season?"

"Haven't thought that far ahead, Bobby. I'll let you know." He paid Bobby and tipped his cap on the way out the door.

Joe pulled out of the parking lot, skidder donut crumbling down his jacket as he took a bite. He flipped on the radio and sang along with the Nitty Gritty Dirt Band, "Fishin' in the dark, … mmm mmm mmm."

The song had him thinking about this past September all over again. He hummed until the music faded out, and then tuned the radio to the pre-game show. As he drove, he didn't hear a word of what the sportscaster said. His mind was filled with thoughts of Sarah.

Seeing her also stirred up the memories of what happened that fall at camp with the bandits, and the men that stalked the woods. He wondered why Sarah and his paths had crossed again, after so many years, and if there was a connection to the mystery that had gone unsolved for so long.

Sarah Molloy

Barone, a cigar hanging from the corner of his mouth, hollered from the open doorway of his corner office. "I want all writers in the conference room in five minutes!"

The writers had become so accustomed to the editor's loud booming voice, they continued typing as if someone had asked if anyone wanted a two-day-old burnt street pretzel. Rich Barone was as terse as New York newsmen come. He had taken the editor job six months ago to revitalize "From Here to There," a struggling travel magazine. Being the editor of a glossy monthly was never something he longed to do, rather, he was forced into it. Since his previous employer, the Daily Record, had suggested he find a new place of employment, Barone ended up taking this job because he was desperate. He'd spent most of his career as a street reporter, and this position was a terrible fit. He lived for covering the rough stories happening in the five boroughs, not editing lame pieces about trendy restaurants, the best beaches for children, and certainly not stories about which bed and breakfast served the best pancakes.

The magazine's owner, a Miami socialite with no interest in the day-to-day management, wanted a temporary editor to turn around the near bankrupt magazine. Barone needed the money to pay alimony to his ex-wives, who both refused to work a day in their entire lives. He figured he'd stay in the role a few months at most, until something better came along. That never happened. He stayed even after being offered the weekend editor job at the New York Pulse, because his ego thrived on being in charge. He found the writers at the magazine to be a much more moldable group than New York City beat reporters, besides the normal daytime hours weren't bad either. The owner kept him on, even with complaints, because he had a certain knack for getting writers to meet their deadlines.

Slowly and reluctantly the writers filed into the two-window conference room on the 5th floor at Broadway and Fulton. The room was close enough to the street for the traffic noise to be distracting, and not high enough to enjoy any of the skyline. The hanging flickering fluorescent light fixture provided an irritating constant buzzing between the honks and sirens down below.

Sarah arrived last. She sat down in an armless, coffee-stained, fabric chair; the one with the wheels frozen in the locked position. It was the only chair left empty, and it was right up front where Barone, "It ends in an E, and it sounds like it," would scream and blow his cigar smoke. The writers all had heard the story of the reporter, now working in a coffee shop, who once failed to pronounce the E. Nobody ever made a comment again, even if the E was supposed to sound like "a."

Barone stormed into the conference room, slamming the door shut with such force the blinds hanging on the inside of the frame rattled and banged for what seemed to be minutes.

He blew out a cloud of white smoke. "This magazine's owner wants a story from Maine. Who has one we can throw in the October issue?"

As it was Friday September 2, the October issue was already in final copy edit. Getting a story together at this late date was something none of the writers wanted to be on the hook for, especially with Barone barking down their neck. They all knew he had little experience fostering stories out of travel writers. He was used to firing rapid questions at beat reporters, and approached travel writing in the same manner as a crime scene investigation.

"Who shot who?" "Were there witnesses?"

"Who's getting a statement from Mayor Koch?"

"What type of story are you looking for, Rich?" asked Gene, whose last piece about four quaint bed and breakfast getaways in New England coastal towns, Barone critiqued as a 'sleeping pill.' Gene had never made it north of Portsmouth, New Hampshire, figuring Maine was more of the same.

Barone ignored him and continued, "The New York Times ran a piece in the Sunday Magazine on some silly sign listing the distances to the Maine towns of Paris, Norway, Peru, Mexico, China, Poland and on and on," Barone said with disdain, holding up the article. "The owner thinks it's charming that Maine has so many towns named after far-away places. Now, from her lounge chair in Miami, she wants us to do a piece on traveling to small towns in Maine."

"When does it need to be done?" asked Lori, who was obviously seven or more months pregnant.

Barone read right through her feigned interest. He knew her well enough to know her question was to ensure he didn't expect her to travel. "Are you not listening, Lori? I already said the October issue."

Lori shrunk in her seat, not wanting to get into the fact that the question of when the piece needed to be done, was different than in what issue it was going to be published. She simply wanted to exit the now smoky, cigar smelling, conference room as quickly as possible.

Barone, continued on, "I need a teaser piece out in the October issue, with monthly installments of the story through spring. That means your first piece needs to be in my hands by September sixteenth. That gives you more than enough time. We've already set the issue, but I'm saving six columns for this story."

He dragged on his cigar and exhaled. "We're losing time here people. Has anyone ever been to Maine?"

Everyone shook their head and mumbled something at the same time.

"Not me,"

"My mom went once."

"Is that part of New England? I've been to Massachusetts. That doesn't count, does it?"

"Never really had a need to go all the way to Maine."

Everyone made some type of excuse, except Sarah, who was particularly quiet. She had tuned out once Barone mentioned the deadline. She knew a couple of weeks was not much time considering research would be needed, and then she'd need days for writing. Barone had already given her an assignment for the next issue, so she figured she was in the clear. She stretched her long legs out under the table, put her head back, and stared at the peeling ceiling. She drifted off, wondering if her resume for the position at the Times Weekend Magazine was getting any consideration.

"What about you, Molloy? Ever been to Maine?"

Sarah raised her head to see Barone looking down at her, his large belly a bit too close to her chair. She tried to move back. The chair wouldn't budge.

"Not for a long time, Rich. I went to Maine with my family when I was in high school."

"Are you holding back on us, Molloy? Where'd you go in Maine?" he pressed, moving closer.

How she hated that he called her by her last name, as if he wasn't acknowledging her personally. But then again, what did he know about being personable.

"I don't remember. It was thirty years ago, or so. I'd have to ask my mom. It was a small town. We hiked and camped."

"That's perfect."

"Rich, you know I'm already finishing a piece for the October issue. How can I go on assignment now?"

"Molloy, are you kidding? You already have a good feel for what it's like up there. You got two weeks. Make it worth the expense report."

Sarah thought, "Go to Maine now? Labor Day weekend?" She had tickets to Phantom for Saturday night, although she still hadn't figured out who might want to go with her.

Barone turned, his hand on the conference room door, and said, "And, Molloy, it's a trip for one. We're not paying for tagalongs." With that, he yanked the door shut making the blinds swing back and slam into the wall. The others stood to leave, relieved they were not picked for the assignment.

Gene hung back and asked, "Sarah, what are you going to write about?"

"I don't know. I'll have to think about it. You know I prefer city stories." She coughed from the lingering cigar smoke. Waving the smell from in front of her face, she wondered if she could research a Maine story from the library. She had nothing but bad memories of Maine and what was a traumatizing time in her teenage life, why go back.

Feeling a bit guilty for not taking an interest in the assignment, which would typically fall to him, Gene tried to be helpful. "I hope you understand why I can't take this on. Cheryl and I just returned from the bed and breakfast trip, and the kids are back in school, and my mother-in-law is not feeling well."

"It's fine. I'll figure something out."

"Do you want me to check with my contacts for recommended B&B's to stay at?"

"Thanks, Gene, but really, I'll be fine. I'll call the travel agent."

At her desk, which was simply a long table she shared with six other writers, Sarah changed from her flats into sneakers, grabbed her bag, and headed out the door. She wasn't going to spend another minute in the office if she was officially on assignment.

Outside on the street, she had no specific plan, so she rode the subway to 51st Street and walked over to Scribners, her favorite bookstore. She picked two travel books on New

England and on an impulse a hardcover of *The Maine Woods* by Thoreau, which was strategically displayed on a round oak table in the travel section. If she wasn't in such a lousy mood, browsing the shelves could have occupied her for the rest of the day. As a writer, she loved to read and would spend rainy days and most Sundays in bookstores scattered throughout the city.

Not wanting to go underground again, Sarah walked back to her studio apartment in the East Village. With every step, she stewed about being sent on a trip. She had to finish the final edits on her October piece and she'd already thrown herself into her next article for the November issue – a piece on artists who wrote poetry for their paintings. Now, she had to leave the city and go to of all places – Maine. She loved the city, especially in September. The temperatures were cooler, there seemed to be fewer people, and the subway smells were not as offensive. Even though the city was experiencing the worst crimewave ever, Sarah wanted to be part of it all. It was the only life she had known since college and she didn't think there was anything more she needed to look for.

When she reached the door to her building, she felt uneasy. A group of men, on the stoop across the street, dressed in black leather pants and jackets, stood staring at her. She hurried with her key and locked the hall door behind her. Slowly, she climbed the four flights to her flat, a 1900s garment factory loft converted into two-room apartments, divided by sheetrock walls that were way too thin for anywhere other than a school for mimes. Closing the door, she leaned back against it, shut her eyes, and sighed. When she opened her eyes again, her tiny studio was still the same size. No window view to a yard with flowers. No pool. No black lab running to greet her.

She kicked off her sneakers, hung up her blue-pleated skirt, put on jeans, and flopped into a sagging arm chair that she had rescued, like a lost dog, from the sidewalk on Bleecker Street.

Opening the travel books, she felt stupid for not having flipped through them back at Scribners. Evidently the editors did not consider Maine part of New England. There were chapters on Vermont, New Hampshire, Massachusetts, Rhode Island, and Connecticut with only one single listing in the back of the book for a hotel in Kittery. Sarah thought that traveling ten minutes into Maine probably wasn't going to make for much of a story.

She picked up the phone and dialed.

"Hello?"

Sarah was glad to hear the familiar voice. "Hi, Mom, how are you?"

"Hello, Sarah. I'm fine. Are you home from work already?"

"Yes. I'm researching a travel assignment."

"Are you going on a trip?"

"Maybe. I could use your help."

"Sure. What can I do?"

"Do you remember the trip we took to Maine when I was in high school?"

"Of course. How could I forget that? You gave us quite a scare. What about it?"

"Where did that happen exactly?"

"That was the year your dad wanted to give us a wilderness experience. I remember the trip well. We endured a seven-hour car ride from Boston to get to cabins on Moosehead Lake, near Greenville. Mind you, the interstates were not what they are now, and we had no air conditioning or radio in that old car. It was a long trip back then."

"Did you like it there?"

"Actually, yes. It took a few years to get over what happened, but your dad and I went back for a couple of our anniversary celebrations. He was somewhat obsessed with…" Her voice trailed off. She didn't see any sense in bringing up Harry's work with Sarah.

"Obsessed with what, Mom?"

"Oh, nothing. He enjoyed hiking in the woods. He often went out by himself for hours at a time. He loved bird watching. Anyway, we found it very peaceful. Is that where you're going?"

"I'm not sure yet. Someplace in Maine though."

"When are you leaving?"

"Probably Tuesday or maybe Wednesday. I have to finish some writing this weekend and I have tickets to see Phantom of the Opera tomorrow night."

"That sounds wonderful. How did you ever get tickets?"

"I wrote a piece on the Majestic Theatre, and they loved it so much, they sent me two tickets."

"That's great. Are you going with that stock broker you've been seeing for the past few months?"

"No. He's going to the Yankee game – again. And to be honest, Mom, it's not working out."

Sarah hoped her mom wasn't going to start asking her about her long-term relationship plans. It's not that she didn't want to settle down and get married and have a house in Mt. Kisco. She just hadn't found Mr. close-to-right yet. All the men she knew were busy making a career for themselves and climbing the ladder. But then again, she'd been doing the same, writing for publication after publication and freelancing on the side. Who had time for a serious relationship? Not her. Certainly not since her most recent multi-year relationship investment had ended when he transferred to head the Singapore division of his financial services company.

There was a long pause before her mom said, "I see. Okay, but let me know where you end up going in Maine, so I know where you'll be and how to reach you."

"Yes, I will."

"All right, dear. I love you."

"Bye, Mom. I love you too."

Sarah hung up and flipped through the travel books one more time. It was hopeless. She found a number for the Maine tourism office and had a pleasant conversation with a lady in Augusta about events happening in Maine. The woman told her that the Annual Seaplane Fly-In was scheduled for the following weekend and read from the visitor brochure, "Pilots from as far south as Gainesville, Florida and sometimes as far north as Alaska will compete and show off their flying machines."

To Sarah, the air-show sounded as good as any Maine event to cover, probably exactly what the magazine's owner was looking for.

"Where is the plane show?"

"Greenville. It's a nice lake and mountain town. I was there once myself."

"Greenville? Really. Thank you very much. Have a nice day." Sarah hung up the phone and rubbed the back of her neck.

The coincidence of an event in the same town she had been to as a teenager clinched her choice of location. Picking up the phone again, Sarah dialed the number for the magazine's travel agent to inquire about booking a flight.

"Greenville, Maine, Miss? Are you sure?"

"Yes, they are having an air show this weekend, so there must be an airport, right?" she asked.

"No, Miss. There are no commercial flights from the airports in the tri-state area to Greenville, Maine. In fact, I am looking in my book and I don't see any flights that land in Greenville, Maine at all. The closest airport near that area is Bangor. Do you want to book a flight there?"

Sarah began to wonder if the information about an air show was incorrect. As she was not a huge fan of flying, she figured driving might be a better option anyway. If the air show was a dud, she could at least drive around Maine looking for a story to satisfy Barone.

"No. Let's skip the flight. Please book me a car and a hotel that has room service," requested Sarah. "And a bar," she squeezed in quickly before hanging up.

Knowing it was going to be a long drive to the middle of the Maine woods, she made plans to spend a night with her mom who still lived outside of Boston. Sarah also wanted to see what more her mom could tell her about that childhood Maine vacation.

* * *

Saturday morning a courier delivered a small envelope to Sarah's flat. She glanced at the printout and read it out loud to herself, "The Loon Mountain Resort, that sounds nice." Before heading out, she called her friend Angie, who she had no problem convincing to see Phantom of the Opera with her later that night.

Sarah spent the next few days in the quiet of the New York Public Library finishing off her October article and her entire piece for November. When she needed a break from writing, she went for a run on Roosevelt Island, walked 5th Avenue, and searched out cafés to have lunch.

It took forty-eight hours before she stopped hearing the unsynchronized key strokes of twenty writers pounding on their IBM Selectrics and to forget the smell of Barone's cigar. With the time she had to think, going to Maine didn't seem so bad after all. It was starting to feel like a mini-vacation and she thought to herself, "Maybe the long drive away from the city will be good."

Tuesday morning, she grabbed a cab to the car rental agency at JFK airport. In the garage, Sarah slipped the key into the lock of a nondescript gray-colored compact car. She sighed as the woman in the next row stepped into a candy apple red Ford Mustang.

Driving away from the city, the midweek traffic was light, and after listening to her Paul McCartney mix tape twice, she spent the remainder of the drive searching for radio stations that would come in clearly. That night she had dinner with her mom and older sister, but was disappointed that neither of them could really tell her more than she had already remembered herself about their "camping" vacation from decades ago. The best source of information came from her teenage diaries, which were still in the nightstand in her old room. She searched the pages until she found her entry for her scare in the Maine woods. After reading it twice, she slipped the diary into her bag.

The following day Sarah followed I-95 north, and six hours later arrived at a town named Abbot, the road sign proclaimed the settlement, "Maine's First Town." She pulled into the parking lot of a small bakery, hoping for a hot coffee, and maybe even finding her first Maine story inside.

A man with a beard down to his chest, wearing a John Deere hat and a camouflage jacket, held the door for Sarah on his way out.

"Evening," he said, with a nod.

"Hello, thank you."

She stepped into the shop and was pleasantly surprised to see a long glass case full of pastries and donuts.

A young man was behind the register and Sarah felt him watching her as she looked over the choices.

"Hi there. Can I help you?"

"I'll have one of these apple fritters, a brownie bar, and a cappuccino, to go please."

"A cup of what?" asked the teenager.

"A cappuccino. A coffee with steamed milk."

"We have regular coffee with cold milk or half and half." He added in a whisper, "I have to warn you though, that pots been sitting on the burner since three this afternoon. Not much call for coffee around here on a Wednesday evening, or any evening for that matter. We're just about to close." He pointed to the clock on the wall. It was almost seven.

"Oh. I see. Just the pastries then."

The kid watched as Sarah pulled away and then went into the kitchen out back. "Did you hear what that lady ordered for coffee, boss? Something called a 'cup o'chino.' Sounds fancy, eh?"

"Obviously a city person, Stevie. Get used to it. They're starting to outnumber the moose around here," said Bobby.

* * *

It was dark by the time Sarah arrived in the tiny town of Greenville. She was worn out from the drive and was looking forward to getting a drink and a nice shrimp Caesar salad at the hotel bar. She pulled into the single-story motel parking lot and sighed. The bulbs on the sign were half burned out. Instead of Loon Mountain Resort, it flashed, 'Loon Mo ta   Res t.' Looking at the green and white one story flat roofed building, with two white plastic chairs on the cement patio in front of each room, Sarah sighed again. It wasn't looking promising that there was going to be a restaurant, or bar inside. As she sat in the car, staring at the not so much of a resort, she was now having second thoughts about her plan. Maybe she should have asked Gene for a recommendation.

Sarah turned off the engine, grabbed her bag, and walked to the end of the building. The door had a hand-painted black and white sign stating, "OFFICE" nailed to it. Before going in, she thought about trying to find a different hotel, but she was sleepy and wanted to rest.

She opened the creaky screen door and walked inside to a dimly lit room, the size of an elevator. A Dutch door, the top half opened, led to a side room where a man, wearing a baseball cap, was watching TV.

Softly, she said, "Hello?" The man didn't budge.

She tapped the little bell that was on the desk. The man didn't move. She tapped it again. Not taking his eyes off the TV, he raised a finger indicating he'd be with her in a moment. Waiting, Sarah thumbed through a stack of three-year-old visitor brochures on the counter.

"Evening, Miss. Sorry for the wait. I wanted to watch the end of that show, Never Solved Mysteries. You ever watch it?"

"No, sorry. My name is Sarah Molloy, I have a reservation." She handed him the fax with the confirmation number.

"I was wondering when you might get in. We normally close the office by six. I'll show you down to your room."

They walked the uneven concrete sidewalk along the front of the building. All the rooms were dark. There wasn't another car in the parking lot.

"You wouldn't by chance have room service, would you?"

The man laughed. "No, Miss. The only room service we have is me showing you to your room."

"Is there a restaurant nearby?"

"Sure, we have a few of them. The Lock, Stock, and Barrel is our Maine-famous diner. The Moose Café is another. The Captain's Galley has a view of the cove. Won't do you any good tonight though, they'll all be closed up shortly, if not already."

Sarah thought, "Welcome back to Maine."

The manager walked Sarah to the last room at the end of the building, handed her the room key with a "Here you are," and then he hustled back to his TV.

Hungry, Sarah reached for the bag with her apple fritter and opened a bottle of Poland Spring water that was on a wobbly round table. A placard read, "Maine's Best Water $2."

She changed into her flannel pajamas and crashed down on the bed, exhausted from the driving. It was too quiet. She couldn't relax. There were no traffic sounds, no sirens, no trash trucks, and no yelling from the rooms down the hall. This was so unlike her apartment. She pulled the copy of *The Maine Woods* from her knapsack. She read until she fell asleep with the book on her chest.

Joe Parker

Lobster Lake – Thursday September 8, 1988

Joe rowed back to shore after a peaceful morning on Lobster Lake. He thought about how he loved fishing in September. The cool nights drop the water temperature and the fish actively feed before the winter. This morning, he had caught two nice salmon and a lake trout, which he released, not because he didn't want to eat them, but he had someplace to be. As Joe pulled the boat up on the grass, he took another look at the ripple-less lake. Gazing out over the water, not another person in sight, he thought it was about as perfect as Maine could get. He hated to leave on such a calm water day, but he was due in town. He needed to meet with the Seaplane Fly-In planning committee. This year he was a volunteer to check in pilots for their flying events.

On his way to the meeting, he stopped at the Lock, Stock, and Barrel diner for lunch. He sat at the counter eating his burger and talking to Buster about the Red Sox, Oil Can Boyd, and what the country would be like once Reagan left office. Two other regulars, Buddy and Don, were seated at the counter and joined in the conversation.

All four of them stopped talking when a lady, they had never seen before, entered and stood by the door. If she was a local, she would have sat down in any open booth, but she just stood there, giving away she was definitely – from away. Joe noticed her baby blue cotton dress and the pink scarf tied around her neck. "She's a bit over dressed," he thought.

Buddy, on the other hand, in his normal volume voice, stated, "Who's Miss Fancy?"

Karen looked up from behind the counter, "Seat yourself, Miss. Anywhere you like. Menus are on the table. I'll be right over."

The men went back to their conversation.

As all the booths were empty, Sarah sat in one closest to the counter and looked over the menu. Its cover had a large photo of a humongous plate of food. The caption read, "Hunter's Breakfast All Day, All Year. Four eggs (your way), four pieces of bacon, four pieces of toast, four hash browns, fruit cocktail. Bottomless coffee. $5.95."

Karen walked over holding a pot of coffee in each hand. "Good afternoon, dear. My name is Karen. Would you like regular or decaf?"

Sarah figured it was not going to go over well to ask for a cappuccino. "Regular please. Would you have half and half?"

"Yes, I'll bring it right over. Is this your first time to our town?"

"Yes, well, no. I mean I was here once, a long time ago."

"Welcome back then. I'm sure you'll find everyone will make you feel like a local before you know it." Karen said this loud enough so the men at the counter heard her.

"Do you know what you'd like to order?"

"Yes. I'll have the Caesar Salad with chicken, please."

"Sure. Coming right up."

When Karen delivered the salad, dressing on the side, with a glass of lemon water, Sarah asked, "Karen, would you by chance know anyone with the last name Parker? They had a camp, north of here."

"You must mean the Parkers on Lobster Lake. How do you know the Parkers?"

"I met one of them many years ago."

"Surely the best person to ask about the Parkers, would be a Parker." Karen turned slightly and said, "Hey, Joe, this pretty lady over here is asking about your family."

Looking over, Joe stopped arguing with Buddy about how the Sox shouldn't have fired McNamara. He rose slowly from his stool and walked over to the booth. The guys at the counter spun around to see what was going on.

Sarah struggled to see the boy she once met, in the man that was approaching her. He looked like she imagined he might, at least the way he was dressed for someone that lived in the woods of Maine. His blue denim shirt, faded jeans, and work boots made him look rugged, but friendly. His graying hair was cropped close to his scalp and by the look of the stubble on his face, he must have skipped shaving this morning. Seeing the scar on Joe's chin, Sarah knew immediately it was the same person she had met so many years ago.

Joe, was drawn to the woman's green eyes. He felt self-conscious about his chin when he realized she was staring at the deep scar. But those eyes, he could have sworn he had seen her before.

"Hi, I'm Joe Parker," he said tentatively, "What can I do for you, Miss?"

"My name is Sarah Molloy, I'm sure you don't remember me, but you saved my life once," she blurted out, her voice a little shaky. Since she hadn't figured on meeting Joe right at that moment, she hadn't had time to think of anything else to say. She stood, put her right hand out, and craned her neck to meet Joe's confused stare.

Joe looked down at her tiny fingers, as if he was not sure what to do. Plus, he was taken by surprise by what the woman had said. He could not recall ever saving anyone's life. He quickly wiped the fry grease from his fingers on his pants, and shook Sarah's hand. He tried to place her face from sometime in his past, but found himself at a loss for words watching her eyes that sparkled like emeralds.

At the mention of their friend being a lifesaver, Buster, Buddy, and Don gathered around waiting to hear the story. Karen sat down in the booth to not miss a word, ignoring the pleas for coffee from the regulars who were arriving for lunch.

Seeing everyone was waiting to hear more, Sarah sat back down. "Many years ago, I was lost near your cabin. Do you remember meeting a teenage girl in the woods?"

With an open mouth, Joe unconsciously slid in the booth next to Karen, directly across from Sarah. Of course, he remembered THAT. For years he could not get the girl he met in the meadow out of his mind. Every time he walked that trail, he could see her face and hear her voice. Sometimes reading the old camp journals he would get to wondering about her. In all that time, he still never thought about the incident as saving her life. Now, all these years later, he could see the young girl in the woman that sat across from him.

After giving those hovering around the condensed version of the story, Joe not so subtly chased them away. "Karen, don't you have customers to take care of? Buster, don't you need to get back to the lumber yard?"

Don and Buddy didn't move.

Joe glared at them. "Don't you two need to go setup for the planning committee meeting?" The guys finally took the hint and went back to sit at the counter where they tried to listen to the conversation.

Once everyone gave them some space, Sarah and Joe talked about her ordeal in the woods and what she had done since then. On the topic of her career, Joe nodded when she told him she was a writer for a magazine in New York City.

"So, you got your wish."

"Did I tell you I wanted to be a writer? And you remembered that?"

"Not only that, but how you wanted to live in a real city, like New York. So, what brings you back to Greenville? This is a long way from Manhattan."

Sarah explained that the magazine wanted to run a series of stories featuring Maine, and she was here to write about the air show festivities.

"Well, Ms. Molloy, we don't refer to this as an air show, but I'm headed up to the airport to check on a few things in prep for the Fly-In. You're welcome to come along."

"So, there's an actual airport here?" Sarah said, surprised.

"Sure, not everyone lands on the lake you know."

Sarah gave Joe a questioning look. "Joe, it's Miss, and besides, please call me Sarah."

"Okay, Miss Sarah, let's go look at some planes then," said Joe, trying to be funny, but also happy to learn that bit of news.

Getting the sense that Joe was a character, she shook her head slightly and raised her eyebrows. "What did you mean when you said, land on the lake?"

"You'll see." He looked over his shoulder, to give a salute goodbye, and saw the guys staring after him, their mouths hanging open.

Outside R.C. jumped from the truck to greet the new arrival. Wanting to have a black lab, since forever, Sarah hugged the dog who was drooling on her new white canvas boat shoes. To draw R.C. away, Joe pulled the saved piece of breakfast bacon from his shirt pocket and told the dog to get back in the truck if he wanted the treat.

Driving up to the airport, Joe talked about the Fly-In, planes, R.C., the town, and a lot of other topics, Sarah only half followed. Her mind was instead wandering about meeting Joe. He was certainly different from the men she was friends with and dated in the city. They wore pressed shirts, ties, and polished Florsheims. Joe was dressed in worn jeans with pieces of stray bacon in his pocket. He seemed nice, with a dry sense of humor, but she quickly realized she was riding down a dirt road, into the backwoods, with someone she didn't know. She hadn't even called to let her mom know she had arrived, and where she was staying. She told herself to relax, this wasn't the South Bronx.

Up at the landing strip, Joe gave her a tour of the small airfield and a peek in a few of the planes. In the unmanned traffic control building, he went over the background of the

Seaplane Fly-In. The entire time, Sarah snapped photos and wrote lots of notes.

"Why is it called a Seaplane Fly-In if they are landing on the lake and not the ocean?"

"That's a good question. It's a matter of semantics. Seaplanes, are more along the lines of flying boats, they land on their hull in the water. Floatplanes have floats and are elevated above the water. You'll get to see both kinds of planes and a few other interesting flying machines over the next couple of days. I suspect we call it the Seaplane Fly-In because it sounds better than the Floatplane Fly-In."

While they were sitting on the folding chairs in the air traffic shed chatting, the small radio transmitter on the gray metal desk crackled to life.

"Greenville traffic, Skycub 1776 inbound, landing runway 3/21, full stop, Greenville traffic."

Joe pointed out the plate glass picture window towards the end of the runway. "There he is."

"Do you need to say something back to him?" Sarah asked.

"No. This is an unmanned airport."

After learning this, Sarah mentally added one more reason, to her list of reasons, to stay out of planes.

They both watched as the plane came in for a landing.

"That's a Piper Cub. It's flown by a couple from Valley Forge Pennsylvania. They come up for the Fly-In every year."

"Joe, do you still have a camp where I was lost?"

"Sure do. I wouldn't give up the family camp for anything."

"Do you think it'd be possible for you to take me back there? I'd like to see that place again. I can hardly remember it."

"I seem to recall you didn't appreciate the woods?"

"That was a long time ago. I was a teenager."

"Well, I don't see why not. I plan on spending the next few nights here in town at Don's place while I help with the Fly-In."

"Don? Your friend at the diner you introduced me to?"

"The one and only. I'll be going back out to the camp on Monday. Can you stay until then?"

"That would be great," said Sarah. "My plans are flexible and I'll be here through next week."

"You must have a great boss if he sends you on assignment up to this beautiful place for work."

"You might not say that if you met my boss. How about you? What do you do for a living that you get to stay here?"

"I was an art teacher for a long time. Now I illustrate for a paper in Bangor and do some freelance work on the side. This gives me plenty of time to spend at camp."

"I'd love to see some of your drawings."

"I can show you when we go out to Lobster Lake. I have a number of sketches I'm working on."

"I can't wait to see them." Then, remembering her arrival last night when all the restaurants were closed, she asked, "Are there any places for dinner you might recommend?"

"Oh sure. Karen's diner, where we met this morning, is always a good option. It's my favorite."

"I was hoping to get some additional experiences, you know, for the write-up," Sarah hinted.

"Oh right. If you want something unique and more upscale country, you might want to try the Moose Lodge. The dining room has a wonderful view overlooking the lake, and I hear the food is top notch."

Sarah perked up immediately. "Lodge? Is it a lodge with rooms to stay in?"

"Sure is. Pricey too, I hear. I've been to the bar a few times, but I've never eaten there."

"It's a lodge with guest rooms, a restaurant, and a bar?"

"Sure," Joe replied, wondering why that made her so excited.

That was enough for Sarah to hear, she decided to change her lodging and didn't care how much Barone was going to scream about the added cost. It would be worth it to get back at him for sending her to Maine at the last minute, although she was starting to be glad to be here.

"Joe, why don't you have dinner with me at the lodge? It would be on me, well on the magazine."

"I don't know, it's real fancy."

"You can't make me eat alone. Besides, it would really help me with my article if I could ask you questions about Greenville, your life experiences here, and what makes this area so special."

"Since you put it that way, it's more of a business dinner. Then, I don't feel so bad about you paying." Joe smiled, and continued, "You know, until today I never knew your name. How did you know mine?"

"I started my writing habits at an early age and always kept a daily diary. The game warden that drove me back to town mentioned your name. The other night, I actually found that diary and read it. From what I wrote back then, I feel I may have been a bit snobby to you. If so, I'm sorry."

"That was a long time ago, Sarah. And besides, I don't recall any snobby remarks." Joe thought it best not to mention that he may have thought she was teenage-girl snobby, in an irresistible kind of way. He continued, "And by the way, that warden was Henry Ford. He was a lifelong family friend."

"He was very nice to me on the drive back to town. Most of all, I remember it was you who calmed me down and made me feel safe."

Joe felt his face get hot and he turned to look out the window, pretending to be interested in a logging truck that was barreling down the road headed towards town. It didn't matter, Sarah had already noticed and was touched he was so humble.

Hoping his face had returned to normal, he said, "It was no big deal. I was in the right place at the right time." Trying to change the subject, he added, "Do you want to go down by the lake? I'll show you some of the floatplanes."

Walking along the shoreline, Joe pointed out the different planes tied up in the water and parked on the grass along the shore.

"That's a Cessna 180, that one's a Beaver, and those two are Piper Cubs."

"And that one?"

"That's a Grumman Goose."

"Why's the engine way on top?"

"Notice it doesn't have floats. It lands on its belly."

"Ah – so a true seaplane then," stated Sarah.

"That's right."

The owner of the plane recognized Joe and waved them over. He let Sarah explore inside the Goose, which had a fully-stocked bar, and beds with seatbelts. It was the fanciest plane she had ever seen. She was starting to think this trip might make an interesting set of articles after all. After a walk along Main Street, Joe and Sarah made plans to meet for dinner.

* * *

Back in her motel room, Sarah called the Moose Lodge to make the dinner reservation and inquire about a room. She was ecstatic to discover that the lodge had one room available due to a cancellation earlier in the day. She checked out of the motel, surprising the manager by paying for the full stay.

Driving up the winding hill to the lodge, Sarah could not believe her eyes. The main building sat high on a hill overlooking the lake with a mountain rising to the sky behind it. Inside, the lobby smelled of apples and cinnamon. The windows went all the way from the floor to a pine logged cathedral ceiling thirty feet high, providing an expansive view of Moosehead Lake. After Perry, the owner, checked her in, he gave her a tour of the main floor, the bar, the dining room, and what he called the writer's room. This charming side nook had a fire burning, plush looking arm chairs, and walls lined with dark wooden bookshelves that went from the floor to the ceiling.

When Perry opened the door to her room, Sarah's eyes took in the antique four-poster bed covered in pillows, and beyond that a stunning view. Perry made a big showing when he opened the double door that led to the private patio, which looked out over miles and miles of lake surrounded by mountains.

"What mountain is that out in the lake?" asked Sarah.

"That's Mt. Kineo. It was formed by a glacier giving it the characteristic shape."

Perry confirmed her dinner reservation for two, and left her to settle in. As soon as he closed the door, she collapsed on the fluffy down king size bed. It was like laying on a cloud. She reached over and looked for the tag. It read, *Cuddledown. Made in Maine.* She closed her eyes and napped for two hours.

After the Fly-In committee meeting, Joe arrived at the lodge to see Sarah seated at the bar talking with Perry, who was also the bartender, while he whipped her up a fancy drink.

Already in love with the four-spout stainless steel espresso machine, Sarah watched as Perry added chocolate liqueur to a cappuccino. On top of the steamed milk, he shaved chocolate, which he told her was made in Blue Hill Maine.

Joe paused at the door admiring Sarah, who was wearing a knee length black skirt, a white button-down sweater, and had her hair tied back in a ponytail. He felt underdressed in his tan khakis and blue polo. Rallying his courage, he walked across the rustic reclaimed barn pine floor.

"Hello, Sarah. You look lovely."

"Hi, Joe. This place is amazing. And they have a cappuccino machine." She motioned behind the bar.

He nodded and grinned, happy to see the city girl enjoying herself.

"Hello there, Joe. Are you dining with this lovely lady?"

"Yes, Perry, I'm one lucky guy."

"Can I get you a drink before dinner as well?"

"I think I'll wait until after dinner for dessert, Perry."

"It's just cappuccino, Joe." Sarah said with a wink.

A server showed them to a table near the large curving front window with a view of the setting sun that was covering Mt. Kineo in an orange glow. The low rays shimmered off the lake surface as the moon rose over Big Moose Mountain.

Joe watched Sarah gazing out the window, drinking in the beauty of the lake and the surrounding scenery. A group of pilots made a loop over Burnt Jacket Mountain taking in the sunset from the air.

"The lake looks so smooth and with the seaplanes, it's like a postcard," she said, almost in a trance.

"I never get tired of the view. The sun paints us a different picture every night."

"Did you know that Thoreau likened Moosehead to a silver platter?" she asked.

"You've read *The Maine Woods*?" Joe was surprised given his recollection of her not liking the outdoors very much.

"I haven't finished it yet, but I'm enjoying the trip back in time. Have you read it?"

"That's one of my favorite books, especially as the snow is falling outside and the fire is warming the old camp. While a lot has changed since Thoreau traveled through here, much has stayed the same." Joe lifted his wine glass to take a sip, but first added, "Thankfully."

Over dinner, Joe answered Sarah's questions about the history of the north woods and the town of Greenville. He proudly talked about the great hiking, boating, fishing, hunting, and back country skiing. When Sarah asked about town events, he filled her in on the festivals held throughout the year. Hoping to plug the town for her magazine article, he added that they had restaurants and accommodations to fit everyone's tastes.

It was clear to her that Joe loved the area and through his eyes, she could see why. He was not only helping her with background for her article, his words were making her fall for this place – or was it for him.

Joe finished with, "Don't misunderstand me, Sarah. Most people who visit here camp or stay in cabins. Not everyone has an expense account."

"I realize that, Joe. I'll write about all aspects. Tonight, however, I'm going to enjoy every bit of this extravagance." She raised her glass in a toast, and sipped her expense account glass of Château d'Yquem with a chocolate terrine smothered in Godiva cream.

Following their dessert, Perry walked over to their table with a tray. "A nightcap of brandy, on the lodge. It goes especially well with star gazing." He nodded towards the French doors leading to the deck.

Taking the hint, Joe carried the drinks and escorted Sarah outside.

Sarah took a deep breath of the cool air. "The moon is so beautiful, the way it's shining on the water. It looks like a spotlight."

"Of course, how else do you expect the planes to land at night? That's the perfect runway light."

Sarah looked at Joe to see if he was serious.

"I'm kidding."

She smirked at him and realized she enjoyed his sense of humor. They stood, side by side, at the deck rail sipping their drinks with Moosehead spread out before them.

"What do you think of our little lake?"

"Little? I don't think so. This is a beautiful location to see it from, that's for sure."

When Joe saw her shudder, he put his jacket over her shoulders.

"Thank you. It seems a bit chilly for early September."

"Maybe a little more than normal. We're in the mountains after all. You never know. It could snow some years."

"Are you kidding again?"

"No. It's not usually measurable, but maybe a dusting."

"I see. I'm glad it's not snowing now. What time should I be in town in the morning?" Sarah asked, as they walked back to the lobby.

"Tomorrow morning it's all about setup for the Fly-In. Pilots will be arriving all day. If you get there around ten, I'll introduce you, and you can do some interviews."

"That will be wonderful. Thank you." She paused, and then added, "I enjoyed spending time with you earlier today and tonight."

"I feel the same, Sarah. I'll see you in the morning."

With his head feeling light, and not from the brandy, Joe arrived back at Don's place to find his friend waiting up to hear all the details. The only details Joe volunteered were about the orange glazed duck he ate for dinner and the expensive wine. His fishing buddy tried to press him for more, but he was too discrete to say anything further. He only said goodnight and went to sleep in his cot.

* * *

Before his alarm even went off, Joe was up at five, ate breakfast at the diner, and then went to help with the pilot registrations. All morning he kept making mistakes on the entry forms. He wrote "Sarah" for a pilot's name more than once, all of which amused the pilots who regressed to school boys and teased Joe about his long-lost crush.

Up at the lodge, Sarah lingered over a leisurely breakfast, taking time to enjoy two frothy cappuccinos. She then sat in the writer's room with a fire crackling, and wrote for the entire morning. She was interrupted only when she watched two tiny spotted deer who nibbled on the flowers right outside the window. Sarah found she was able to think and write so easily in the peace and calm of that room. She hated to get up and leave, but she did have interviews to do.

In town, Sarah spoke with pilots, shop owners, residents, and visitors to get their perspective on the town and the Fly-In event. Over lunch, at the Captain's Galley restaurant, she read Joe a few paragraphs of her article and asked him to check her facts about the planes.

"Sarah, this is excellent, with one needed change."

"What's that?"

"I would advise you to stay away from calling this event an 'air show.' While you might see a few stunts from these hotdoggers, there are no Blue Angel maneuvers here."

No sooner had he finished his statement, when a pilot came almost out of nowhere and did a restaurant fly-by. The plane dipped its wings first to the left and then to the right.

"Whoa, he almost hit those telephone lines. Is he in some kind of trouble?" asked Sarah, a nervous pitch to her voice.

Joe laughed. "No, not at all. That's Don waving hello to the crowd. He had plenty of clearance."

"Do you know him well?"

"Don? Sure do. We've been friends since we were old enough to hook a worm. He's lived here all his life. Heck of a bush pilot that guy. If you want to go to the pilot's banquet with me tomorrow night, you'll get to know him. His wife Linda is a sweetheart. She'll be there too."

"I'd love to go, thanks," replied Sarah.

That was exactly the response Joe was hoping for. He was enjoying her company and hadn't felt the way he felt, well since his wife passed away, so it had been years.

By the end of the long day, Joe wanted to get away from the crowds and he invited Sarah to have a quiet supper with him, or as he said it, "Suppah." He told her he knew a great place near a remote pond.

Being pleasantly surprised by the way this trip was turning out so far, Sarah envisioned a gourmet restaurant serving up a dinner by the water. She readily agreed.

"Wonderful. I'll pick you up at six. Dress casual. Jeans and a warm sweatshirt will be fine. It's country rustic." Joe drove off before Sarah could ask for additional details on where they'd be eating.

While Sarah returned to the lodge to work on her story, Joe ran errands picking up supplies. He borrowed fishing gear from Don and glasses, plates, and napkins from Don's wife, Linda. He made a quick stop at the Trading Post for some other necessities, and then went to pick up Sarah.

* * *

"So, what's the name of this place we'll be eating at? For my article."

"Oh – this is not a place for your article. The locals wouldn't want it to be overrun with out-of-towners."

Sarah was now really intrigued and figured it had to be a hidden gem. Her interest turned to concern when Joe parked along a dirt road. There were no houses, restaurants, or lodges anywhere in sight. There wasn't even another car parked anywhere on the road.

She wasn't sure what to think when Joe grabbed a large duffel bag and two fishing poles from the back of the truck.

"Ready for a north woods dinner?" he said, starting down a path.

Sarah raised her eyebrows and tilted her head. Joe simply smiled back and motioned for her to follow him. The two hiked a well-maintained trail until they reached a picnic table at a remote camp site along the shore of a pond surrounded by huge pines.

"This is Papoose Pond, not a cabin on it," said Joe, handing Sarah a rod.

"I've never fished before," confessed Sarah.

"If you want to eat, you'd better hope you're good at it," he half joked.

Seeing Sarah struggling to get her line past the rocks, he put down his rod and walked over. Standing behind her, he held his hands over hers and showed her the arm motion needed to get a good cast. After a few tries, she had the hang of it. By the time the sun was getting low on the horizon, Joe had two nice trout in his basket, so he walked over to give Sarah a few tips.

"Don't reel the line in so fast. Give them a chance to grab it," he whispered. After some patience she pulled out a nice sized trout.

"My first fish!"

"Congratulations. That's a nice one. Here, I'll take if off the hook for you." With his back to her, and grin on his face, he said, "Sarah, why don't you get the fish cleaned up, and I'll start the fire."

"What? I don't know how to do that."

"Just kidding. How about you gather up some kindling for the fire, while I start on the meal?"

With Sarah busying herself with the fire, Joe cleaned the fish, and then brought a pot of water up to temperature for washing. To her surprise, he handed her a bar of lavender soap and a plush towel.

Tending the fire, she was charmed watching Joe preparing their dinner. When he took out the bottle of white wine and a cheese platter, she realized this north woods man was intent on making an impression.

Joe poured her a glass of wine and returned to cooking the potatoes in a skillet with a piece of bacon and some onion. Next, he steamed asparagus with a sprinkle of salt and then pan-fried the trout. As the fish cooked, he set the picnic table and lit a candle.

"Is this a true woodsman dinner? Or is this all show for a city girl?"

"You might be on to me, but I wanted you to have a nicer time in the woods than the last time you were here."

Dinner was served with perfect timing to see a loon couple glide slowly across the pond. The beautiful birds called out to one another with a chorus that echoed off the hills.

"This fish is amazing," exclaimed Sarah.

"Fresh caught are always much better than fish that traveled to a grocery store by way of truck. The fire, the setting sun, and the loons, make for a great atmosphere too."

Reaching into the cooler, Joe pulled out two pieces of Maine blueberry pie for dessert.

"You've thought of everything, haven't you?"

"I tried."

After Joe covered the remaining hot coals in the fire pit with sand, they went to sit on the rocks near the water's edge to watch the sunset.

Sarah started to say, "This was…," when Joe put a finger in front of his lips and pointed. A moose and her calf were stepping into the water for their own evening dinner on the opposite shore.

Quietly opening her camera case, Sarah captured the moment on film, and Joe sketched the scene in his journal. They watched the two moose until it was too dark to see. The only light came from the crescent moon's reflection off the pond.

"This was an amazing night, Joe. I've never had a dinner like this. Thank you."

"You're very welcome. I'm glad you enjoyed it."

"I can't believe it's not a totally black sky and there are so many stars out again."

"And yet another wonder of being in the north woods. With so little here, there is so much to see."

"Now that it's dark, how are we going to hike back to the truck, Mr. North Woods?"

Joe reached into his duffel bag and pulled out two headlamps.

"You really did think of everything."

As they drove back towards town, Joe turned on the radio. "Mind if I check to see if they mention how the Red Sox are doing?"

He scanned the stations for the news, but stopped at the country station. The lyrics for *Fishin' in the Dark*, filled the truck. Joe wondered if Sarah was feeling the mood of the song just like he was.

Sarah smiled out the side window, uncertain of the feelings she felt. She thought about the fabulous dinner, the stars, the smell of the pine forest, the warm camp fire, the loons, the moose, and of course, Joe. It was all so wonderful. Maybe it wasn't all that bad up here in Maine after all....

Lobster Lake

On Saturday, Joe was up at dawn excited to get over to the American Legion for the pilot's breakfast. The weather was clear and the winds were calm, a perfect day for the Moosehead Lake Seaplane Fly-In. It would be the busiest day for Joe. With a full day of events, he would be answering questions, playing gofer, and doing anything needed to help keep the event running smoothly. As he drove down Pritham Avenue, he couldn't focus on what he had to do; his head was clouded with thoughts of Sarah.

Buddy and Buster were standing in the parking lot when Joe pulled in. "So how was the fishing last night, Joe?" yelled Buddy. Buster let out a loud laugh. Joe, not one to fish and tell, waved to the guys, and went right in to get his double stack of pancakes and bacon.

* * *

Sarah slept later than she had in a long time. Stepping into the fluffy flannel slippers she bought at the trading post, she couldn't remember the last time she had an uninterrupted night's sleep. Her breakfast of a French press coffee, fruit, and croissants, served with local Maine berry jam made right there at the lodge, was delivered to her room. She sat in the wide bay-window seat looking out over the lake amazed at how wonderful this trip was turning out. Taking a bite of perfectly ripe melon, she thought about how sweet it was going to be submitting the expense report to Barone. She was getting terrific material for a series of articles on the north woods, she was relaxed, and she even had found time to work on her novel. She wasn't missing her busy city life at all, and she wished she could live at this lodge forever.

* * *

By ten o'clock thousands of people had descended on Greenville. White vendor tents were set up in the town square selling everything from Allagash ash furniture to Maine maple syrup. Food trucks were lined up in the parking lots tempting everyone with fried dough, gourmet donuts, crab cakes, and local apple cider. Pilots did fly-bys and buzzed over the spectators sitting on the pier. The warm September sun was shining for the event without a cloud in the sky.

Joe sat at a table near the announcer tent chatting with pilot friends while they registered for events. Since he was distracted scanning the crowd for Sarah, more than once he put pilots in the wrong event.

"Hey, Joe, what gives?"

"About what, Dunn?"

"You've got me down in the wrong event," said Johnny, pointing at the sign-up sheet.

"Oh, sorry about that, my error," replied Joe, fixing the entry form. He then went back to keeping an eye out for Sarah.

* * *

Arriving in town, Sarah made a stop at the *Happy Kamper* store for a new hat, and then wandered through all the action. Walking over the grassy hill along the lake, Sarah watched the faces of the children excited over the planes. She could hardly believe there were so many people in this no-traffic-light town. Just two nights ago, she could have counted the people she saw walking down the main street on one hand. Now, Greenville was more crowded than Central Park for a summer evening concert.

Sarah made her way through the sea of lawn chairs to find Joe. He waved to her as she came walking around the corner of the hangar. Her strawberry blond hair was flowing from under her cap. She sure made Joe's heart skip a beat in her white collared shirt, denim shorts, and hiking boots.

Helping her set up her tripod and camera, he said, "Nice Red Sox hat."

"I wonder if they will win this year?" Sarah said. She flashed him a smile, pleased he noticed.

"What? A New Yorker, and you're not a Yankee fan?"

"Don't you remember, I grew up in Boston." Sarah didn't mention she had just purchased the hat, and if he pressed her, she wouldn't be able to name a single player.

"How could I forget? You made a big deal of being a city girl the day I met you in the woods. I also remember you were not a big baseball fan," replied Joe.

Sarah raised her eyebrows and thought, "There are plenty of things you don't know about me, Mister."

Buddy was running the public address booth, and seeing Sarah standing by Joe, he announced her arrival. Pointing down from his wooden perch, used also as the air traffic control tower for the lake landings, he said into the microphone with his booming voice, "And ladies and gentleman all the way from the Big Apple, and not the convenience store, I mean New York

City, Miss Sarah Molloy is here covering our Fly-In for a big travel magazine. How about helping me give her a north woods welcome." The crowd gave Sarah a big Greenville yell and applause.

Sarah waved, but not being used to the spotlight, quickly sat down.

Noticing Sarah blushing, Joe said, "Must be the hat."

Between events, Joe introduced Sarah to a couple of the pilots who were responsible for starting the Fly-In fifteen years ago. Having to run off and deal with competition logistics, Joe introduced Sarah to another friend of his.

"Sarah, this is Game Warden Andy Green. He can tell you some stories about Henry while I take care of the crisis."

"Nice to meet you, Sarah."

"Nice to meet you, too. So, you knew Henry Ford?"

"Oh yeah. Henry was a legend in the warden service. He covered more ground up this way in a day, than most of us can in a week." Between the pilot competitions, Andy made her laugh as he told her story after story about Warden Ford.

"It wasn't all fun and games, Henry also nabbed some bad characters during his career. The year I became a Game Warden, back in fifty-six, was the year Warden Ford solved the biggest case we ever had up here."

"1956? That's the year I was last here," said Sarah.

"Is that so? Long time between visits."

"Yes, unfortunately. What case did Warden Ford solve that year?"

"You haven't heard? The bandits and the big bust?"

"No, I haven't"

"Oh, would you look at that." Andy pointed out towards the raft in the middle of the cove.

The crowd was in hysterics because a pilot fell in the water during the bush pilot canoe race. Sarah wanted to ask more about the crime he mentioned, but they were distracted watching the wet team trying to tie the canoe back to the plane's float.

The day flew by as Sarah interviewed people, took pictures, and watched the events with Joe by her side. Around five o'clock, Buddy announced into the PA system, "Well folks that's the end of our competition for today. These pilots need to get cleaned up for the big Maine lobster dinner up at the airport. We hope to see you all back here tomorrow morning at nine sharp. If you've never seen planes drag race before, then you're not going to want to miss that. And please support the vendors on your way out. Fly-In t-shirts and hats make great gifts."

With the flying events over for the day, Sarah drove up to the airport to meet Joe for the banquet. They sat at the committee table with Don and his wife Linda, and the other volunteers. Everyone wanted to know what Sarah thought of the Fly-In.

"So, what event was your favorite so far, Sarah?" asked Buddy, cracking open his second lobster. Sarah flinched as water squirted out and hit Buster in the arm. Buster didn't even notice; he was too busy dipping his lobster tail in a bowl of butter.

"Hmm, each event had its moments. I'd have to say, the unpredictability of the bush pilot canoe races was exciting.

Seeing those guys fall in the water was hilarious. And when that one canoe came loose and fell off the plane's float, I wasn't sure what they were going to do."

"That Dunn crew really tried to cut the corner this year. They usually have no problems winning. It was all in good fun though," Buddy added.

"I also liked the grapefruit bomb drop. It was funny to see how close some teams were able to get to the target and how far off the others were. What happens to all those grapefruits?"

"Oh – Karen collects them when they float down to the end of the cove. She has enough fruit for her Hunter's Breakfast special for weeks."

Sarah couldn't tell if Buddy was serious or not.

Once everyone had finished eating, the airplane hangar was turned into a dancehall, and the band took the stage. Joe showed Sarah how to do the two-step and after slow dancing to, *"Could I Have This Dance,"* Joe led Sarah outside to cool off. They mingled at the bonfire, and then took a moonlight walk around the airstrip. While walking, they made plans to go for a canoe ride in the morning. Some pilots had tents pitched along the edges of the field and were sitting at their camp fires. Many of them called out to Joe to introduce Sarah to them. It had been a long time since they had seen him with a lady friend.

When they were all talked out, Joe walked Sarah to her car. "Are you still up for the morning canoe ride?"

"You bet. I'll meet you at seven, but you better appreciate I'm leaving that comfy bed, lovely breakfast, and, of course, that cappuccino machine."

Joe laughed. "That's hard to compete with, but I'll see what I can do. Goodnight, Sarah." Joe was taken a little by surprise when Sarah reached for his hand and gave him a hug.

She whispered, "Thanks for a terrific day."

* * *

After their morning canoe ride, Joe treated Sarah to breakfast at the diner. They then watched the seaplane drag racing, and then checked out the items for sale at the craft fair. Sarah purchased a signed book from a Maine Game Warden, turned author. Glancing at the book's cover, she had the impression the book was about making cider, but that didn't matter, she thought the warden was a real funny character and wanted his book anyway. Joe and Sarah enjoyed the rest of the day, socializing with the pilots who were all in good spirits.

That night Don and Linda held a barbeque for their pilot friends and the committee members. By now Sarah knew most of them, and jotted down notes as they told their stories. She kept looking at Joe to check if some of the adventures these guys had were really true.

Joe vouched for the tales. "Yep. Every story these guys tell happened. You'd be amazed at what can happen out here where not much is going on."

"Even the one about the bear napping in the plane?" asked Sarah.

"Yep. Scared the bejesus out of Don when he opened the door to get ready for a flight. Ever since, he locks the plane up when he's not near it."

"I'm going to have a hard time deciding which stories to include in the articles and which I have to cut."

"Why cut any? You could have a stream of articles to last a good year."

"I guess you're right."

The stories and the campfire started to wind down around ten, and Sarah asked Joe to walk her to her car. "Are we still on for tomorrow to go out to your camp?"

"Absolutely. The weather's looking to be perfect. If I pick you up at nine, will that give you enough time to sleep in and be pampered up at that lodge?"

"I guess I can make that work." She playfully rolled her eyes, gave him a hug, and kissed his cheek.

Joe sat on the boulder at the end of Don's drive and watched the red tail lights disappear down the winding camp road. He sat there even after the car turned the corner. He picked a long blade of grass and tore off small pieces as he thought about the day. He felt something special with Sarah, but he wondered if he was making more out of it, than it was.

R.C. started wagging his tail and let out a single quiet bark at Joe.

"What's the matter, buddy? You're afraid of the dark, aren't you? Okay, let's get inside."

* * *

When Joe picked up Sarah the next morning, she was wearing hiking boots, jeans, and had an LL Bean backpack over her shoulder. Joe couldn't help but think how sexy she looked with her hair pulled back in a pony tail.

"Good morning, Miss North Woods."

"Good morning, Joe."

"I trust you slept well in the king size bed with eight pillows and the overstuffed down comforter?"

"Yes, I did. It was so peaceful. The mountain breeze was blowing through the windows all night. As soon as my head hit the pillow, I went right out."

"Sounds like our lake and mountains are agreeing with you."

"Maybe they are." She laughed, seeing Joe smirking.

"Well let's get a move on. We've got a flight to catch."

"Wait. What was that?"

"You'll see." He opened the truck door and told R.C. to move out of the way so Sarah could get in.

Sarah wasn't so sure about getting into a plane, especially after she had seen how these pilots up here flew. Planes that played boats concerned her even more.

Joe parked his truck in the grass lot and they walked to the pier with R.C., who followed along, sniffing and running in circles.

Down by the water Don and Linda were standing by a floatplane with a tan and blue stripe.

"Good morning, Joe. Good Morning, Sarah," yelled Don.

"It sure is. Good morning to you, too" said Joe, walking along the dock.

"Nice plane," Sarah said, being positive, even though she was still apprehensive about flying. She took out her notepad.

Don almost took his plane apart explaining every intimate detail to Sarah, he figured she might spotlight his plane in her article. Sarah wrote furiously and made special notes about Don's career as a bush pilot.

When the tour was over, Don said, "Okay everyone, pile in, it's time to go."

Joe helped Sarah up on the float to step into the plane. R.C. leapt from the dock right through the open door as if he went for plane rides every day.

Sarah asked on last question to Don after they were all seated. "So, there's only the one engine?" Everyone laughed.

Don had his plane tricked out for touring. He handed each passenger a headset so they could talk to one another without having to yell over the roar of the engine. As they taxied down the lake, Joe said into the microphone, "Please stow all personal belongings and remain seated. Photographs are encouraged. There will be no cabin service on this flight, unless you brought your own flask. In case of a water landing, realize that this is normal."

The water on east cove was choppier than it had been the past couple of days. The plane bobbed up and down jerking Sarah in her seat. She began to wonder if this was such a great idea. As Don accelerated down the lake, Sarah was reminded of skiing over moguls, which she didn't care for all that much. The plane squeaked and rattled. Sarah was surprised at how smooth the ride was once the plane lifted off the water.

Don flew the plane over the town and said into the headset, "This is our favorite lake to fly over in the entire country." Gazing out the window, Sarah tried to take it all in. She could certainly see why Don felt that way.

Joe acted as tour guide pointing out Big Squaw, Burnt Jacket, and Kineo. "See that mountain over there, Sarah? You and your family were camping close to the base of that mountain the year you vacationed here. That's Big Spencer."

Don flew over Northeast Carry and up towards the north side of Lobster Lake.

Sarah placed her finger on the window. "What mountain is that over there?"

"Ahh, that's Katahdin."

"Oh! I'd sure like to hike that mountain."

Joe, was encouraged with her change of heart about the outdoors. "If you visit again, we can plan to do that."

Linda looked over at Don and raised her eyebrows. He mouthed back, "What?" not catching her subtle point about the conversation between the two passengers in the rear seats.

Don made a pass over Lobster Lake, to be sure no canoes were making the trip over the open water. The lake was a popular crossing for those wishing to follow Thoreau's 1846 trip along the West Branch of the Penobscot River.

With no paddlers in sight, Don brought the plane down and taxied toward a cove with a sandy shore to beach the Cessna. The men secured the plane with rope to a couple of large pine trees to keep it stable.

Linda grabbed the cooler. "How about we eat here at the lake and then walk over to Joe's cabin before our hike?"

"That sounds terrific to me," answered Sarah.

The guys shrugged, figuring anyplace to eat would be good with them. Sarah spread a blanket on the sand, while Linda unpacked ham sandwiches, potato salad, and home-made pickles.

"This looks wonderful, honey," exclaimed Don.

A loon family floated by inspecting the new visitors. The mother loon hooted at her young one to keep up. Sarah fit right in with the three old friends as if they had known her for years.

When Sarah went to chase after R.C., Linda whispered to Joe, "I really like her. She doesn't seem to be a city girl at all."

Joe didn't say anything, but he knew what Linda was getting at; Sarah was surprising him as well.

Passing the plate of her homemade chocolate chip cookies, Linda turned the conversation to how Joe and Sarah originally met. "So, Joe, we heard some rumblings around the hangar yesterday that you saved Sarah's life. How'd that happen?"

Joe turned red in the face. He was still not convinced he had saved Sarah's life. He figured he didn't do anything more than anyone else would have done.

He responded, a bit matter-of-factly. "Sarah was turned around in the woods not far from here, I walked her back to our cabin where Warden Ford was already waiting, and he took Sarah back to her family."

Don jumped in. "There must be more to it than that."

Sarah nodded. "Joe, you should tell us about the fort and the deer and how you ran down the mountain. I'm sure you remember much more than I do. I was in a state of panic. I don't remember it all that well, except that you came to my rescue."

"I guess as I think about it, that was an interesting year."

"How about you tell us as we hike?" asked Sarah.

"I don't see why not. We can stop in at the cabin on the way around the loop," Joe said.

The men checked the ropes securing the plane before they started down the pine needle covered trail. Joe began to tell them how he remembered the events of that year.

"It was 1956, I was sixteen. I remember it well because that was the year I was allowed to hunt alone, and we had some real crazy excitement up here that fall hunting season."

"Wait. I thought you found Sarah during the summer?" interrupted Linda.

"I did, I did. But it's all part of the story the way I remember it."

"Give the man a break, Linda," joked Don. "He just ran into this lovely lady after thirty-two years of thinking about her." He gave Joe a sideways grin.

Joe saw Sarah give him a wide-eyed look and blush.

She wondered, "Had he really been thinking about me all these years? And what does Don know, that I don't?"

"Okay, what was the crazy excitement that fall then?" Linda asked, ignoring the romantic spark between Joe and Sarah.

Joe stopped walking. "As it happened, it had to do with a robbery, more than a million dollars. It was a big heist."

"A robbery of that amount? Here in Greenville? Not a chance," Linda said.

"No, Linda, the robbery wasn't here. However, there may have been a connection to *our* north woods. It was the same year Sarah was lost and Warden Ford nailed Red and the Lobster Lake Bandits."

Joe's voice took on a haunting tone as he continued down the trail, telling the story. "Dad and I packed up the truck, and headed to camp for a few days of hunting, we never could have anticipated what we'd stumble into…"

The Boston News

January 18, 1950

$2.7 Million Stolen

Last evening, while most residents were in their warm homes, eleven men robbed a money depot in Boston's North End. At first estimate, authorities report that over $2.7 million dollars in cash and securities were stolen. This is the largest robbery in United States history.

The FBI, Boston Police, and Private Investigators are piecing together the information and clues left at the scene.

The gangsters, who all wore masks, bound and gagged the guards. Nobody was hurt in the incident.

Up to Camp

Bangor Maine – November 1956

Stan stood in the front hallway and yelled up the stairs. "Come on Joe, we want to get there before it gets dark. The sun will be down around four-thirty tonight."

Joe rummaged through his bag one final time. Chewing gum, Hershey bars, comic books, compass, knife, and a picture of his mom. Even though Mom did not hunt, each evening Joe and his dad would get back to the cabin and she'd be there. She would listen to their stories, as they enjoyed the hearty chicken pot pie she cooked for them.

Joe and his dad always anticipated their fall hunting trips, but last year, neither of them could bear to think about going. This year, encouraged by the words in her final note, they were trying to go on. They both knew Louise would want them to continue with their traditions and the family connection to camp. This trip could be a huge step in the healing, no matter how painful it seemed right now, and how much they missed her.

Waiting for Joe, Stan grabbed the paper off the front seat of the truck. He took one last look at the weather forecast. Without electricity at camp there was no radio, and they had to live by the five-day weather forecast in the Bangor Daily.

Stan was cautious in watching the north woods weather this time of year. Once the heavy snow came, the road to camp would become impassable by any vehicle until the spring melt.

The logging companies only plowed the Golden Road up to the south end of Caribou Lake, and that was only when they got around to it. Since they couldn't log until the ground was good and frozen, they might not plow until January.

Looking at the paper, Stan noticed the conditions for their trip were expected to be cold, below freezing at night, and crisp in the high thirties during the day. The forecast looked perfect for fall hunting. No precipitation was expected. Stan thought it looked to be typical Maine November weather, meaning it could change at any moment. He'd have to pay attention to the skies and his instincts. The plan was to spend four nights at the camp, unless of course they were to bag their deer early. Deer, or no deer, they were expected at his sister-in-law's house on Thursday for Thanksgiving dinner. He placed the paper behind the truck's front seat to take along. Getting impatient waiting on Joe, he honked the horn.

Joe came running out of the house, leapt from the porch, climbed into the cab of the truck, and slammed the door. His black lab, Sparky, was already there, taking up the center of the seat.

"A hunting we shall go," Stan said, as they drove away.

Joe fiddled with the radio and tuned it with excitement as Tennessee Ernie Ford crooned out, *The Ballad of Davy Crockett*. Joe would often run the trails around camp singing his own version as, "Joey, Joey Parker, king of the wild north woods."

The radio signal didn't last long. They were able to pick up an AM station from Bangor for a little while, then there was nothing but static. Joe turned it off and asked, "Dad, can we get a car like Jimmy Johnson instead of this truck?"

"What kind of car does Jimmy's dad drive?"

"A '55 Ford Thunderbird. Bright blue."

"Isn't that a two-seater?"

"Yes. Very fast too."

"Where would Sparky sit?"

Joe thought about that for a moment and let it pass. Pressing his case, he continued, "It has a folding top you can take down. We'd look cool in it."

"How do you think it would hold up on the road to camp?" asked Stan, playing it cool. He certainly would not mind a sporty roadster. He also knew it was not practical for many reasons. Stan was also wise to Joe. Many of Joe's friends had started driving and most of them had bought their own cars. Joe himself had been saving, working two jobs so he could have enough money to buy one. He worked at the grocery store after school, and on weekends at the ice cream counter inside the pharmacy. He planned to save enough money by spring, although he wouldn't have enough for a Thunderbird.

"Yeah, I guess you're right, Dad. A sports car would bottom out and be stuck on the camp road all the time."

"I am glad you understand that, son."

They talked about what supplies they needed to buy at the store. Stan called out items and Joe wrote them down on a piece of cardboard that he picked up off the floor of the truck.

Ice	eggs	tomatoes
milk & cheese	coffee	potatoes
sugar	cereal	corn
butter	carrots	apples
bacon & ham	peanut butter	flour
sausages	beans	bread

Joe added chocolate bars, cookies, and soda pop, even though his dad hadn't mentioned those items. After the list was made, they talked about their plans for hunting and fishing. Before they knew it, they had reached Greenville.

Stan pulled into the store parking lot. The hand painted sign over the front door read, "Trading Post. Last Stop Food and Much More." The Trading Post sold everything from hunting and fishing gear to truck parts.

"If the Trading Post didn't have it, you didn't need it. At least not up this way," Stan would say.

Joe always tried to get the cashier to take things in trade, like the trading posts he read about in his history class. He had offered deer antlers for comic books and pieces of Kineo flint in exchange for candy. He had yet to get them to trade for anything but money.

The parking lot, all twelve spaces, was jam packed with pickup trucks. A few more trucks, towing campers, lined the road. It appeared to Stan that a lot of hunters were planning on making it a busy week for the area. One truck in the lot caught his eye. The red Ford pickup belonged to Red. That probably wasn't his real name, but it's what his partners in crime always called him. The men always seemed to be up to no good. They were loud, drove too fast, and stirred up trouble wherever they went.

Stan knew that while it looked busy here at the store, once everyone was out in the woods, with millions of acres around, there would be a slim chance of even seeing another hunting party the entire week. He had to hope that would be the case with Red and his gang, the less they saw of them, the better.

Inside, the aisles were full of men filling carts with the three B's – bacon, beans, and beer. In addition to the items written on the cardboard, Joe and Stan selected a couple of steaks for their dinner. Walking up and down the aisles, Stan avoided shopping in the same sections as Red. He did notice Red opening a bag of chips, which he proceeded to eat while walking through the store.

On the way to the checkout, the bakery section caught Stan's eye and he grabbed a blueberry pie for dessert, Louise's favorite. An empty chip bag was stuffed between the boxes of donuts on the shelf.

"Unbelievable."

"What is it, Dad?"

"Nothing. Let's go pay."

With the supplies stowed in the bed of the truck, and the meat packed on ice in the cooler, they gassed up and started out again towards camp. It was still another hour and twenty minutes, give or take, until they would pull down the grass path that led to their cabin.

Less than twenty minutes of the remaining drive would be on paved road. After that, the first stretch of dirt wasn't too bad. Past that point, all bets were off and the traveling was slow and unpredictable. If the road was paved and straight, instead of winding and rutted dirt, they could drive the miles much quicker, even in their old truck. Although, if it were a paved road, they wouldn't have a camp there.

Cruising down the Golden Road, Stan and Joe were in a conversation about the Red Sox, when in the rearview mirror Stan noticed two sets of headlights closing fast.

Joe noticed his dad looking in the mirror and swung around in the seat to look. "Whoa, those guys are flying."

"Yep, wonder what the problem is." Stan jerked to the side of the road to let them pass. A red Ford, and a green truck following right behind it, went flying by, leaning on their horns the entire time.

"That was Red and his gang, wasn't it?"

"Yep."

They watched the trucks slide around Crash Corner.

"Where do you think they're headed?"

"I'm sure not anywhere near we're going to be." Stan pulled back into the road and hoped his hunch was correct.

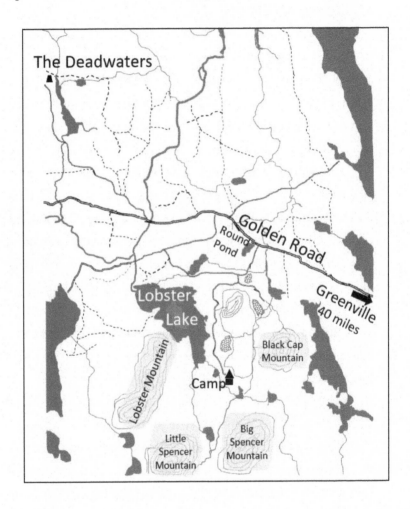

The sun was behind the trees by the time they hit the Round Pond turn-off. From there they had to travel another ten miles on what Joe's mom called the deer path. It was worn down first by the deer, maybe a moose, the occasional logging truck, but mostly from the Parker's own pickup.

On many first-of-the-spring season trips to the camp, there were often washouts on the road from the brooks and streams crisscrossing the entire area. When coming to one of these roadblocks, the Parkers would have to park their truck on one end of the wash-out and hike for a mile to their camp. Joe and his dad would then spend the better part of the summer repairing the log structures that passed for bridges, many of which would wash away with the next spring runoff.

It was a vacation that took work, but it was well worth it, not only for the beauty, but knowing that three generations of Parkers had called this area, southwest of Katahdin and east of Moosehead Lake, camp.

Since their last trip back in August, the late summer rain storms had done a number on the road surface and it was as rough as a washboard, or as Stan called it, north woods cobblestone.

The old truck bounced and squeaked. Luckily, there were no trees blocking the road and none of their homemade bridges had been washed out.

A deer ran out across the road, catching Stan by surprise. He hit the brakes hard and Sparky slid off the bench seat onto the floor. For the remainder of the ride, Joe sat at attention after almost hitting his head on the windshield.

Breaking the silence, Joe brought up a memory. "This deer path sure is in bad shape this fall." It was the same phrase his mother would use, only changing the season each time. His dad smiled, a sad smile, knowing the reference.

"Well, Joe, this is the first year you'll be on your own. Are you excited?"

Even though Joe had been waiting for this trip all year, he was a little apprehensive. As he was now sixteen, this would be his first-year hunting separate from his dad. To prepare, they had already developed a communication strategy on where they would meet, and at what time. These were precautions mostly, as Joe figured there wouldn't be any problems. There never were at camp. And besides, Joe knew the woods around Lobster Lake like it was his own bedroom.

"I'm sure looking forward to it. But I do want to hunt together some of the time."

Stan appreciated that Joe still wanted to spend time with him. "We can arrange that easy enough. We'll have the woods around camp all to ourselves. We can hunt solo in the mornings, fish in the afternoons, and hunt together before dusk."

It was dark by the time they turned onto the unmarked grass lane to Parker cabin. The truck's headlights reflected off four eyes along the tree line. Getting out of the truck, Joe and Stan caught sight of the bouncing white tails high tailing it into the brush.

"I bet tomorrow those deer will be near impossible to find," Joe said, as he walked up the creaky porch steps.

A rush of cold air escaped into the night when Stan opened the cabin door. Inside, it was chilly, with a musty scent of pine.

Stan lit the gas lamps, turned on the propane-powered refrigerator, and then built a fire, while Joe unloaded the supplies from the truck.

"Dad, should I leave the cooler out here on the porch?"

Stan knew leaving any food on the porch this time of year, was at best an invitation for raccoons, and at worst a gift to a bear looking to put on a few extra pounds before his winter nap.

"No, that could be inviting trouble. Bring it to the back closet, it never gets warm in there. The fridge won't be cold until morning."

"Okay."

After dinner, they cut into the blueberry pie, and went over their plan one more time. Joe would head north along the Beaver Creek Trail and hunt from the meadow. Stan would head northeast to hunt from Bug Bog. They would meet at the base of Rum Ridge around noon.

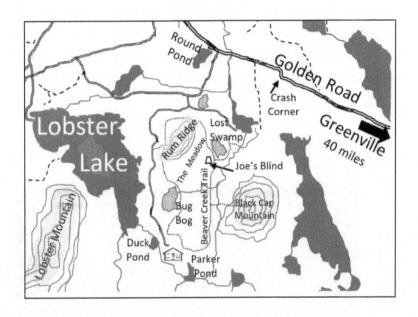

The paths through the woods were known to them to be good game highways. Rarely did other hunters venture down the road past Round Pond, the road conditions not worth their effort. Stan and Joe knew better. For the Parkers, hunting the terrain around Lobster Mountain meant an exciting challenge with bigger game. They knew each meadow, ridge, and swampy area from years of exploring this piece of the north woods.

Even knowing the trails around the camp, they both were experienced enough to know that it was easy to get lost, especially since the surroundings start to look the same very quickly. Every year, to make sure Joe knew this was serious business, Stan would retell the story of the hiker that died of starvation six-hundred feet from the Appalachian Trail (AT) back in 1948. "And remember the hiker story I told you about, Joe? The young man had left the trail briefly – to look for water. Whatever happened, he couldn't find his way back to the trail."

"Yes, Dad. I remember. You told me the hiker had lost his compass and never stopped to replace it."

"That's correct, son. The poor man's remains were found several years later. A note written using charcoal and a stick was found in a bottle and told of the hiker's last days. Remember, the AT then, as it is now, was about four feet wide and fairly well maintained. Whereas, the narrow trails around our property are maintained mostly by the deer, with a little of our help. Be sure to keep your bearings at all times and never go anywhere without your compass. And remember, Joe, as soon as you leave the trail, it all starts to look the same."

Joe nodded and told his dad he understood. Joe was confident in his woodsmanship, but he also took the woods seriously. Just this past summer, he had seen firsthand how panicked and disoriented a person could become when surrounded by nothing but the woods. He drifted off wondering how that girl was doing now.

He thought about her a lot. She was so different from any of the girls he knew. She wore makeup, hated the woods, and couldn't even get across a steam without falling in. But boy, she was beautiful.

"Joe, are you paying attention?"

"Huh, Dad?"

"I was reminding you of the signal."

"Oh, yeah. I got it."

To not be distracted by a gunshot, from other hunters, that could carry for miles out in this area, they devised a signal. If either of them was successful, they were to fire one shot, pause, three shots, pause, one shot. They would then meet at the Rum Ridge trail and circle back to the deer.

They played a game of cribbage and relived the hunts of years past. The antlers on the walls of the cabin served as reminders for each hunting tale they told. A little after nine o'clock they headed to bed to get their rest for the morning.

Being Watched

Joe's wind up alarm vibrated itself off the narrow pine shelf and onto the floor. Kicking off the covers to silence the clock, he discovered how cold it was in the camp. The heat from last night's fire had escaped hours ago through the uninsulated pine walls. He dressed quickly, somewhat because he was excited to get going for the day, but mostly because he was freezing. By the time he had thrown on a pair of jeans and his boots, his dad already had the oatmeal heating on the stove. No bacon this morning. The smell of bacon on a hunter would send the deer straight across the mountain. Not even a fire was crackling in the woodstove, the scent of which would linger and give them away to any deer half aware it was hunting season.

On the way to the outhouse, Joe caught a glimpse of the old metal Maine Moxie thermometer hanging on the porch column. The mercury was trying to pull itself towards twenty. The wash water he had dumped on the ground last night had formed a miniature ice-skating ring.

At 6 a.m. sharp, still barely a hint of daylight in the sky, with their bags packed and rifles over their shoulders, they were out the door. Stan gave his son a few words of last-minute advice.

"Now remember, Joe, stay on the trail, keep your compass with you at all times, and be safe with that loaded rifle."

"Okay, Dad, I will. Don't worry, I'll meet up with you in a few hours."

Stan watched as his only son made his way down the trail they had traveled all the years prior, always together. He stood looking, even after he could no longer see Joe. He then turned and went in the direction towards Bug Bog.

* * *

Joe felt strange to be walking alone this morning. Sure, he'd walked the Beaver Creek Trail by himself plenty of times before, he'd even had his rifle with him on many of his walks. During the summer he'd stop to take target practice at pieces of wood, or his empty soda can set on a stump. Last spring, he fired a shot in the air to scare off a bear he noticed up ahead on the trail. This time was different. It was hunting season. Hunting had always been with his dad – side by side.

Joe kept to the shadow of the trees, creeping quietly along. He had seen plenty of deer grazing this area all summer and fall. This morning, however, the deer had checked their calendars, and once they realized it was the last few days of hunting season, they all were hidden well in the brush. Lost in his thoughts, Joe was not sure he would even take a shot the first day out. At first, this sounded crazy, but Joe loved being in the woods, and even more than that, being around camp. A quick hunt would mean they would pack up early to get the meat into the freezer back at home. Of course, if Joe happened to spot a trophy buck, the ones camp legends are made of, he certainly wasn't going to pass up that kind of opportunity.

This morning, Joe planned to take his time to get to his hunting spot in the meadow. He figured at his current pace, he'd be there by seven thirty. He was enjoying the hike and listening to the sounds of the fall woods.

A lone gust of wind clicked branches together on a bare birch tree. A snowshoe hare hopped into the middle of the trail, stopping just long enough to seem to wonder about Joe. Then he hopped off. A couple of squirrels, chattering loudly, chased one another in a circle and then went up a tree.

Other than that, the woods were quiet, and Joe day-dreamed as he walked. At the sound of a twig snapping, he could not remember the last few hundred yards he had hiked. He stopped and waited. Then he heard a thrashing, and thirty yards ahead caught sight of a dark shape veering up the trail to the peak of Black Cap Mountain. He quickened his pace to get to the trailhead, remaining cautious as he walked.

The trampled ferns marked the spot the animal had traveled. Joe peered up the overgrown shadowy trail; it was a trail he hadn't walked in years. Even with the trees bare of leaves, it was difficult to see much of anything. Whatever had been moving around must have come to a stop. He knew that if he took the trail, and it was the trophy buck he always dreamed of, any game shot up there would be a challenge to get back down. The trail was steep with a lot of rocks to climb over and he didn't have time to make a fruitless diversion this morning, not even for a short scouting expedition. Although, a voice in his head told him that the sense of adventure, and the unknown, were two of the reasons he loved the woods to begin with.

With his curiosity peaked, Joe headed up the trail to try and see what took off in such a rush. It was much darker, and even colder, than on the main trail. The tall pines, hemlocks, and dense spruce were thick and created a canopy that blocked the early morning sun. The trail had been washed down with the latest rain storm making it muddy in spots and icy in others. Maintaining his footing on the rocks and the exposed slippery roots was a challenge. There were prints scattered about in the semi-frozen mud, indicating it was well-traveled by the local inhabitants. He easily identified deer, bear, rabbit, and fox tracks crisscrossing back and forth. A large moose print had a smaller print partially inside of it. It looked fresh.

He stopped to quiet his breath and waited. He knelt down to examine the paw indent in the mud. It was characteristic of a cat with a large pad and four smaller round pads to the front of that. From his investigation, Joe decided that the shadow he saw must have been a bobcat. This morning was not the time to be stalking a cat. Joe turned and quietly headed down, trying not to slip on the wet ground. He bent his head under the low hanging branches and stepped back on the Beaver Creek trail.

The startled animal froze in a pouncing stance. Joe turned toward the meadow, not even noticing what was a few steps behind him. As he took a step down the trail, the hair on the back of his neck stood up. He felt like someone, or something, was watching him. He slowly turned and found he was looking right at a lynx, its black tipped tail twitching slightly. Joe figured the cat must have gone up the trail and circled back around in the woods in stealth mode.

The lynx was not shy at all and did not back away or make for cover. The two prior times Joe had seen a lynx, the cats never remained still to look back at him. To avoid spooking the cat, he didn't move for what seemed to be minutes, then he slowly raised his arm to his rifle. The lynx slowly rotated its head, staring, but not moving.

Joe was absorbed in watching the animal and taking in all the details. The cat's coat was a rich silver with hints of golden brown reflecting in the streaks of sun that passed between the trees. Joe's eyes focused on the cat's paws, which were so large, he imagined them as furry catchers' mitts. The animal's ears, which were standing straight up, looked too small for the size of the body. The eyes, cold-black dots in the center of yellow green, looked directly at Joe, without a hint of fear. The stare was mesmerizing.

Slowly, he un-shouldered his rifle to be prepared to fire a shot to scare off the cat. He waited for the lynx to back down. It wasn't until Joe took a half step forward that the cat turned, and slowly walked off into the brush, disappearing without a sound.

With his heart pumping, Joe exhaled and continued down the path, intent on getting back on schedule. He could tell by the droppings and nibbles on the branches that the deer were actively walking in the area, and recently. He crossed a stream he had long ago named Little Beaver Creek. It was all but a dry bed of rock this time of year. A few minutes later he arrived at the south end of a small meadow. He glanced at his watch. It was almost eight. Walking another two-hundred yards, he settled into his three-sided log hunting blind.

Joe had spent weeks during the July heat building the blind, anticipating this very fall hunt the entire time he chopped, sawed, and set the logs. His simple structure was barely four feet high, but perfect to stay hidden from the deer. Set inside

were three fat logs, set on end, one along each wall for seats.
Not that Joe was expecting company. He figured if he was
going to be doing a lot of waiting, he may as well include
seating at any angle he needed to observe. At his seated
shoulder height, he had created openings giving him a clear
view of the meadow. A few maple sticks were wedged between
the logs to use as hangers. On these whittled branches he hung
his binoculars and canteen. When Joe had finished building the
blind, and he proudly showed his dad, Stan remarked that the
blind was the fanciest hunting structure anyone in the Parker
clan ever built.

The birds that had announced his arrival finally settled
down and accepted his presence. A red squirrel was not so
cooperative and continued a rhythmic screech from a branch
above Joe's seat. Joe pulled a Spaceworld comic book from his
pack to pass the time. It took thirty minutes for the squirrel to

quiet down. The meadow was so still, Joe could hear his own breathing.

* * *

Two miles to the west, Stan had reached Bug Bog. The bog was aptly named for the black flies, mosquitoes, gnats, horse flies, and ceratopogonidaes which were so nicknamed no-see-ums, since aside from being invisible, nobody could pronounce their full name anyway. The insect residents of the bog would lie in wait for their dinner to come to them. However, like the tourists, the pests were seasonal. This time of year, the bog was completely deserted. The cold nights of October had finished off the last of the holdouts, tourists and bugs alike.

Stan took a seat on a downed pine in the cover of the thick brush running along the outskirts of the bog. Almost immediately he heard something approaching with the cautious rhythmic steps of a four-legged prize. He readied his Remington 141. It had not yet occurred to him that an early success for himself, might not be much of a trip for Joe. His breathing slowed. He wondered if he had picked the right spot to sit. The wind was starting to pick up and chilled the back of his neck. Turning up his collar, he realized his scent was being carried right towards the approaching animal.

He looked through the sight of his rifle towards the sound and spotted a worn-down game path coming from the woods, directly into a stump-less spot of the bog. The perfect morning watering hole. As he watched the path, the sound of the crunching earth came to a halt. Behind him the leaves rustled. He caught sight of a bird scratching at the frosty earth for breakfast. Stan waited, not making a move. A minute passed without a sound. Stan thought, "Maybe whatever it was had scented me and left."

A second later, a large bull moose casually stepped off the bank and into the shallow muddy water. The bull had a huge rack and easily weighed over nine hundred pounds. Stan lowered his rifle. If it was moose season, and he had the good fortune of having a bull permit, it's unlikely he'd have this opportunity. Then, he thought about it a bit more. Even if it were moose season, and he had a permit, taking this big guy back here in the bog would mean a heck of a job hauling it out. Stan and his father had made that decision too many times, always forgetting in the excitement of the hunt the work that would follow. As Stan grew older he was now much more selective on a location when it came to big game season. A deer back in this area wouldn't be much of a problem, dragging out a moose was a totally different story.

Stan slowly unzipped his pack, and removed his Kodak Tourist II camera, a gift from Louise the last Christmas they celebrated together. "State of the art," she'd said.

As quietly as he could, he moved a branch to get a clear shot. The loud click of the shutter brought the moose's head up from eating the bog weeds. The bull peered directly in Stan's direction, nose in the air.

When Stan clicked the film forward, the moose shifted on his huge legs. As soon as the shutter released, the moose raised his ears, turned, and walked into the woods. Stan immediately advanced the film and took two more pictures, that when developed would be nothing but a moose moon. Enlargements would later hang in the camp under a sign Stan carved out of a maple log. It would read, "Phases of the Moon."

For the remainder of the morning, Stan waited and didn't see another creature. He collected his stuff, and continued his advance to Rum Ridge. As he walked he realized he didn't even want to get a deer this morning, this was Joe's trip. If anyone was going to get the first deer, he wanted it to be his son.

When he reached the trailhead, well before the scheduled meeting time, Stan figured he could hike up to the top before Joe even broke for the trail. From the summit he'd have a view of the meadow, and with binoculars he could observe any deer making their way toward Joe. He thought about what a feeling it would be, to watch Joe have success the first day hunting alone.

Reaching the top of Rum Ridge, Stan dropped his pack, and pulled his canteen off his shoulder. Even though it was not yet near eleven o'clock, he was hungry. He rummaged through his bag for the sandwich of sliced ham and cheese he made this morning. He had stuffed two of the sandwiches in Joe's pack, knowing one wouldn't be enough for the boy. As he unwrapped the sandwich and took a few bites, he gazed down on the meadow where Joe was sitting. He strained his eyes to make out the location of the stick shelter. Stan could recall where about in the meadow the blind would be, but the shadows from the trees made it difficult to see. He dug into his pack and removed his binoculars. He waited until he finished his sandwich before lifting them to his eyes. A critical few minutes that later he realized may have been a poor decision.

Triple Trouble

Caught up reading his comic book, Joe barely watched the meadow. The woods were so still he figured his hearing was tuned to any crunching an approaching deer might make anyway. In the Spaceworld story, the aliens had invaded the earth and proceeded to abduct all the movie stars of Hollywood. Joe often thought about visiting Hollywood, and if he was lucky, maybe even catching a glimpse of John Wayne. As he read, he was lost between the two worlds of aliens and movie stars, and completely oblivious to the shadowy form entering the meadow to his left.

Finishing the comic book, he quietly rummaged through his backpack for a snack. Biting into the ham and cheese he thought it was probably the best sandwich he ever had in a hunting blind. Taking a second bite, he looked up at Rum Ridge. It was from the rock ledge last spring that he had decided on this meadow for his blind. Back in June, with the sun coming up, he hiked to the top of the ridge, and noticed the steady traffic of deer on their daily rounds through the meadow.

Today, he wondered where they all had disappeared to. He thought maybe he should have scouted a location in the fall instead, or he could have scared all the deer with his approach from Beaver Creek. With barely a noticeable breeze, Joe used a wet index finger to find the wind was blowing directly from the west, straight from the direction of the ridge. It was the perfect flow of air to keep his scent behind him. There was nothing he could do but wait. He pulled another comic book from his bag.

* * *

After finishing his sandwich, Stan searched the meadow with his binoculars. He located Joe's blind after scanning the woodline several times. The blind was certainly hidden from human eyes. Being hidden from the nose and ears of the four-legged species might be a different story. He zoomed out and slowly panned to the left of the blind. Nothing was stirring. He panned to the right. At first, he passed it, thinking the shadow was a downed tree or large stump. But quickly his mind put the image together. His heart beat a little faster. His breathing became heavy. He focused in on a large black bear, who was moving slowly along the cover of the trees, headed directly for Joe.

Zooming in on the blind, Joe was sitting with his head down; Stan guessed most likely reading a comic book instead of keeping his eyes peeled. Looking back towards the bear, it had closed to within fifty feet of Joe. Based on the direction the bear was moving, he would stumble right into the blind if Joe didn't happen to make a sound to give the animal reason to veer off. Stan knew, hearing or smelling danger, the bear would prefer to get away, rather than confront a human. The worst scenario would be for Joe to inadvertently surprise the bear with a sudden motion. A surprised bear could be unpredictable.

Stan wondered if he should fire a warning shot. That certainly would get both Joe's and the bear's attention. It would also ruin any chance Joe would have of seeing a deer in the meadow this morning. Stan would have to explain later why he was in fact observing from up on the ridge. He didn't want Joe to feel he was being spied on, or worse, being kept an eye on. That was not Stan's intent at all.

None of that would matter if the bear closed within twenty feet of the blind, he'd have no choice but to fire off a round. When Stan thought it couldn't get any worse, it did. Out of the woods came tumbling not two, but three, bear cubs. Based on their size, Stan figured the cubs were close to ten or eleven months old. The cubs ran out into the center of the meadow tackling one another and rolling in the grass, reminding him of puppies. The mother bear remained cautious, staying close to the trees, and watching for danger. Stan looked through his binoculars at Joe.

Luckily, the cub commotion was enough to get Joe's attention. Stan saw Joe's surprised face fade to a smile as he watched the young bears. He was proud to see that almost immediately, Joe realized that the mother would not be far away. He watched as Joe looked around until he spotted the mama bear. Stan watched with pride as Joe did everything as he was taught when it came to bears.

* * *

Joe watched as the mother bear walked into the center of the meadow, laid down, and scratched behind her ear. The smallest furry black cub ran up from behind her and jumped on her head. She playfully pawed at his back and knocked him to the ground. The cub made a grandstand of her push and rolled as if she had used her full force. Not wanting them to be startled, Joe whistled a tune and scrapped two sticks together. Instantly, the mother headed into the woods. The curious cubs stood on their hind legs and looked around for the source of the sound. Within a moment they darted after her.

Joe was relieved the bears had moved on without incident. Realizing how late it had gotten, he packed up to go and meet his dad. Before leaving the blind, he clipped a bell onto his belt loop. With the bear and her cubs in the area, he was taking no chances to come between the mama and her babies, somewhere on the trail to Rum Ridge.

View from the rock on Rum Ridge.

* * *

Stan watched Joe leave the blind and head towards the trail. Amazingly, the bears returned a few minutes later to forage and play in the meadow. More relaxed knowing where the bears were, and that Joe was headed in the other direction, he sat down on the ridge and ate an apple. He turned to his right and looked down at the lake, thinking about the fishing they'd be doing in a couple of hours. He thought to himself that it didn't get much better than this. He observed the three cubs for a few minutes and then headed back down the ridge trail to be at the base before Joe arrived.

* * *

Joe hurried along the trail, he wasn't concerned about staying quiet to hunt, he was too excited to tell his dad about the bear cubs. The section of the trail from the meadow to the base of the ridge was in rough shape. It had been at least three years since they had done trail maintenance this far from camp. Joe had to watch the brown blazes on the trees closely as the underbrush was starting to retake the path. He also had to climb over a couple of fallen hemlocks. In some spots, there were so many blow downs, he had to leave the trail and make his way around through the woods, being extra careful to not lose his way. Joe knew that his dad had chosen a specific color brown to keep their trail inconspicuous, but with the difficulty spotting the blazes, he considered next spring repainting them bright orange.

Approaching the Rum Ridge trailhead, Joe noticed his dad sitting on a boulder drawing in his journal. He stopped and waited, not knowing if his dad was drawing scenery, or capturing an animal that might scurry off. Joe knew his dad loved to draw. The camp journals were full of pictures he had sketched, along with writings about the subjects he drew. Joe always thought his dad would have made a great writer for an outdoor magazine. As it was, Dad was a sought-after illustrator. Publishers would send Stan drafts of stories, and he would create scenes and bring animals to life on the pages.

A scratching noise on the ground revealed the grouse that was posing under a bush. Joe could think of better uses for that bird than a drawing, especially since they only had cans of beans for dinner if the fish weren't biting. Once the grouse made its way into the bushes, and Stan closed his book, Joe gave a yell.

"Hey, Dad, you'll never guess what happened earlier over in the meadow. There was a mother bear and her cubs." He was so excited telling the story of the bear encounter, he completely left out any mention of the earlier lynx sighting.

Stan said, "I'm proud of you son. That is exactly the way I would have played that situation." He didn't let on that he had watched the entire scene unfold from up on the ridge.

Putting his sketch pad back in his pack, Stan continued, "I bet those three bear cubs will be sticking closer to their mom the next few days."

"I suspect so. They're likely not used to anyone being around," Joe agreed.

Watching his dad zip up his pack, Joe realized he had not mentioned there were three cubs. It was then that he noticed they were standing directly across from the trailhead to the top of Rum Ridge. He looked from the trail to his dad but didn't say anything.

Together they hiked the trail out to Rum Ridge Road. Along the road, next to the old double pine tree, they grabbed their fishing rods that Stan had stowed the prior night on the drive in. Placing the rods along the trail meant they didn't have to hike back to the cabin, and neither of them had to worry about carrying rods on their morning hunting trip. They walked along the road until they reached Lobster Stream and then followed the path that ran along the bank. By one o'clock they were at Duck Pond, one of the few ponds in northern Maine that remained open to fishing until the end of November. Stan and Joe appreciated the late season fishing that gave them the opportunity to catch a fresh dinner.

Along the shore of the pond, in a little cove, the Parkers had long ago constructed a primitive camp site. Stan and his brother had built a 'hang out' table completely from a maple tree that had toppled during a summer microburst. This was not a picnic table, as they did not bring in picnics. The table was used to hang out around while taking breaks from fishing or cooking up some of the days catch. It was rough cut, all by hand with a chainsaw, ax, and bow saw.

A fire pit, made from the rocks found around the pond, was covered with a grill made from the iron grate of an old locomotive. A stainless-steel coffee pot was left in a small metal cabinet, the color of real rust, for anyone who happened by the makeshift camp to use. Stan collected kindling to build a fire, and then made coffee with the water left in his canteen. Joe pulled out a couple of chocolate chip cookies and handed one to his dad. After their snack, they split up along the shore of the pond, within sight distance of one another.

Within minutes of casting, a fish grabbed Joe's lure and took off. Joe let out the line a little and then held the tension. He had a fighter. Once the fish slowed, he started to reel it in.

The pole bent in an arc as Joe expertly pulled back, and then brought the rod forward while spinning the line. Trying to throw the hook, the fish took a jump out of the water. Joe was quick and reeled in the slack. He pulled out a nice lake trout, which was a good start to the makings of a fine dinner.

Stan motioned a clap in Joe's direction, making Joe smile. They fished for an hour or so. By the time they called it quits, Stan had two fish, Joe had four. The sun was getting low in the sky and the cool fall air was turning colder. It would drop below freezing again tonight. Stan checked the fire, dumped water over the last few coals, and covered it with sand to be sure it was out.

Back at the cabin, Joe took Sparky for a quick run down to the stream. On the way, he saw three nice size does walking in the clearing on the opposite shore. That would figure. Luckily, old Sparky was clueless to the deer. At his age there would be no way Sparky could keep up with the pace of a running deer. He would tire out in a quarter of a mile. Just the same, Joe would not have enjoyed chasing after the dog to call him back after he had already been hiking all day. He was hungry and he wanted to sit by the fire and warm up.

By the time Joe and Sparky returned from their walk, Stan had the woodstove roaring and the fish cooking. The trout along with a few red potatoes and green beans made a satisfying meal. After the dishes were washed and put away, Stan put the finishing touches on the grouse sketch from earlier, and Joe finished reading his comic book. They both were in bed early to be well rested to do it all over again the next day.

Memories of Mom

In the morning, eager to get an early start, Joe was up before his dad. He started preparing their breakfast and getting supplies ready for the day. While the water boiled on the stove for the oatmeal, he packed each of them a snack bag with apples and peanut butter sandwiches.

Hearing all the noise, Stan pulled himself out of bed. He stopped in the kitchen doorway with a satisfied smile.

"You're up early, Joe. Thanks for getting breakfast started,"

"No problem, Dad. I was anxious to get going this morning and couldn't sleep."

While Stan finished the morning preparations, Joe took Sparky out for a run down to Kidney Pond. He hated to leave the dog home all day, but even at his age, Sparky had the patience of a puppy when it came to sitting still. It was better to let him sleep in the cabin, rather than trying to keep him quiet out in the woods.

Before heading out, Stan and Joe checked their supplies and filled their canteens. Stan took the opportunity to give Joe a little father to son talk, north woods style.

"And, Joe, I don't need to remind you to be diligent about those bears. If they were there yesterday, there's a good chance the meadow is on their normal daily rounds. A mama bear protecting three cubs can get unpredictable."

"I know, Dad, I'll keep my eyes peeled." Joe thought again about how he had never mentioned there were three cubs in the litter.

"It's probably a good idea as you walk down the trail, to whistle or wear the bear bell your mom gave you. At least until you get close to the blind anyway. You don't want to scare off the deer."

"I think I'll stick to the whistling. I'm a bit old to be wearing a bell. Besides, I tied the bell on Sparky's collar before I let him out last night, just in case something was out prowling around the cabin."

"Oh, that was a good idea." Stan grinned, but didn't mention he had noticed the bell tied to Joe's belt yesterday when they met at Rum Ridge. He picked up his pack and said goodbye to the dog. "Okay, Sparky, we'll be back before dinner."

Sparky, knowing the routine, was already curled up on his blanket and had no response.

Stan latched the door and they headed their separate ways down the paths. Their plan was the same as yesterday – to meet at the base of Rum Ridge around noon.

* * *

Joe decided to hike at a brisk pace to get to the blind before the sun came up over the trees. Maybe the deer made their rounds through the meadow earlier, rather than later. He walked the one and a half miles in less than thirty minutes, not bad for carrying a full pack he thought. Settling in on his log stool, he realized he had worked up a bit of a sweat. He took off his heavy field coat and hung it on a curved maple branch hook.

He was hesitant to take out a comic book, not wanting to be distracted should a bear, or three, wander near. There wasn't much to do but wait. Facing the meadow, he kept twisting his head to check the side of the blind that faced the trail. As he sat there, miles from anyone else, nothing but the forest surrounding him, he had a new appreciation for his mother's favorite saying, *"With the two of you boys, I need to have eyes in the back of my head!"* In her mind, Stan and Joe were always getting mixed up into some kind of trouble around the camp. To them it was all a big adventure and what made for good camp stories.

Watching for deer, and worrying about bears, or something else sneaking up behind him, Joe daydreamed about his mom's favorite 'eyes in the back of her head' story. She would retell the tale at least once a summer, either over breakfast on a rainy day, during a canoe trip lunch stop, around the evening camp fire, or anytime they had first time visitors. The setting for the story was their late afternoon hike over to Lobster Lake the summer Joe was eight. Mom had relived the day so many times, Joe had her version of the story memorized. Even now he could visualize his mom, sitting on a log next to him this cold November morning, telling him about the scare on the trail.

She would start out by saying, "Do you remember the afternoon we headed to the lake for our swim?"

During that particular walk, Mom, as usual, was out front, leading the way and keeping an eye on Sparky who was only a puppy. The dog knew to stay on the camp road, he knew where the trail veered off to the left, and he knew at the end of the trail was the lake, his favorite stick, and if he was lucky, a few ducks to menace. The ducks being the better swimmers would have great fun tormenting Sparky. It was as much a sport for the ducks as it was fun for the pup. The puppy, full of spirit, would run out ahead of Mom, round a bend and then to be sure Mom was still coming, he would stand in the middle of the road with his tail wagging. As soon as he knew she was still there, he would take off again sniffing the side of the road. Louise on the other hand was not in the habit of turning around to see if the stragglers behind her were keeping up.

It was on that day, when Stan, Joe, and Don were walking slowly, talking about the fishing the night before and debating what type of lures the fish might bite on that afternoon.

Joe, always wanting to catch the big one, turned to his friend. "Don, what'd you use to hook that big trout yesterday?"

Don, being a year older than Joe, was in Joe's eyes an expert fisherman. He was also Joe's best friend at camp, or anywhere for that matter. The two were almost inseparable during the summers, and Don would spend weeks at a time at the Parker camp. While he lived in Greenville, he preferred the wilderness near Lobster Lake, his love for the woods instilled in him from his father, who was a Maine Guide. The Parkers appreciated having Don around as it gave Joe, an only child, someone to hang around with.

"It was a *wavy worm*."

"Did you buy it at the Trading Post?"

"Nah, my dad made it."

"Oh."

Don reached into his fishing vest and pulled out a green feathery lure. "I've got an extra. You can have it."

"Thanks!" Joe's eyes went wide as he examined the intricate design of the lure. He couldn't wait to get to the lake and try it out.

By now, the road had made a few twists and turns, and they had no way of seeing Mom and Sparky. When they reached the path that led to Lobster Lake, Stan stopped short and motioned to the boys to not make a sound.

The three of them watched as the limbs on the trees at the side of the trail moved up and down. The air was totally still, not a breeze blowing, and Stan was not sure what to think. He thought it could be a turkey. Or it could be a fox. Or worse, it could be a bear. He never knew what they might stumble across out here in the woods. Whatever it was, it continued to move the branches up and down.

Joe and Don waited, fixated on the moving bushes. Time felt as if it were standing still. Slowly the image came into view.

First a leg. Then the shoulder. Then the head.

Looking right at them with big brown eyes was a moose calf. Her ears were pinned flat along the side of her head. The calf looked curious, as if she wanted to investigate what THEY were up to. It certainly was in no hurry and had no fear of them.

Joe whispered, "She looks young. Where do you think the mother is?"

They didn't have to go looking. A deep grunt came from behind them on the road. In unison they turned. The mother, not looking curious, but rather agitated, stood in the center of the woods road. At shoulder height, she was taller than Stan. She grunted again and raised a hoof, scraping at the weeds on the hump that ran down the center of the road.

Stan slowly lifted his right hand to get the boys attention. "Let's just walk through the brush here and come out on the other side of the calf. We need to move out of the line between her and her baby. If she charges, get behind the biggest tree you can, as quick as possible. Walk slowly, backwards."

As they moved a step back, the mama moose took a step forward. Step for step she followed. Bucking her head as if to motion them along. Her hoof kept pawing at the ground.

The calf was curious, her stare never left Joe as he stepped into the weeds. Then she started to follow him, tracking him along the path.

"Dad, what's this calf doing?"

At that moment a curious puppy came running around the bend. Sparky stopped in his tracks startled at the sight of the two huge animals. A moment later, Mom came around the corner and froze when she saw the calf, and beyond the calf, Stan, Joe, and Don, standing in the roadside weeds. On the far side was the cow looking about ready to charge. Everyone stood still waiting for someone, or some moose, to make the next move.

Sparky decided he needed to take control of this situation. He bolted to Joe's side, for backup, and started barking up a storm at the calf. The calf looked down at this tiny pup, not much bigger than a raccoon, stumbled back, and ran behind her mother. At the sign of victory, Sparky's high pitch barking became more brazen. Reunited, the mother turned and trotted down the road, calf right on her heels.

Mom then spoke up, "With you boys I need to have eyes in the back of my head. Why you can't keep up I'll never know."

She turned, whistled, and headed back towards the lake, Sparky at her side. She yelled over her shoulder, "That whistle is for ALL of you. Let's go!"

Joe's mom would sometimes bend the story to the point that she rescued them by scaring off a mad moose. Even Sparky would groan at that version.

While daydreaming about his mom, the rustling of some leaves brought Joe back to the present. He was not sure how long he was deep in his dream, all he knew was that some time had passed and he was again not paying much attention to his surroundings. He sure could use a set of eyes in the back of his head about now, making him decide that next summer he was going to add a back wall on the blind with a small door.

A woodcock scurried into the meadow, and strutted to about the same spot the bears were yesterday. That started him wondering. While three cubs were not atypical in the area, he was curious how his dad had known there were three of them. Joe's eyes found the rock ledge at the top of Rum Ridge. He had not realized, until now, how unobstructed the view was from the ridge to his hunting blind. Grabbing his binoculars, he zoomed in on the top of the ridge. He could easily make out individual trees. If he could see that clearly to the top, someone up top could certainly see him.

Joe recalled that yesterday, when he met up with his dad, Dad was sitting and writing in his journal across from the Rum Ridge trail. A smile crossed Joe's face when he considered that his dad may have pulled a fast one. Then Joe wondered why his dad would be spying on him.

All of a sudden, Joe felt he was being watched. He drew in a deep breadth when he thought he saw something duck behind a tree in the direction of Beaver Creek, directly behind the blind. He told himself his suspicions were getting to him, and it was probably the wind moving a branch. Feeling a chill, he put his field coat back on. He drew up against the far side of the blind to stay out of direct view from someone, or something, that might be back on the path.

Sitting sideways on his log to watch the meadow and the trail at the same time, he nibbled on a piece of beef jerky. His mind started to race trying to formulate if he saw a person or an animal.

Finding Poachers

Setting out, Stan decided to walk along the road. He figured he could get to Rum Ridge quicker than following the woods trail climbing over downed trees, or navigating iced-over tree roots.

When he passed Duck Pond, he heard a low rumble. At first, he figured it was a Piper Cub flying in the distance. Then he realized it was unmistakably a vehicle, and it was headed his way. Thoughts ran through his mind as to why someone might be driving out here this time of year. There was the chance it could be a hunting party – or even Red and his crew.

Stan stopped and listened. The vehicle didn't sound large enough to be a logging truck, but he thought it could be a company supply vehicle. Those guys drove like maniacs. The beds of their trucks were always crammed full of gas cans to deliver to the chainsaw gangs out in the woods.

The driver was going at a pretty good clip, based on the pitch of the engine, so Stan moved out of the narrow road that was not wide enough for both a vehicle and him. He made his way through the pine saplings and stood behind a boulder. The vehicle came barreling over the hill kicking up stones. Seeing the green sedan, Stan recognized it immediately. The road dust, which had been following the car, started to pass it as Henry slowed down. When Henry hit the brakes, the dirt road may have well been ice the way the cruiser went into a slide – going right past Stan. A cloud of dirt hit Stan before he could cover his nose and eyes.

The local Game Warden, Henry Ford, no relation to the automobile manufacturer, lived back towards town. The Parkers were introduced to Henry through Stan's father, George, who had known Henry long before he became a warden. When Stan was little, his father would take him for ice cream at the pharmacy, where Henry worked behind the soda fountain serving up sundaes and root beer floats. Later in life, Henry and Stan became hunting partners, enjoying their time out in the north woods together.

Since Henry grew up in the Moosehead area, he knew every back road, trail, and hidden pond. He loved being a game warden and said his job was a dream come true, especially since he was assigned to patrol his home district. It wasn't a hard district to get back then, no other wardens wanted to live this far out in the woods. If by chance they entertained the idea, their wives were sure to put a stop to the fantasy. Henry's wife, Alice, on the other hand, didn't need any selling. She picked out her new fishing pole and winter underwear before Henry was even guaranteed the job.

Henry jammed the car into reverse and backed up. His sedan was beat up, dented, scratched, and dirty. To be a Maine Game Warden in the early 1950s you had to supply your own vehicle. Henry had bought a used state police cruiser that was headed for the junkyard. After he finished restoring the engine, he painted the exterior a dark evergreen. He thought it helped him blend in with the woods when he was doing surveillance. The first morning Henry left on official business, Alice said the car looked almost brand new. By the time Henry came home that evening, he had already had a flat, the muffler had been ripped off, and the rear passenger side quarter panel was dented from taking the turn by Crash Corner a little too fast. Even the logging truck drivers would shake their heads when they saw Henry driving down these dirt roads in his not-meant-for-off-roading vehicle.

The driver's side window rolled down, a hand shot out, and a finger pointed at Stan.

"I thought I saw your truck drive through town the night before last. Why didn't you let me know you were coming up? Where's Joe? And that old dog of yours? How long ya staying?"

Stan was use to the interrogating style of his friend, it was always the same, no matter if he was talking to Alice, a friend, or a poacher, he was all questions, all the time. It was a wonder someone could get a word in to answer.

Stan walked over to the car and shook Henry's hand. To Stan, it appeared Henry hadn't changed in twenty years, other than a few more wrinkles and more gray hair. Although, maybe he looked the same because Stan always saw him wearing his green warden cap and uniform.

"Good to see you, Henry. Sorry, we thought we'd have time to stop in on our way up the other night, but we got a late start. Joe's off hunting on his own this year. He's sixteen now you know. How's Alice?"

"Where's the dog? How long ya staying?" Henry repeated, not letting Stan off on answering every question.

"Sparky's back at the cabin. These long early morning walks in the cold are hard on him. And with his lack of patience, he doesn't make a good hunting partner. We plan to be up through Thursday morning. We have an invite to Louise's sister's house for turkey dinner this year."

Now that Stan had answered Henry's interrogation, he answered Stan's question.

"Good to hear the boy and dog are well. Alice is great. We've missed seeing you around. She has her hands full this fall. We have an injured moose who is enjoying the easy life of three square meals a day and a clean bed of hay every night. We don't think she's going to ever leave the pen in our yard. Why don't you get in out of the cold?"

Stan put his gear in the backseat of the cruiser that was already packed with Henry's extra jacket, a sleeping bag, rifle, fishing pole, and rain gear. Given the outside temperature was only in the high twenties, Stan was glad to be in the car.

Henry pulled a thermos out from behind the seat. "Would you like a coffee, Stan?"

"Sure would. I didn't make any this morning."

"There's a spare cup there in that sack on the back seat."

Henry filled Stan's cup and topped off his own. They slowly drank their coffee and talked, catching up on the news since last seeing one another in September. Stan told Henry about the mother bear and her three cubs. Henry filled Stan in on the success of hunters over the past several weeks of the season.

Henry reached into a paper bag he had next to him on the seat. "Alice made these sweet buns this morning, give one a try."

Stan took a bite and was reminded of the sweet treats Louise would stuff in his day pack for his fishing and hunting trips.

"Delicious. You have a good woman there. She can run your wildlife park and cook."

"Yep, she's a keeper all right. But this morning she gave me all sorts of heck for making a ruckus when I came in at one in the morning waking her up. She complains, but I know she wasn't sleeping. She never closes her eyes 'til I'm home. The life of a game warden's wife it is."

"Why were you out so late?"

"Routine night hunting surveillance. Didn't see anyone." Henry started into his second sweet bun. "So where's Joe off hunting?"

"Remember the blind he built in the meadow over by Lost Swamp?"

"Oh yeah. He should be safe there."

Stan frowned, thinking that was a curious response to Joe's location.

"Why wouldn't he be safe anywhere around here? He knows these woods almost as well as I do."

"Not as good as I do, young man," Henry was quick to interject. "I wouldn't be too worried, the meadow's in an unknown and not easy to get to location. We've had several characters up here the past few weeks. Last year, I suspected the same bunch of some shady hunting practices. I never could catch them, but I had a tip they were night hunting last week with their truck headlights. I happened to be at the tagging station the morning they came in. They swore they shot the deer they had in the back of their truck at first light, but the deer had to be dead a good six to seven hours."

"Do you have a hunch they're hunting up here around our land?"

Even though the woods belonged to the logging company, a conglomerate from a province in Canada, Stan always referred to the land around the Parker camp as "ours." With no other cabin around, they were the only family who lived out here, if only for the summers.

The Maine pulp and paper company that originally issued Stan's dad the lease, wrote it for ninety-nine years. So, when Royal Pulp and Paper purchased the unorganized territory land, they asked Stan to name a price.

"Your check can't fit that many zeros," Stan responded in a letter. There was no chance he was giving up the property, especially figuring they'd be the only ones here. Stan, being a natural negotiator, was able to add another ninety-nine years on the lease in exchange for filing a land report twice a year. He couldn't believe his luck. All he had to do was keep tabs on wildlife activity and watch for species that might cause tree destruction, stuff he did anyway while out hiking.

Henry responded, "Those poachers could be anywhere up here. I was parked out by the trading post this morning and I saw them drive by. I followed at a distance, but after we were on the Golden Road, I lost them. There aren't too many roads they could have gone down up here, but taking any one of them would give them good cover for hours. It's not easy chasing their half ton pick-up in this here boat that almost drags on the ground."

Without even taking a breath, Henry continued, "Have you heard? The warden service is thinking about issuing cruisers. Sedans no less. Those guys in Augusta have no clue about the roads up here. We need trucks. They can give the cruisers to the state police. Those guys drive those nice paved roads on the interstate. I need a working vehicle up here."

Ignoring Henry's rant, Stan asked, "Have you seen these guys around here before?"

"Oh sure. And so have you. Remember the crew we nicknamed the Lobster Lake Bandits last summer?"

"Those guys? The 46' Ford, red flannel, and long johns in the middle of summer. Sure, I remember them. They blew by Joe and I on the Golden Road the other night."

"Hmm. They're a wild bunch. By the way, that tip you gave me last summer about the buckets they stored under the alders along the stream was terrific. How'd you know about that?"

"We were eating lunch at the Lock, Stock, and Barrel when I overheard the four of them talking up a storm about how they fooled the game warden. It was the day we dropped off that rabid fox." Drinking another cup of coffee, Stan filled Henry in on how the fox assisted in locating the Bandits.

Stan and Joe came across the fox on their way to the lake for their evening swim. They were hustling to catch up to Louise and Sparky, who as usual were way ahead. Stan and Joe never made it to the lake because the infamous fox chased them all the way back to the cabin. Louise added this story to her collection of 'eyes in the back of her head' tales about her boys.

The menacing fox snarled from the porch steps, and wouldn't let them leave. Stan had to get his rifle and put the animal down. He boxed up the fox, and the next day delivered it over to Henry's place.

Henry and Alice Ford had a yard that doubled as a makeshift zoo. Over the years, Henry had built pens from any wood and fencing he could find. They had corrals in the back yard, side yard, and along the driveway for injured animals to recover in. At any one time, the Fords might be caring for deer, turkeys, foxes, dogs, turtles, and raccoons – sometimes all at once. The garage Henry had built, to house his personal warden vehicle in the winter, had long been converted to stalls and meshed bird cages. They had owls, ravens, and even an eagle once recuperating in the garage turned animal hospital. Alice deserved much of the credit since she stayed home and cared for the animals while Henry was out patrolling day and night sometimes.

Louise always told Alice that she must love and adore the man with what she put up with. Alice didn't think anything of it. She loved living in the north woods, and being the wife of a game warden suited her. She'd help anyone with whatever they needed. Locals and tourists would stop by to ask Henry all sorts of questions they figured a game warden should be able to answer. Being Henry was usually out on patrol, or fishing, Alice became a woods educator and animal nurse all in one.

A stall once even held a bobcat, or attempted to. The bobcat, which had been hit by a car, was brought to the Ford's to recover. Alice asked Henry what he intended to do with the bobcat once it regained its strength. Henry was never one for worrying that far ahead. It didn't matter, because the next morning when Alice opened the garage door, the bobcat jumped down from a rafter and bolted out the door. Feathers from two recovering turkeys and a grouse were left on the floor. Henry was upset that the bobcat robbed him of a nice poultry feast. Alice reminded Henry that if he wanted such a meal he had better get out on the trail and do his own hunting, there would be no eating of those under their care.

Alice drew the line on caring for certain species after someone dropped off two adult skunks. They left the package on her porch and drove away. The spray narrowly missed her when she opened the lid. The stink lingered for weeks, even after washing down the porch every day with bleach and tomato juice. She made Henry paint a sign and nail it to a tree in the driveway. It read, "NO SKUNKS ACCEPTED!"

The day the Parkers delivered the fox, Stan turned into the Ford's driveway and reading the sign, he half joked, "I wonder if with what we are dropping off, Alice is going to make Henry update that sign. Hopefully, she doesn't turn us away after this long drive into town."

Getting to the Ford's from camp was a fifty-mile round trip that would take all day, partly due to the dirt roads, but mostly because Louise and Joe would spend hours looking around in the Trading Post. Joe would shop for lures and talk to the Maine Guides who hung around the sporting goods counter. Louise would pick out fabrics for her sewing hobby.

Seeing the Parkers pull into the rocky-gravel driveway, Alice gave a wave from near the deer pen where she was spreading hay. As soon as they were out of the truck, she gave Louise a big hug. If Henry and Stan were like brothers, Alice and Louise were as close as sisters could possibly be.

Joe ran over to the pen where three small deer were lying down. The smallest doe walked over to the fence to greet him.

Handing Joe a carrot from her apron so he could feed the fawn, Alice told the Parkers that a family out hiking had brought her this newest addition. The vacationers, not used to the ways of the woods, had assumed the fawn had been lost.

"I had to explain to them that the mama deers purposely leave their young hidden in the brush, and it was not abandoned at all. But now that they had touched the deer, and put it in their car, the fawn could not go back to the woods. At its young age, it could not survive without the care of its mother. Sometimes I think I need to offer nature classes to the tourists before we allow them in the woods. Let's go sit down out of this sun."

Alice led them onto the back porch where she poured lemonade and brought out cookies she had baked that morning. Not wanting to jump right down to business, Stan didn't bring up the fox in the box right away. He sipped his drink and asked, "Is Henry expected around today, Alice?"

Alice's face became serious. "I suspected this wasn't purely a social call. I was wondering when you were going to get around to mentioning what was in the box in the bed of your truck."

"We had a run in with a fox."

Alice stood and started towards the steps. "We can't leave it sitting in the summer sun, Stan!"

Louise touched Alice's arm.

Alice's face grew grim. "Oh." She looked at Stan.

Stan nodded.

"If it has passed, why drive it all the way here and not just bury it out in the woods?" asked Alice.

"It appears that the fox may have been rabid. It was behaving strange and chased us all the way from Lobster Lake back to the cabin. It would not go away or leave the porch."

"That does sound strange. Henry has mentioned a rise in rabid animals this year. The state wildlife management is not yet sure why."

"He mentioned that to me a few weeks back. He asked me to keep a watch out, and if I had to kill any animals behaving strange, he wanted to have them to be tested."

"Great, more drop-offs to be excited about." She continued, "Henry said he had to go check on a fishing party up near Ripogenus Dam. They were over their catch limit twice already. They gave him some sad excuses as to how they lost count. He said if he finds them over again, that'll be their third strike, and he's gonna pull their licenses and fine them. Told me this morning he'd be back by supper."

"Do you want me to put the box in the shed to keep it out of the sun?" asked Stan.

"Sure as heck wouldn't want it in my kitchen, now would I?" Alice said with a hint of sarcasm.

Louise and Alice drank a second glass of ice-cold lemonade and chatted, while Joe helped out filling water troughs and adding straw to the stalls.

Stan, meanwhile, placed the box in the shed and latched the door. He then wrote a note and dropped it in the message box that Henry had secured on the porch railing. It was a homemade pine box with a hinged lid. The painted lettering on the side read, "Messages for the Warden."

Stan wrote:

> One rabid fox. From near Lobster Lake.
>
> Stan Parker, August 15

Before heading back to camp, Stan took Louise and Joe to lunch at the Lock, Stock, and Barrel diner. A crew of rough looking men were at the next booth laughing and having a grand old time. Stan couldn't help but hear them as they talked about duping the game warden. They laughed to one another about how easily "ol' Ford was fooled" when they hid some of their catch in buckets under the alders by the shore. Stan grew suspicious and listened closely.

After lunch the men were standing around their trucks when the Parkers came out of the diner. Stan made a command decision to try and find out a bit more about these men.

"Nice Ford. What's it a '47?"

"'46 Half Ton," said a burly man in a long sleeve red flannel shirt and green work pants, obviously annoyed that Stan could make such a mistake.

As Stan considered his next move, he felt a bead of sweat roll down his back. The midday summer sun was baking the packed dirt of Pritham Avenue. Stan wondered how this Paul Bunyan of a man was not even breaking a sweat.

The man bellowed on. "Bought it exactly a year to the day before Henry himself died. April seventh. Great man and great truck."

"Not like the local Ford. Right Red?" said the youngest with a smirk. The others laughed, except Red, who scowled in the kid's direction.

"Those are some nice poles in the bed there. You guys on a fishing trip?" Stan asked.

"Yep, up on Lobster Lake, right near the stream outlet," volunteered the youngest, this time taking an elbow in the side from Red for the remark.

"Must be good fishing this time of year up that way. Good luck." Stan politely ended the conversation now that he had the information he needed. On their way back to camp, he detoured back to Henry's place.

Alice met him at his truck. "Henry's not back Stan."

"That's okay, Alice, I just need to add something on the note."

"You can tell me, I'm not that forgetful."

"I really want him to read it."

He hustled over to the message box, Alice right on his heels.

He pulled out his note and added a final sentence.

One rabid fox. From near Lobster Lake.

Stan Parker, August 15

P.S. – Lobster Stream outlet – fishing – <u>check under the alders.</u>

"What does that mean?" Alice quizzed, reading over his shoulder.

"Henry will understand. See you soon, Alice." Stan headed back to the truck, proud of his detective skills.

Sitting in Henry's cruiser, with the heater blasting, Henry nodded and refilled Stan's coffee cup.

"I remember that fox. The lab sent me a letter saying it tested positive for rabies. Luckily, we didn't get too many more cases last summer. Hikers simply don't know what to do when they happen along one of those crazed animals. The situation can get dangerous. Warden Tapper was bit by a raccoon once, and had to get the shots. I pray I never have to go through that."

Henry then remembered about Stan's note. "And by the way that was a great tip you left me. I sat there drinking a lemonade on the porch that night trying to piece together what the heck you were trying to tell me. It's bad enough I have all these investigations going on and you leave me partial clues to chase down. It's a good thing law breakers are not all that smart. It would make my job out here a lot harder."

Stan laughed. "Did you find them?"

"Sure did."

"Well, there you go. It was enough of a clue then wasn't it?"

"I reckon so," Henry said, with a laugh.

"I was headed out to meet Joe up by Rum Ridge about noon," Stan told Henry. "Do you think I need to worry about him and instead head over to the meadow?"

"If you did, you'd likely scare off any deer in the area and blow his chances today. Those guys are lazy as all heck. If I was to find their truck parked along here somewhere, they wouldn't be too far from it. I haven't seen anyone yet this morning. The problem I have is checking all the side trails that are big enough to hide a vehicle from me. And that's exactly what I'd suspect from a gang of poachers."

Henry shook his head, and looking off into the woods went on. "They might be sitting off the road, in the brush laughing, as I drive by. They love to tell stories over at the diner on how they fooled ol' Ford." Henry paused, and then added, "I wouldn't worry too much about Joe back by his blind."

"Well, I'll tell you something. Yesterday, I went up to the ledge at the top of Rum Ridge, and with my binoculars I could see Joe sitting in his blind. I felt a little guilty about spying on him, but I wanted to see his first solo deer hunt."

"That's understandable. If you want, we could walk up there together right now to have a look. It's a short hike. That'll give me a good view of the perimeter roads too. Who knows, I might see something interesting."

Stan nodded. "It'll be good to have company on the hike." Taking a drink of coffee, Stan asked, "Henry, if you were to come across Red and the Bandits, what are you going to do?"

"Ah, nothing really, unless I was to find some incriminating evidence on them. Mostly, I want them to see I'm here to keep them honest. Last night, I parked out by Lazy Tom Bog thinking that might be a place they would light up with their headlights. The only bandit sighting I had all night was a family of raccoons walking along the road as if they owned the place."

Stan noticed a look of disappointment on Henry's face.

Henry took a final gulp from his thermos cup, and continued about his surveillance techniques. "Sometimes I get lucky, other times I'm just waiting around. Let's go take that hike. It'll do me good to get out of this car and walk a bit."

Henry flicked the remaining coffee sludge and grinds that were stuck to the bottom of the cup out the window. He started up the car, made a U-turn, and accelerated back towards Rum Ridge. Stan grabbed the dashboard as the car kicked up gravel.

Bird Calls

To get his vehicle far enough off the road, Henry pulled up on an incline near the trail. Stan had to push with all his might to open the heavy door and step out. He had to jog to keep up with Henry, who was leading the way as if he had an urgent appointment on the top of the mountain. Reaching the summit in record time, Stan couldn't believe that Henry wasn't even winded. The man was in great shape.

The two old friends knew the Lobster Lake Bandits were a sly bunch, so they crept along the ridge keeping to the cover of the trees. Thinking like the expert woodsmen they were, Henry and Stan took spots behind neighboring large white pines to keep out of sight. Each peered down into the meadow with their binoculars.

"That's strange, Joe's looking out the back of the blind," Henry said.

"I see that. He's looking toward the creek trail. I wonder what's up. Could be the bears again."

Henry moved behind a tree closer to the edge of the ridge. "Bears or bandits, neither a good scenario. Red is harmless, but likes to put the fear into people."

Stan scanned along the edge of the meadow and even with the sun almost directly overhead, the dense trees were difficult to see through.

* * *

Joe turned up his coat collar. The biting wind was blowing directly through the openings he had left for viewing ports. Other than the wind whistling through the branches, everything else was quiet and still. It was too cold for even the year-round winged residents to get moving this morning. With all the hardwoods bare of leaves, the sun shone down into the blind. Even this late in the year, the slight warmth of the rays felt great to Joe.

Sitting along the side wall, Joe could watch the field, and with a slight twist of his head, he could see out the rear of the blind. He thought if a bear was to corner him, he could jump out over the wall. Then looking at the feeble structure, he had second thoughts about the logs being able to support his weight, especially given the structure was built from fallen trees and thick limbs.

Joe spent last summer dragging the wood that had fallen on the Beaver Creek Trail to the meadow. Each morning he would pack a lunch, grab an axe, a bow saw, and whistle for Sparky to come along and keep him company. He'd cut the largest logs to length, added notches at the ends, and fit each one together. He wasn't after a tight-fitting cabin, but he needed it to not blow down before hunting season. He knew if he paid enough attention to the details, the blind would last several years. With the cold temperatures, he was glad to have his shelter.

As the wind blew through the pines, Joe heard a bird, but to his trained ear he knew immediately the call was only a bad imitation. A chill ran down his back as a second, even worse imitation call, responded. Joe was one hundred percent certain it was someone making the calls, and not a bird. His dad had taught him many bird calls over the years. It was their way to alert one another when they were out hiking, so as not to spook an animal before the other could get a look. They each had a call they had mastered. He would know his dad's unique call amidst a migration of gold finches singing, as his dad would know his. They would often sit at the camp fire practicing. Each was so proficient with their calls, they had tied for the 'Best Bird Call' at Woodsmen's Days five years in a row.

After the Parker family winning streak, the organizers asked if they would honor the town by being judges for the competition. The head chairperson said, "With your talent, you both will be excellent judges." Stan knew it was to give others a chance at winning the contest. Joe was disappointed that he would no longer win the prize – a coupon book for five free ice cream cones from the Dairy Shack. Stan convinced him it was an honor to be a judge, and then he surprised Joe with a homemade coupon book worth five ice cream cones and a bonus sundae.

With his trained ear, Joe listened and wondered who was making the poor bird calls. The first had come from the north side of the meadow, near Lost Swamp. The second came from behind him, out on Beaver Creek Trail. He figured it must be two hunters, yet it unnerved him to know there were other people, people he probably didn't know, so close to him. He was mostly concerned to know how many there were, and if they were safe hunters.

The first caller, called again, making what Joe thought was a pitiful dove call. The second caller, who was attempting an owl, if the owl had a frog in its throat, came from behind the blind on the trail. If this was the annual competition, these guys would be booed off the steps of the school house. People around here took their bird calls and moose calls seriously. The locals made no attempt at being nice to competitors who couldn't carry a call.

Joe strained his eyes looking for movement or anything out of the ordinary. The sun was casting shadows making it difficult to see. Suddenly, he realized he didn't imagine something ducking behind a tree earlier. Through the trees, he spotted a man directly across the trail from the back of the blind. Shivering, Joe stared, trying not to move.

The silence was broken with the rumble of a vehicle on the Golden Road, headed in the direction of town.

* * *

Up on the ridge, Stan said to Henry, "I'll be right back. That coffee has me needing to visit Mother Nature." Stan backed away down the trail.

Scanning with his state issued, low power binoculars, Henry spotted a dust cloud on the road behind Lost Swamp. Whoever was driving was headed in the direction of town. He moved his binoculars ahead of the cloud by a few hundred feet to a clearing where he could see the road. His heart beat faster anticipating that it would be the Bandits. Within seconds, the '46 red Ford pickup entered his field of vision. The driver, which had to be Red, must have had the accelerator pressed to the floor. The truck was only visible for two seconds before it disappeared again behind the trees.

Stan was coming out from behind a tree as Henry was passing him, all packed up.

"What's the rush?"

"Just saw the Bandits!"

"In the meadow? And Joe?"

"Nah, far off by Crash Corner in their truck. Heading out the Golden Road."

"Okay, be safe. I'm going to stay up here a bit. I still have a couple of hours before I need to meet up with Joe." The two shook hands and Henry was down the trail in a flash. He was a warden on a mission.

Looking down from Rum Ridge towards Lost Swamp

Henry ran down the Rum Ridge Trail at a pace way too fast for his age. He was at his car in under ten minutes. This was a record he'd be sure not to tell Alice about. He jumped into his cruiser all out of breath. His heart was pumping hard, partially due to running down the mountain, but mostly due to the adrenaline of the chase. He fumbled in his right pocket for his keys. Nothing. He checked his left pocket. Nothing. Then he checked his coat. Nothing. With panic setting in that he'd dropped the keys somewhere on the trail, he looked down and noticed them dangling from the ignition.

He turned the key. Nothing.

"Son of a poacher."

He pumped the accelerator twice and tried again. The old engine whined and complained but finally turned over. With a strong hunch Red was up to no good, he pressed down on the gas pedal and shot down the road determined to find out where he was headed.

* * *

Red was driving down the Golden Road near the Caribou Lake boat launch, when Junior yelled out, "Look out!"

Red had been speeding right down the center of the road, not paying attention as he tried to light a cigarette. The oncoming black truck swerved to the side and crashed directly into a stand of new growth balsam and fir saplings. Red never even slowed down.

"That'll teach 'em to pay more attention." Red laughed as he looked in the rear-view mirror.

There was no way Junior was going to mention that it was totally Red's fault. Junior looked back over his shoulder, feeling sorry for the man who might now be stranded on the side of the road.

The driver of the pickup backed slowly out of the ditch. His truck was running rough. He stepped out to assess the damage. Walking around the back, he noticed a section of his tail pipe in the weeds. He picked it up and threw it in the bed of the truck. He had no time to deal with that now. Right now, he had an urgent tip to chase down.

He proceeded down the Golden Road, headed towards Lobster Lake, his truck putting along with a double backfire every so often.

* * *

Stan leaned on a tree and focused on the blind. He could only see the top of Joe's green hunting hat. Taking the binoculars away from his eyes, he rubbed the lenses with the bottom of his shirt, to clear a smudge. When he looked up, a deer was walking directly across the center of the meadow. He looked through the binoculars to get a closer look. It was a nice size doe. She had apparently been eating well all summer and fall. The deer's coat was a deep amber with the characteristic patch of white running from her neck to under her chin.

He zoomed on the blind and thought, "Why wasn't Joe setting up for a shot? Was he reading his comic books again?"

The doe walked off into the woods.

Disappointed that Joe missed the shot, Stan focused his view on the road to get a glimpse of Henry in hot pursuit of Red's truck.

Instead of seeing Henry, Stan was surprised to see a black pickup truck. It was a truck he'd never seen before. He jerked his head back in surprise when he heard two shots ring out in the direction of the road. He laughed once he realized that the truck he was watching was backfiring. So much for a peaceful day hunting.

* * *

Joe never saw the deer that crossed the meadow because his eyes were focused on the person crouched down, binoculars in hand, looking right back at him. He was going to yell out, "Hello?" when the dove call came again, this time twice in a row. In hunter code, this meant, "What's keeping you!" The man rose, glared into the blind at Joe, and took off down the trail, making no attempt to be quiet.

Joe took a deep breath. The woods were silent once again. This lasted only a couple of minutes until Joe heard the rumble of a loud vehicle. Whatever type of car or truck it was, it putted roughly and was backfiring. It had the growl of a motorcycle but the timing of a lawnmower. Joe surmised it was missing a muffler by the PaPaPa, PaPaPa, rrr, BangBang sounds it was making. He knew there was no way the person he saw on the trail could have made it to a vehicle already.

Joe wanted to know who the man was that took off down the trail. And if, whoever was driving around out on the road was not the bird callers, then who else was out here? All this activity had Joe on high alert. He was completely ignoring the meadow and the reasons he was here – deer. He thought that not since he and his dad unsuccessfully chased an elusive buck for three hunting seasons, had there been so much suspense at camp.

When Joe heard another vehicle back behind Lost Swamp, he forgot all about hunting, stood up, and listened as the sound drifted off into the distance. With all the racket, he figured he'd have no luck hunting. He checked the time; it was already ten o'clock. Taking a long drink from his canteen, he gazed up at Rum Ridge. If his dad was going to make for the ridge, Joe knew he'd be up there by now. He sat back down on his log.

As the minutes ticked by, he sat still, listening for any odd sounds. After finally convincing himself the birdmen were gone, he headed towards the Rum Ridge meeting point.

* * *

The two bird callers leisurely strolled to their truck they had hidden down a skidder path near the swamp.

"I think I may have frightened that kid."

"What'd you do, Al?" asked Moose.

"Nothin. I was only looking through my binoculars at him when you let out the bird call to come meet you."

"Did he get a good look at you?"

"Nah, I was behind a tree."

"You'd better hope not. Red will kill us if someone identifies us out here."

"Speaking of grumpy Big Red, we'd better head to town and meet him and Junior at the diner. You know how sore he gets if we're late."

"Yep. First help me dump these barrels in this pond so we can tell Grumpy Red we took care of this batch."

When they finished, they jumped in Al's green pickup and sped towards town.

* * *

Stan saw Joe gather his stuff and head for the trail. Not wanting to get caught spying, he hiked down and headed towards Bug Bog. He wanted to give Joe enough time to reach the meeting point before he walked back.

Going Fishing

To save time, but mostly to not run into anyone who might be lingering on the Beaver Creek Trail, Joe walked diagonally across the meadow to pick up the ridge trail. As he walked, he thought about that man he saw. The distance through the trees was too far to see the man's face clear enough to describe him. He now wished he had been brave enough to pick up his binoculars and look right at the man. He told himself the man was another hunter, who chose not to disturb Joe's hunt. It would be common hunter courtesy not to call out and scare off any game.

Joe reached the base of the ridge trail at eleven o'clock. Sitting on a cold boulder, Joe had a feeling that his dad might be up top looking down on the meadow. He dropped his pack a bit off the trail, leaned his gun up against a tree, and took a drink from his canteen. Thinking he could catch his dad and give him something to explain, he headed up to the ridge.

He jogged up the trail with his binoculars in one hand and his canteen in the other, making it to the top in under ten minutes. Standing in the sun on the rock ledge, he felt warmer. He laughed to himself as he noticed a large doe right in the center eating what was left of the wildflower stubs. Within a moment another two does walked across the meadow, coming from directly behind the blind.

He reached for his shouldered rifle.

"Crud!" Immediately, he remembered he left it down at the bottom. He would have liked to spot the deer through his scope. If the wind was calm, he might have even taken a shot. Making a shot from here on the ridge, would become camp legend. It figures. He wondered if the deer were watching *him* and waited for him to leave.

He sat down on the smooth rock and enjoyed the heat of the sun for a moment. It was one of his favorite spots. He thought about how much being at the camp, the meadow, and lake meant to him. It was the best place in the world as far as he was concerned. Noticing the time, he picked up his canteen and binoculars, and headed back down to meet his dad.

* * *

Today, Joe was the one waiting at the meeting point before his Dad arrived.

"How was the hunt today, my boy?" said Stan, walking up to Joe.

"It sure was interesting. No bears. No deer. But I had some strangers out on the creek trail."

"What? Who were they? Did you recognize any of them?" Stan's interrogation put Joe on edge.

"Nah, Dad. I didn't really get a good look through the trees. I think there were two of them based on the bird calls they were sending each other." Joe downplayed his earlier apprehension.

"I met up with Henry Ford earlier. He was scouting some possible poachers." Stan kept his voice calm so as not to alarm Joe.

"Oh. How is Henry? I wish I could have seen him."

Joe enjoyed Henry's company. Henry often told Joe how in his job, he was able to help animals, protect nature, and teach people how to respect the wildlife and the land. In Joe's memory, some of the best campfires they ever had were when Henry was there to tell his tales. He told stories about bears, skunks, deer, and moose, all made funnier because the animal characters were often mixed up together somehow in the same story. The stories Joe wanted to hear most were about poachers Henry had caught red handed. The element of danger and surprise intrigued Joe as a young boy, to the point that he was not sure if he would be afraid of a poacher, or ticked off should he ever meet one.

"You know, Dad, when I was in the blind this morning, I heard three different vehicles. I bet one was Henry's green turtle."

Joe and his dad had nicknamed Henry's green sedan, "The Green Turtle." Although, they'd never let Henry hear them talking about it that way. It was so dented on the sides and top it looked like a turtle shell. Henry was particularly sore about the dents in the roof. There was one large dent that was so big you could notice it sitting inside the car. Henry had come across a blow down on a road he needed to drive down for no specific reason. He parked the turtle too close to where he was sawing. As he cut through the last of the trunk of the pine, a rogue wind, as Henry tells the story, came up with such force the tree jumped and landed on the roof of his cruiser. The tree hit the roof with a thud, leaving the windshield and windows unharmed. Henry then had to climb up on the roof to saw the limbs apart, his boots leaving further imprints and dents.

"I suspect one of those vehicles was certainly Henry. He said he was chasing down the Lobster Lake Bandits, so you probably heard Red's pickup as well." Stan did not let on that he and Henry were together up on the ridge earlier.

"A third vehicle was definitely missing its muffler," Joe remarked.

"You don't say. I suspect Henry will swing back and fill us in on what's going on. If not, we'll make a quick stop at his house on our way home Thursday morning. It'll also be nice to see Alice. Why don't we head over to the pond and catch our lunch."

"Okay by me. I'm pretty hungry."

They started their hike down the trail. The fall sky was a light blue, with large white clouds breaking the sun now and then. A wild wind was blowing, making the trees along the trail whip and sway. Stan considered what Joe said about hearing bird calls, and a vehicle that was missing its muffler. He wondered who it might have been in the black truck he heard backfiring on the road earlier, and if it wasn't anyone from the Bandits, then who else might it have been.

Joe and Stan fished from their hangout spot on Duck Pond. Within minutes Joe had caught a brook trout and placed it in his basket. Stan reeled one in right after that. While Joe continued to fish, Stan prepared their lunch. He peeled and diced two potatoes he had stowed in his sack this morning. He placed them on a skillet with a bit of rendered bacon fat.

With the fish in the pan cooking, Stan watched Joe fishing. The pond looked like a painting with the sun reflecting off the crystal blue of the water. The only sound was the rhythmic whoosh of the waves against the rocky rip rap shoreline. He looked down to flip the fish.

"Dad!" Joe screamed from down by the rocks.

Stan jerked his head quickly to see Joe jumping from rock to rock holding the line in his hand. At the end of the line a fish was swinging to and fro. Stan was shocked. Joe knew better than that. Running with a fish on a hook was a sure way to lose a meal. Never mind that Louise would have scolded him for running across wet slippery rocks. When Joe reached the fire pit he held the fish up for Stan to see.

"Wow, that's not a good catch from Duck Pond."

Which was exactly what Joe was thinking. At the end of Joe's line hung an eight-inch perch. Duck Pond was a prime spot for trout, catching a perch here could spell disaster for the pond.

"Dad, do you think they migrated here on their own?"

"That's unlikely. They would have had to be introduced to this pond. In all the years we've had this camp, and your grandfather before us, that's the first perch ever caught here."

"Do you think there might be more?"

"It's a certainty. Where there's one, there's many." Stan was not happy about the perch being in the pond. If the perch were here, he knew it wouldn't be long before they would swim up into Lobster lake, if they hadn't already done so. Not much could be done about this today. He would have to talk it over with Henry to see what he knew. No sense stewing over the catch, a perch was a good tasting fish, and pulling it out meant one less to disturb the native trout population.

With the fish frying, the potatoes sizzling, and the coffee percolating, the crisp fall air was soon filled with the smells of a great meal. As much as the hunting, Joe looked forward to eating outdoors. He was going to miss not having fresh fish to eat the next couple of months, at least until ice fishing season anyway.

After eating, they fished for their dinner. Joe pulled out three more perch, and his dad caught two.

"Guess we can have fish chowder tonight, huh, Dad?"

Although alarmed at the catch, Stan had to admit he enjoyed eating perch.

They walked back to the cabin, put their catch in the fridge, and took Sparky out for a walk. The entire walk, Stan couldn't stop thinking about who it was that Joe might have seen on the trail earlier. Along with that, he worried about the perch in Duck Pond, and he worried about Henry out chasing Red and his gang. Henry was no longer a young duckling.

With daylight fading and the sun disappearing behind the mountains, it was getting cold, so they picked up the pace and headed back to warm up in the cabin.

"I'm starving," Joe said, as they walked up the porch steps.

"You just ate two fish and a full plate of potatoes a few hours ago." Stan was impressed with his growing son's appetite.

"Yeah, but they were tiny once they were cleaned. Besides, I've been up since five o'clock and out here hiking all day."

"Then, let's get cleaned up and cook up those perch. I'm looking forward to that fish chowder."

The two worked fast together making their supper. Joe, as the prep chef, chopped onions, carrots, potatoes, and celery. Sparky sat at Joe's feet, begging for pieces of carrot.

Stan lit the old propane oven, and while it heated, he cooked a slab of bacon in a pan. He saved most of the bacon for the morning, less two strips that he and Joe had to eat right then, one Sparky played dead for, and two crispy pieces he set aside for topping the chowder. To the bacon fat he added diced potatoes, the vegetables, and seasoned it all with salt and pepper. Once the vegetables had cooked, he added the fish.

While the chowder base simmered, he whipped up a batch of his no-rise, quick drop biscuits. In a large bowl he added a cup of flour, a quarter teaspoon of salt, a tablespoon of sugar, two teaspoons of baking powder, some butter, and a cup of milk. He beat the ingredients with an ancient bent fork until most of the lumps were gone. He reached for the oversized spoon that was hanging on a black iron hook next to the sink. As he held it, he could see his own mother standing in exactly the same spot, with the same spoon, grabbed from the same hook, to drop large balls of the same dough recipe, on the same cast iron pan he was using. Once he had six biscuits in the bacon-fat greased pan, in the oven they went for fifteen minutes at 450 degrees, which was an imprecise temperature for the old oven, but close enough for camp biscuits.

While the biscuits baked, Stan added milk and a can of corn to the chowder pot, and then together they peeled apples. Joe dumped the apples in a baking pan and covered them with a topping he made from sugar, flour, oatmeal, and butter.

Once the biscuits were done, Stan placed the pan of apple crisp in the oven to heat through. Closing the oven door, Stan thought about how he was always amazed at watching Louise and her skill in the kitchen. He learned the art of camp cooking from her, knowing his was a crude imitation.

Stan served the fish chowder with the bacon crumbled over the top of each bowl. They both dug in and enjoyed every spoonful of that trout and perch chowder, using the biscuits to wipe up what was left in their bowls. By the time they sat back in their chairs the entire pot of chowder had been emptied.

"That was a great meal, Dad. It really hit the spot. Mom would have enjoyed your cooking."

Stan missed Louise's cooking, but not as much as he missed her company. She could whip up a better tasting meal in half the time, all while listening to his plans for restoring his dad's birch bark canoe, and at the same time she'd be helping Joe with his homework.

"She was a good teacher. Glad you liked it. The perch give the chowder a good taste, but I'm not too pleased they're in Duck Pond." Stan thought again about how to get a word with Henry about the perch. If neither Henry nor Alice were at home Thursday morning, he'd leave a note in the warden message box.

"The crisp will be ready in about five minutes. Sorry we don't have ice cream to put over it."

"Are you kidding me? If we can have fresh chowder and apple crisp out here in this beautiful country on a hunting trip, we're lucky enough. Who needs ice cream?"

The words brought a smile to Stan's face. Hearing Joe say how content he was around camp made Stan feel very lucky indeed.

"Let's play some cards before bed. I'll give you another chance to try and beat me at rummy," kidded Stan. Joe always beat his dad at cards, the kid had a way of remembering every card that had been played, a trait he must have inherited from Grandpa George.

The all-day hunting, the fishing, and the chowder, followed by the warm apple crisp, knocked the boys out good. They could only keep their eyes open for two hands of cards.

"Dad, I'm beat, let's finish this game tomorrow."

"Sounds good to me. I'm exhausted myself."

Stan loaded up the woodstove with enough logs to last until morning, and they settled in for a much-needed rest.

Thanksgiving Eve

If Sparky hadn't started whining to go out at 6:05, Joe and Stan would have slept the morning away. After trips to the outhouse, which felt more like an icebox, Stan broke down and started the fire. It was so cold his teeth were chattering, so he took the risk the smoke smell on their clothes wouldn't spook the deer. They pulled the kitchen chairs close to the fire and sat down to breakfast. The wood crackled and popped, filling the cabin with the sounds of a fall camp morning.

In addition to the oatmeal, Stan heated the left-over apple crisp, and made himself a pot of coffee. Joe warmed a mug of milk and added three huge tablespoons of Ovaltine.

"Dad, what do you say we switch paths today? I'd like to try some hunting over by the bog."

"What about using that fancy blind you spent so much time making this past summer? Don't you want to hunt from there?"

"I've been sitting over there the past couple of days. I could use a change of scenery."

Stan took a slow sip of his black coffee. He thought about the man Joe saw on the trail. Maybe Joe was nervous about being out in the meadow alone. Stan realized that if he was the one down in the meadow, and not up on the ridge, he had no way to keep an eye on Joe if there was trouble. Although, he concluded he would not be much use to Joe if he was up on the ridge and something happened anyway. All these thoughts rushed through his mind as he contemplated how to answer.

Maybe he was being overly cautious. They were in the north woods of Maine after all, where the only thing to ever happen was not much of anything.

"Sure, son. I wouldn't mind having a comfy seat in that nice blind of yours. But don't go blaming me if the meadow fills up today with all the deer and you miss out."

"We can only wish." Joe finished up a big spoonful of apple crisp and wrapped his hands around the warm mug of hot chocolate, trying to get the blood flowing to his fingers. Even sitting near the fire, in his jacket and knit cap, he was still chilly this morning. "Seems a lot colder than the forecast said it was going to be."

"I was thinking the same thing. The wind must have shifted bringing us cold air from up north."

Watching the flames flicker in the firebox, Joe went into a trance thinking about what he might hear or see in the woods today.

Stan inventoried the cupboard shelves. He wondered what to throw together for their backpack snacks. Their supplies were getting low and the pickings were slim. He wasn't overly worried about it. By noon tomorrow they'd be eating a turkey dinner at his sister-in-law's in Old Town. He was hoping to bring some fresh venison for his brother-in-law, but that all depended on their luck today.

Stan scraped the last of the peanut butter from the jar to make sandwiches. Along with an apple and a Hershey bar for each of them, these would have to do until they could catch some fish later. He couldn't help but think that Louise would never have cut supplies this close; she always packed more than they needed for any stay at camp. He could hear her saying now, "You never know. We might get hit with a freak thunderstorm. Trees could come down. We could be delayed in getting back to town for a week."

Of course, she was right, she always was. Getting stranded happened to them more than once over the years. Torrential rains had washed out the roads and their small bridges over the streams, microbursts had dropped a half mile long swath of trees across the road back in 1951, and the next summer the old truck's carburetor gave out, forcing Stan to walk to town for help. Luckily, Louise had stocked the cupboards with plenty of canned fruit, vegetables, and tuna. Stan was always glad she was one to think ahead. If she saw the shelves now, she would not be too pleased at all.

Stan looked on the bright side. He knew the two of them would figure out how to survive out here if they had to, even if it meant eating fish and grouse for a few days. Besides, the paper called for clear weather right through the weekend. He told himself they'd be fine, especially now that they had a pond that was likely full of perch, which was still bothering him, but they'd be easy to catch if need be.

Through the window, Stan watched Joe throwing a stick for Sparky. That old dog sure loved to fetch, even if Joe had to make shorter and fewer throws. The old boy did more of a walk back with the stick than a run. Watching them, Stan had a flashback to when Joe and Sparky were eight years younger, a time when Sparky would be running circles around Joe. The young pup used to love jumping through the piles of dried leaves. Now he was content to sniff and meander along the border of the yard. Stan knew this bit of morning exercise would have the dog sleeping the entire time they were out hunting.

Hearing Joe calling Sparky to get inside, Stan finished packing their bags. With a goodbye to their best friend, the father and son team headed out the door for their final day of hunting this year.

"Now remember, son, keep your eyes and ears peeled today."

"I will. You too, and good luck."

Stan placed a hand on Joe's shoulder and said, "Joe, I hope you get a big one." Joe smiled and nodded as he buttoned up his coat and headed off quickly toward the bog.

Stan turned and walked the trail along Beaver Creek. The sky was gray with thin clouds making for a dreary day. Miniature frost heaves in the dirt crumbled under Stan's boots. As cautiously as he stepped, there was no way to be quiet this morning. Not that it mattered, his mind wasn't on hunting. The mystery man Joe spotted yesterday on the trail, the same trail he was walking today, weighed on his mind. Who could the person have been? And who was he signaling to with the poor imitation bird calls that Joe heard?

Walking along, his thoughts drifted to Henry and if he found any of the men from the Lobster Lake Bandits yesterday. What weighed on him most, were the perch and how they ended up in their little pond. It would only be a matter of time before the only fish they'd be catching would be perch, and there isn't a whole heck of a lot of fun in that. If the fish had reached

Lobster Lake then what about Moosehead Lake? Stan didn't even want to think about the problems then.

* * *

Joe walked the path to Bug Bog. He looked forward to a slower and more relaxed hike this morning. He took his time on the winding trail, stepping over the rocks and the trees that were still down across the path. It was slow going listening to every rustle of the wind and bristle of the pine trees. He kept wondering if he would come around the corner and meet a deer, a bear, or the man from yesterday.

When he reached Bug Bog, he sat down on a log bench his dad helped him build for his mom. She used to love coming to the bog in the early spring before the bugs became so annoying that she felt like she was donating blood and not bird watching. She'd sit for hours watching the migrating birds returning to the woods and listening to their calls. When Dad knew Mom was sitting in the bog, he would take Joe and they would sneak around the far side, keeping out of Mom's sight. From there he'd let out a bird song. If he could fool Mom's trained ears, he knew he was getting good. Over lunch back at the cabin, Mom would tell them about the wood thrush, red eyed vireos, and magnolia warblers, she had heard. Then she would say smiling, "And Stan, you need to work on that ovenbird a lot more before the annual competition. Your pitch was good, but your timing was too fast." Joe sure missed the antics of his parents.

Sitting on his mom's bird bench, without the walls of even his tiny log blind, the slightest breeze sent a chill down Joe's back. As he sat, he saw the head of a bull moose rise from among the mountain holly, rhodora, and huckleberry plants. It was probably the same big guy his dad had spotted the other day. He watched as the big bull nosed the air, smelling something was not right. Joe sat still, wanting the moose to calm down and not be rushed away. The moose took a few steps toward the woods, stopped, then bent down to continue eating the bog weeds. The warmth of the bog still provided a good array of greens, even if the nightly frost was wilting what was left. No matter how many times Joe had seen a moose, there was nothing that compared to watching a thousand-pound animal up close. Once the moose had eaten his fill, he turned, stepped out of the bog, and headed toward the road.

Joe was relieved the moose went the other way. While he liked observing the large king of the woods, he was not all that comfortable with getting close to them during the fall. He had started to be much more cautious around these finicky woods creatures after several close calls.

While he sat waiting for a deer to come his way, Joe thought about all he had learned over the years about the biggest members of the deer family. The first was not to come between a moose mom and her calf, unless of course you are in the company of a brave little puppy. The second thing he had come to realize about moose is that they prefer taking the easy paths if they can find them. Being so big, and particularly for the males with their large antlers, staying out of the brush and trees makes traveling a lot faster. He had come upon moose more often on the logging roads, than anywhere else around camp. A couple of times he stumbled on what could have only been a moose march with five, six, or even seven of them out for a stroll together. He knew they weren't the brightest creatures in the woods and during hunting season they weren't usually stealthy in their habits. It was that time of year, when the opportunistic hunters could wait along a logging road, usually in their nice warm truck cab, and a moose would walk right to them. The third, and most interesting moose fact that he'd share with his friends when they asked about his scar, was if you're in a canoe and racing a swimming moose, you will lose.

This he learned recently. His dad told him later that he was spared the brunt of the attack thanks to moose having such poor eyesight. It happened the September before last, when Joe was fifteen, and he set out to go fishing on his own.

That morning, Joe was canoeing on Lobster Lake in the narrows by Little Claw Cove. He cast his lure into the water and noticed a moose on the shore. Knowing moose can be unpredictable during rut season, he planned to keep his distance. Joe wasn't sure what to think when the moose didn't fade away into the woods, as most would have. Rather, the moose stepped, or rather dove, into the water and started swimming. Joe stopped his paddling and watched the moose. At first, he thought the moose was headed to Big Island. It took a few moments to realize that the bull was headed straight for Joe's canoe. By this time, the wind had turned the bow of the canoe and it was pointing directly at the oncoming moose. Joe struggled to turn the boat away, but the wind was fighting his every stroke. By the time he had steered the canoe toward the point at Big Claw, the moose had closed to within twenty yards. With no weight in the bow of the canoe it was riding high catching the wind and slowing Joe down even more. He turned to look over his right shoulder. The moose was now only a few feet away. Joe stared right into the eyes of the moose and could not help but notice the size of the rack rising out of the water. He dug his paddle deeper in an attempt to put some space between him and this crazy bull. It was no use; the wind was too strong, and Joe didn't have enough strength to out paddle the animal. Joe was shocked at how fast and nimble this half-ton moose was in the water.

A foot from the stern, the moose blew out a breath Joe could hear. For a split-second Joe thought about a comic book he had recently read that depicted the Loch Ness monster, and he thought this moose might be the north woods version. As the moose brought his front leg out of the water towards the canoe, Joe yelled, "Get away from me you dumb moose!"

The moose, startled by the yell, changed course. Joe then realized that the moose had no idea he was chasing a canoe. In the excitement of the moment, Joe over compensated on his stroke. The wind caught the bow and tipped him into the water. The paddle whacked him in the face and he felt a sharp pain on his bottom lip and chin. The moose was spooked by the commotion and veered toward Big Island.

Remembering not to panic, Joe made a fast move and grabbed the rope that was tied to the stern of the canoe gunnel. He tightened the strap on his life jacket, thankful he heeded his dad's advice to always wear one. He swam dragging the canoe behind him. The late September water was cold, but not yet deadly. He slowly made his way the thirty yards to shore. When he reached land, he laid down on his back. That's when he noticed he had split his chin and blood was dripping down onto his chest. He took off his wet shirt and put pressure on the gash. Given the depth of the cut, he realized he had to get back to camp, and quick.

Joe searched for the canoe paddle. When he didn't find it in the canoe, and it hadn't drifted to shore, he suspected the wind must have taken it out into the center of Big Claw. With no paddle, he had no way of canoeing back to the other side of the lake.

He turned and looked towards the woods. His dad's voice came to him as he was about to attempt hiking out, *"Always remember, Joe, if you are stranded in the woods, and you don't have a compass or know the trails, you are better off staying put."*

Joe didn't have a compass and he knew of no trails that passed near this section of the lake. He'd be bushwhacking, without gear, through the forest in a location where he'd never hiked before. He slowly lowered the shirt from his chin. It had turned a dark maroon color. The cut must have been deeper than he first thought. He realized he was going to have to wait for help, so he focused on getting dry.

As he had been taught, he had a dry bag of supplies tied to the center beam of the canoe. He took out the matches and built a fire. His first order of business was to stay warm. He stripped off all his remaining clothes and draped them over sticks he fashioned into drying racks. Then he collected all the dry drift wood he could and sat close to the fire to warm up. He rotated himself and the clothes every few minutes. Sitting on the sand, buck naked, he imagined what Robinson Crusoe must have felt like when he was first shipwrecked and stranded.

Joe, being somewhat modest, hoped nobody would happen by until his clothes were dry, even if they were a rescue party. He tended to his chin. The bleeding had slowed, but only slightly. Once his pants were semi-dry, he put them back on and walked back to the tree line. With one hand still holding his rag of a shirt to his chin, he used his free hand to snap off live spruce and hemlock branches. He piled these on the flames. The green foliage made a huge plume of white smoke. Using a large hemlock branch, he broke the smoke column every few seconds. He had no idea what, if anything, such a signal might mean, but it certainly wouldn't look like a normal fire plume to anyone nearby. He could only hope his dad, who was fishing over on Duck Pond, would spot the smoke and recognize it was a signal.

Stan was trying to reel in a trout that was being particularly difficult when a pileated woodpecker let out one of their characteristic cries. Stan turned to try and spot the bird's perch, and in doing so, noticed the white smoke.

Slowly, he came to the conclusion that the smoke was coming from the far side of Lobster Lake. He knew that Joe had taken the canoe over that way to fish. When he realized the smoke was rising in broken columns, he wasted no time in going to find out what the problems was. He stuck his fishing pole between two trees, figuring the trout would have to be patient until he could get back.

He ran over to the shore of Lobster Lake, launched the rowboat, and set out across the water. It took him almost an hour to reach Joe's location. He was relieved to see his son was okay, but was very concerned about the cut on his chin.

"I'm glad to see you used your survival skills. This could have been a much bigger problem."

"You taught me well, and I remembered your advice to keep calm and stay put."

Stan extinguished the fire and loaded the boat. "Let's get you back to camp, so your mom can take care of that chin. Medical skills are not something I can pass on to you." He tied the canoe to the stern hook, and pushed off.

Joe told his dad more about the moose as Stan rowed back across the lake.

"That moose probably had no idea you were a person in a boat. He probably thought you were a long-lost female friend of his. They have terrible eyesight and they're not that bright you know, especially this time of year – they only have one thing on their minds."

Louise took one look at Joe's chin and realized he was going to need stitches. Joe figured they would drive into town to see the doctor, but was dismayed when his mom took out her needle and set to sterilizing it on the stove.

"We have no time to get you to town. It's already past five o'clock. This has to be stitched up right here and now."

While Joe's mom had some experience working as a candy striper at a hospital during high school, Joe was certain she had never given anyone stitches before.

Mom made him drink some whisky, which Joe thought was worse than the pain. She then rubbed more of the alcohol on the wound before she started stitching.

"This is going to hurt, Joe, but I only need to add a couple of loops."

And, she was right, it hurt something fierce. Joe grabbed the arms on the chair and cried for more whiskey. As he had seen in a Western movie, he bit down on a stick.

Stan, not one for seeing blood, or hearing anyone scream in pain, took Sparky for a walk.

When it was all over, Joe was proud of his mom and how she took such good care of him. However, he would have the scar for the rest of his life. The next day they drove to town and the doctor told Louise she was right to stitch him up. He added, so that Joe could hear, "Had I done those stitches there would have been a scar as well. You did a fine job, Mrs. Parker."

That day, Joe learned several lessons about moose, wilderness preparation, and the agony of getting stitches without pain killers. His greatest lesson was to always tie a spare paddle inside the canoe.

The moose that had left the bog was about the same size as the one that caused Joe to tip. Running a finger over his scar, he wondered if maybe it was the same moose. Joe sat shivering on

the bench listening to the quiet. With the cold wind kicking up
he thought that if he were walking he'd stay warmer. He ate a
biscuit left over from last night's dinner, and then continued to
Rum Ridge. He planned to hike up to the top, to check on his
dad.

It was barely eight-thirty when Joe reached the top of the
ridge and saw the commotion down below. He unzipped his
pack and pulled out his binoculars for a closer look. The three
bear cubs were having a great time playing in the meadow. He
searched and noticed the mother bear was standing at the edge,
on the far side. He scanned over to the blind – there was no sign
of his dad. He slowly moved the lenses south of the blind along
the wood line. He thought his dad might be watching the cubs
from a safe distance. If he was behind a tree, it would be
unlikely Joe could spot him. He moved the field of view back
to the blind and scanned north.

His rotation took him half way to the top side of the
meadow, when he gasped. He pulled the binoculars away from
his eyes and dropped back behind a tree. He found himself
shaking and not because of the cold air. Joe's mind was racing
and he thought, "What should I do now?"

Strangers in the Meadow

The binoculars shook in Joe's trembling hands. To steady himself, he knelt on the cold rock, and slowly raised the binoculars to his eyes again. Turning the dial to focus the lenses, he could tell the man wasn't one of Red's gang. It was someone he'd never seen before. It appeared the man was watching the bears. Joe began to worry about where his dad might be. He panned to the north and then to the south. There was no sign of him.

* * *

From the south side of the meadow, Stan watched the bears. When he had arrived, ten minutes earlier, they were already wrestling with one another. He knew he couldn't get to the blind, so rather than scaring the bears off, or worse, triggering a bear encounter, he looked for an easy tree to climb.

Being up a tree with no escape route was probably not the best place to be, but he knew to keep his distance, and he made sure he could see the mother bear at all times. He unpacked his camera hoping the cubs might come close enough for the small lens to pick up something more than a big black ball in a field. He had no idea how long the mama bear would allow the cubs to linger and play, so he reclined against the tree trunk to watch the wild bear show. From his perch he was safely out of sight and completely unaware there was a stranger on the far edge of the meadow.

* * *

Looking through his binoculars, Joe tried to figure out the man's purpose in the meadow. The stranger seemed out of place. He wore high black boots laced up over his olive-green pants and a matching field coat. The coat had side and breast pockets with gold metal buttons, which were reflecting the sun, when it shined through breaks in the clouds. The man's hat was not a ball cap, but reminded Joe of a newsboy's cap. In Joe's first year of high school he had studied about the New York City Newsboy strike of 1899. The text book had a picture of a rough looking crew of boys holding stacks of newspapers, all sporting a similar looking hat to the one the man was wearing. Joe thought it would be neat to have one of those caps, although he wouldn't go hunting in it.

The man was smoking a cigarette, his face stoic and serious. Joe thought he resembled John Wayne, as Ethan Edwards in *The Searchers*, a film he saw with his dad and his friend Jimmy at the drive-in last summer. Joe wondered if maybe the man was wearing a side arm under his coat, maybe a Colt, just like John Wayne. Realizing his imagination and his love of movies were distracting him, he forced himself to focus on the situation.

Near the man's feet was a pack. It was not a pack of a hunter or a hiker. It was also olive green, matching the man's pants and jacket. Joe looked for a hunting rifle or fishing pole. He couldn't see anything but the bag. Joe concluded that the man was not dressed like a hunter and he had none of the gear a hunter might carry. And no hunter was going to be smoking while stalking game. Joe was getting wrapped up in his thoughts as he tried to figure out who the man was, what he was searching for, and if maybe it was one of the men from yesterday he had heard making the bird calls.

Joe continued searching for his dad, but was having no luck. As he panned back toward the center he noticed the mama bear was standing on her hind legs. She was staring in the direction of the stranger. The bear probably caught scent of the man, or more likely, his cigarette. She walked across the meadow, in the opposite direction, heading towards Bug Bog. The three cubs followed her into the woods. Everything was still, even the wind.

Joe panned back to the north. The man was still there, but now Joe had a bigger problem. The man had his own binoculars pressed to his eyes and was looking straight up the ridge. He was focused right at the tree where Joe was sitting. The eeriness of being watched made Joe shiver. He moved back into some berry bushes, laid flat on the ground, and asked himself, "Where's Dad?" At the moment, Joe couldn't think of anything else to do but wait. He had to think. But right now, he was too cold to think.

Trying to stay low and keep out of sight, Joe had a different feeling from the last time he saw a stranger in his meadow. It was a day this past summer, when he hiked up to the ridge to scout a place to build his blind. Crouching behind the berry bush, he remembered what he spotted down below, and it wasn't a deer, a bear, or a man.

It happened the July morning Joe had been sitting on the edge of the ridge, his legs dangling, eating some wild blueberries he had packed for a snack. The day had started out beautiful with cool temperatures and clear blue sky. Suddenly, the weather changed. The sun began heating the mountain air, a sure sign that thunderstorms might crop up. A dark storm cloud passed over Black Cap Mountain in the east. A dense fog overtook the valley. The chickadees, starlings, and nuthatches all went quiet.

Joe knew the worst place to be, should lightning develop, would be at the top of the open ridge. He remembered his dad's warning about lightning storms, *"If you're caught outdoors, find a low area or ravine. Try to find a spot with a group of small trees surrounded by taller trees. You don't want to be the tallest thing around. Crouch down, stay on your feet, minimize your contact with the ground."*

He watched the cloud for a minute, while he considered his escape down the ridge to find shelter. Joe began to gather his gear when as quick as the clouds had appeared, they blew away, leaving only the wind behind. The birds started to sing again.

He was identifying the song of a cedar waxwing, when a girl came running into the meadow. She was yelling something with her hands cupped around her mouth, but the wind was carrying her screams away from his position high up on the ridge. He zoomed in with his binoculars to try and read her lips.

She was screaming, "Mom, Dad, Mom, Dad," over and over. She looked panicked.

Joe tried to get her attention. He yelled down, "Hello, Hello." She didn't look up or even glance around.

Joe decided to make a run for it to try to get to her. He immediately started sprinting down the trail. Leaping over rocks and roots, he figured it might take him twenty minutes to reach the meadow. He only hoped he could run fast enough to get there before the girl wandered deeper into the woods. He worried she would get even more disoriented, making it harder to find her.

He knew he had to act fast, and that meant running the Lost Swamp Trail, which wasn't the straightest line, but it would be easier than trying to cut through the woods directly. Pushing through the forest and thickets would mean a lot of lost time. Once in those thick woods, even he would have to stop and check his compass often, or risk getting turned around and losing valuable minutes.

At school, Joe was part of the cross-country team. He was one of the most agile runners in the junior class. He accredited his ability to read a course, even the first time he ran it, to his experience in the woods. He could anticipate the way the ground would move under his feet. He was adept at jumping rocks and timing his stride to miss large tree roots in his path. He would spend the summer running the trails at camp as a workout for the fall season. Leaving the camp porch, he'd run the trail along Beaver Creek to Lost Swamp, then he'd cross over towards Rum Ridge, then down to Bug Bog and back on to camp.

Lost Swamp

Joe was winded when he reached the meadow. Always wanting to improve his running time, Joe automatically looked at his watch. He had made it in under fifteen minutes, pretty good he thought. Removing his Red Sox cap, he wiped his forehead with his shirt. The girl was sitting at the far end of the wildflower field on the logs he had started to pile for building his blind. He could hear her crying. He walked halfway towards her and stopped. He didn't want to startle her. She seemed much older than him.

As if she sensed a presence, she turned with a cautious look in her eyes. Wiping her tears on her blue shirt, with the letters NYU on the front, she stopped crying, and took a deep breath.

"Hi, I'm Joe. Do you need help?"

"I'm lost. I think," she said, her voice cracking.

Joe thought she was beautiful. Her hair was strawberry blond down to her shoulders, her curls were creeping out from under her Boston Red Sox cap. Joe thought, "She might go to NYU, but at least she was a fan of the right ball club."

Joe stepped closer. "What are you doing out here?"

"I was hiking with my family. My dad thought it would be good to get out of the city and go to the country. The only things here in the country are trees and more trees. If I wanted to see trees, I could have gone to the park. Now look where this has gotten me." She started to cry again.

"Where are you staying?"

"These rustic camps my mom says are charming. To me they are old wooden cabins with spiders. They're on some bay, I think it was named "Spensive Bay," which from the looks of everything there, it should have been called Cheapskate Bay."

"I think you might mean Spencer Bay. There are some nice hunting camps over there. That's a long way from here. Did you walk that entire way?"

"No! Of course not. My dad thought it was necessary to get in the car, go to the country, sleep in the cabins in the woods, then get in the car to drive even deeper into the woods to get even more country. All to go for a hike. And here I am lost. I'm probably going to die out here."

Joe tried not to laugh. "You're definitely not going to die. I know these woods better than anyone and you are not lost. This is my backyard."

"You live here? Why? Nobody has a yard like this."

"This is where we have our camp. It's technically not all our yard, but it might as well be. And I love it here. Everyday there's something new and amazing."

"You want amazing, you should see Central Park. All the trees are pruned, the paths are paved, and the buildings rise up around it," exclaimed the girl.

"Sounds terrific." He didn't hold back a sarcastic tone, which the girl was quick to notice.

"Can you help me get back to my parents?"

She had lost interest in small talk and was obviously upset at Joe's disregard for the beauty of Central Park.

"I can help you get out of my meadow, to find your parents we'll need a car. For that we'll have to get my dad."

Joe picked up her oversized purse, or maybe it was a miniature backpack, he wasn't sure.

She reached out and grabbed it from him. "I can carry my own stuff."

"Sorry, I was just trying to be helpful."

"How far is the road?"

"The road your family drove in on is about a mile from here. It's the only one in and out. But we are not going that way."

"What? Why the heck not?"

"Because we could get there and have to walk all the way around and not see anyone. It's best if we head back to my cabin. My dad can drive you back to the place you are staying."

"Oh. I guess that makes sense."

"So, you're from New York City?"

"I wish! Why do I talk like a New Yorker?"

"I thought, well I thought, because of your sweatshirt. It says NYU and your comment about Central Park. Your accent reminds me of my math teacher. She moved to Maine from a place called Revere Beach."

"I'm from Cambridge."

"Where's that?"

"Near Boston. Not so far from Revere. And Revere is definitely not in New York. You don't get around much do you?"

Joe frowned, not sure what to say. The girl continued, in a tone Joe felt was bragging.

"I go to Browne & Nichols High School in Boston. When I graduate, I plan to go to Columbia University or NYU to live in a real city."

Joe had been to Boston once, back in middle school. As far as cities go, it seemed real enough to him. His dad had considered taking a teaching job in Quincy for higher pay. He took Joe and Mom down one weekend to see what they thought of the neighborhoods. He remembered his mom trying to be positive. They stopped to eat at a lunch counter near Fenway Park where his mom broke down crying. She said she didn't care for the extra money if it meant living in a city. Joe's mom had been born in Jackman, a town where everyone knew everyone, and there was plenty of space to roam. One of the reasons she fell in love with Stan, and married him, was because the two of them enjoyed the great north woods of Maine.

Joe remembered his dad hugging her and saying, "It certainly seems this move would be less of everything we really enjoy. I don't want to move either."

And with that, they piled back in their pickup truck and headed north. Joe really didn't have an inclination to want to be in the city, but he wondered what it would be like to be inside Fenway with thousands of other people. That would be more people in one place, at the same time, than he had seen in his entire life.

"My dad is probably so upset right now knowing he lost me."

"How did you get separated from them?"

The girl looked down, not sure what to say, it was a little embarrassing. She was too upset to care, and she was mad at her parents, so she blurted out her story, not even stopping for air.

"I had to go to the bathroom, which of course there are none out here. Not even outhouses on the trails. And my dad said I needed to go behind a tree. I didn't want to do that. But I had to go really bad. My family was standing right on the trail. All three of them. My dad, my mom, and my sister. I told them to go on ahead up the trail a little so I couldn't see them. But I heard them laughing, so I thought they could see me. So, I walked into the woods farther. After, I walked back to find the trail. It took a lot longer to get to where I thought I started. But there was nobody there. Then out of nowhere, clouds, or mist, I don't know what it was, engulfed the entire trail. Everything was foggy. I yelled. I could hear them faintly yelling back. I thought they were playing tricks on me. So, I walked through the woods, getting scratched by branches. I yelled for them, but I couldn't hear them any longer. I turned around and walked back, thinking I must have gone the wrong way."

She trembled as she spoke, "It all looked the same. I kept walking, hoping to find them. We had hiked up, so I kept going down. But the mountain didn't always go down. I'd go down, then have to go up. I knew I was lost. I had to climb over logs and walk in the mud."

She pointed at her shoes as evidence of her story.

Joe thought she shouldn't have been hiking in such shoes, unless the hike was down the aisle at church on Sunday. "In those situations, it's best to stay still and remain calm. They likely would've been able to find you if you hadn't been a moving target."

A woods trail near camp.

"Well that's not what happened and this is where I ended up. Now I'm covered in mud, I've been eaten alive by mosquitoes, and I've lost my family. How did you find me?"

"You're in my deer meadow."

"Your what? Is that your play fort back there?" She pointed at the pile of logs.

"Those logs are for my blind. It's not a fort. It is used to hunt from. I was scouting the deer from the ridge for hunting season when I saw you." Joe pointed up to the top of Rum Ridge.

"You kill deer? That's horrible!" She turned away.

Joe thought it was probably not the right time to talk to this girl about hunting's benefits to the ecosystem and the health of the deer herd.

"We'd better get a move on back to my cabin to get my dad." He led her out of the meadow and onto Beaver Creek Trail.

"This is a nice wide trail. Not like the one my father took us on. It was full of weeds, logs, and rocks. I'm not sure it was a trail at all."

"My dad and I cleared this trail and we maintain it every year. It runs along Beaver Creek, and then straight on to our cabin."

"If I get out of here, I'm never going in the woods again."

"I can say with one hundred percent certainty you'll get out of here. As for never going in the woods again, I sure hope you don't mean that. If you spent time here, I'm sure you'd come to love it."

She rolled her eyes. "Unless the MET or the Boston Opera House will be opening here, no thank you."

"I'm not a big fan of the Mets, but I like them more than the Yankees," said Joe.

"The MET has nothing to do with a baseball team." She laughed. "It stands for the Metropolitan Opera House." She swept her arm and motioned to the trees. "There's not much art happening around here. I guess I don't need to tell you that."

Joe wondered what her limited view of artists and writers might be. He thought about asking if she had ever read Thoreau or seen photographs from Ansel Adams, but then thought it would not be polite if she hadn't. He figured it was better to let it go given her current state of panic.

Joe caught her staring at the scar on his chin several times. He felt self-conscious about it and tried to keep his head half turned from her. At the same time, he felt drawn to her eyes and didn't want to look away. He noticed they were green, sugar maple leaf green. They sparkled, not from the earlier tears, but naturally. Her eyebrows were perfectly shaped and her lashes, dark black. She was wearing makeup that left a little black streak along the corner of her eye. No girls he knew from Bangor High wore makeup.

"I like your Red Sox cap."

"Oh no! I forgot I had this on. It's not mine. I don't play sports. It's my sister's. My mom thought it would be good for me to wear to keep my hair up. I wore it to keep the bugs out."

Joe searched for things to talk about. "Have you gone fishing on Spencer Bay?"

"No. I don't fish. My dad went one morning."

"Did you have a campfire?"

"Some people did. There were too many bugs. I stayed inside. Not that it mattered. The bugs found their way through the screens, biting me while I was doing my nails."

Joe was quickly running out of things to say, she obviously was more interested in looking good, than looking at what the woods had to offer.

When they reached the crossing at Little Beaver Creek, he offered to take her hand and help her across the mossy rocks.

She scowled at his hand. "I can manage just fine."

Stepping from boulder to boulder, she lost her footing and slipped.

"Ahh. Now I'm all wet. Why did you bring me this way? There were no rivers the way I came."

By then, Joe had reached the other side of the creek where he stood trying not to laugh.

"Can you give me a hand?" she yelled as she slipped again while trying to get her footing.

"Seems to me you're managing just fine. That is if you intended to go for a swim." Joe shook his head and smiled. He easily walked back out over the rocks and helped her up. He offered her his hand.

As she took his hand, she looked into his dark brown eyes for the first time.

When they reached the other side of the creek, she noticed he still was holding her hand. "Thanks, I'm okay now," she said, glancing down at their hands.

Joe let go of her soft fingers. "Not a problem, it gets slippery."

"So, do you live around here all year long?"

"No. We stay here at camp in the summer. Our home is in Bangor."

"Where's that?"

"It's about three hours east of here."

"Is it a city?" she asked intrigued.

"I guess by Maine standards it might be considered a city."

"How much farther is it to your cabin? My legs are hurting and my pants are all wet from falling in that river."

Joe laughed. She didn't find it amusing, and scowled at him.

"I'm not laughing at you. It was funny that you called Little Beaver Creek a river. That creek is about as small as creeks come. If you want to see a river, you should see the Penobscot right after the ice break in the spring."

Little Beaver Creek

"I have no intention on being here until the spring. How much farther do we have to hike?"

Joe thought she was cute, even if she wasn't in a great mood. "It's another half mile, or so."

Joe noticed an eagle flying along the ridge of Black Cap Mountain. He pointed to the sky. "Look at that!"

The girl looked, but did not seem too impressed. "What? That bird up there?"

"That's an Eagle."

"Looks like a big bird to me. I can't really see much of it."

Since she was no lover of being outdoors, Joe tried to think of something they both might be able to talk about. "Have you read any of Thoreau?"

"Sure. We had to read Walden in ninth grade. Then the school dragged us on a field trip to see what supposedly was his cabin in the woods, which it was not. The only thing there were some foundation stones lying around."

"Thoreau also wrote the book titled, The Maine Woods. In it he describes his trip that took him not too far from here. He paddled on Lobster Stream, which is right over that way." Joe pointed.

"I don't care too much for Lobster."

Joe thought about elaborating on his point, but wasn't sure what to say. They finished the hike back to camp in silence.

When they reached the cabin, Joe saw Henry Ford leaning against his cruiser talking with Dad. Joe gave them a wave.

"Here comes Joe now. Maybe he saw something while on his hike," Stan said.

"I'll be...," said Henry, when the girl came into view behind Joe. Henry removed his hat and scratched at his head.

"Hello there, young lady, you don't look too lost to me. I'm Warden Ford and your parents are worried sick about you."

"You found my parents?"

Henry laughed. "They found me when they came flying into town in a panic, blasting their horn all the way down Lily Bay Road. The warden service is organizing a search party back in town right now. I came out here to talk to the Parkers, the best search party we could have around here. Looks as if Joe proved me right on that count."

Joe's face flushed red.

Henry's car didn't have a CB radio to alert the state police, who probably had already shown up back in town to save the day and take all the credit. The department had only started issuing the two-way radios to wardens this year, and he hadn't been down to the warehouse to pick his up. He figured it wasn't going to be any use to him anyway. Who was he going to talk to? He was too far from town and the signal out this way would be blocked by all the mountains. Alice said he should ask for two radios so he could at least keep her informed of his location. He had decided to delay the trip to Augusta for now.

Henry gave Joe a pat on the back and turned to the girl, "Okay, Miss, I'd better get you back to town." Henry wanted to hurry to alert the search party. If they headed out before he was back, he'd have a heck of a time rounding them up and they'd be out searching for nothing until darkness fell.

"Oh, thank you. Can I stay at a hotel in town? It has to be better than the cabin we are renting. It's dirty and the bathroom is a wooden shed across the yard."

Stan and Henry laughed.

Joe thought to himself that he wished she could stay at their cabin and learn to appreciate the woods.

Henry opened the passenger door for the girl and she hopped in. Stan put his arm on Joe's shoulder as the cruiser pulled away. When Henry was half way down the drive the cruiser stopped.

The girl leaned out the window. "Thanks for finding me."

That was all. She ducked back inside the car and Henry sped away.

"Good job, son. Her parents are going to be very grateful. What was her name?"

"I don't know." Joe felt a hollow feeling in his stomach and he didn't understand why. That girl was a little obnoxious, and she hated the woods, but Joe still felt connected to her in some way.

The following week, the local paper ran an article titled, "*Boston Girl Lost in the Woods Near Lobster Lake.*" In the story, the reporter wrote that it all ended safely when she was returned by Warden Ford to her parents a few hours later. The article never mentioned the girl's name or anything about Joe. He cut the article out of the paper and pasted it into the 1956 camp journal, right where he had written two entire pages about his meeting the girl.

A few weeks later, Joe overheard his dad and Henry talking. "The wardens, the state police, and volunteers, including the local Boy Scout troop, were about to leave town to start a search when I pulled up with that young lady."

"I bet they were glad to see her."

"You bet. The mother came over and gave me a big hug. But you're not going to believe who I saw on my way to town when I was bringing her back."

"Who?"

"It was just my luck. That Lobster Lake Bandit crew went screaming past me in their truck. Nearly ran me off the road. They had a truck bed full of barrels. If I didn't have the young lady with me, I'd have swung around and chased them."

"Huh – wonder what they were up to."

"Who knows."

Stan noticed Joe leaning on a tree nearby listening. "So, Henry, what was that girl's name?"

"You know, I can't recall. I think her family name was Mallard or Maloney. I can't say. Everyone was so glad she was back, the troopers and I never even filed a report seeing we never officially started the search party."

Disappointed Henry didn't know the girl's name, Joe kicked at the ground with his foot. He thought about the girl for the rest of that summer. All summer long, he kept his eyes out for anyone with strawberry blonde hair around town, in the trading post, or at the Dairy Shack when he went for ice cream. She never did turn up again. But he never forgot her.

Joe was staring out over the meadow, lost in his daydream about the girl from the summer, when he caught a glimpse of his dad walking. Joe reached for his binoculars and inched closer to the edge of the ridge. His dad was strolling along without a care in the world.

Joe's heart started to beat faster. He had to think. His mind raced trying to find a way to warn his dad that he was walking right toward the strange man, who was still standing on the opposite side of the meadow.

The Informer

Staying low on the smooth ridge rock, Joe looked through his binoculars and watched his dad walking down the center of the meadow. He looked to be whistling, probably to keep the bears from wandering back in. It was obvious to Joe that his dad had no knowledge of the man standing against the tree in the shadows.

Joe focused in on the stranger in the cap. The man had his binoculars pointed directly at Dad. Joe zoomed in to see his dad's face. He wanted to yell and warn him. But then he considered, "About what? A man standing by a tree with a newspaper bag?" Joe relaxed a little knowing his dad could take care of himself against any man or bear.

That thought kept Joe calm until the man receded to the path along the creek. Joe's imagination started to run wild and he worried that the man was going to circle around to get a jump on his dad. He took a deep breath and pushed the air out; he was frustrated he couldn't think what to do next. Several minutes later he noticed a dust trail out behind Lost Swamp.

Looking back down at the meadow, Joe watched his dad settle into the blind, pull an apple out of his pack, and take a bite. Joe decided to wait at the top of the ridge and keep a lookout, just in case.

* * *

Henry never did catch up with Red, or any of the other Bandits, yesterday afternoon. He drove around so long he had to coast back into town running on fumes. This morning he was up earlier than usual, anxious to find out what that gang was up to. After breakfast, Henry left Alice to her chores of caring for two raccoons, an owl, and the injured moose. On his way north, he made a stop at the Lily Bay General Store to catch up on the news, which meant the local gossip, and to refill his thermos with hot coffee.

"Morning, Bonnie. What's new?"

"I've got some good information for you, Henry."

Bonnie, who was Alice's sister, was always on the lookout for tips to pass along to Henry. She considered herself the warden's unofficial informer. She also became his unofficial dispatcher. Since Henry was mostly on the road, and Alice was taking care of animals, there was no one in their house to answer the phone. So, the locals would stop in the store to do their shopping, and use Bonnie to get messages to Henry when he stopped for coffee.

Most recently, Bonnie had relayed a message to Henry from Brent Hill, who complained he couldn't get down to his boat due to a wild animal standing ground on the dock every morning. Brent wouldn't tell Bonnie anymore about the animal, he wanted Henry to come out and take a look himself.

When Henry finally had a free morning, he stopped over at Brent's camp to see what the fuss was about. Henry was a bit perturbed to discover the animal in question. Standing on the path to the dock, he found a red squirrel squeaking away.

Henry turned to Brent, a two-hundred-pound, six-foot man, and asked, "What do you want me to do about a squirrel, Brent?"

"How should I know. You're the game warden. That there squirrel won't let me, or the dog, get anywhere near the dock. The darn thing has it such that Lady won't even come out of the house if she hears that squirrel."

"Have you tried peanuts, Brent?" After that, Brent had to keep a supply of peanuts in his pocket to bribe the local wildlife and pay the toll before he could get to his boat.

Occasionally though, Bonnie would have some useful news for her brother-in-law warden. This morning was one of those rare occasions. Henry drank a cup of coffee and ate a blueberry muffin, as Bonnie told him that Red and his gang had stopped in the store the night before.

"I overheard them saying they were all "perched out" and needed something other than fish for dinner. They picked up two cases of beer and all six steaks I had left in the meat case. When I was ringing up their stuff, I asked the leader a few questions." Bonnie retold the conversation she had with Red to Henry.

"You boys got a camp up here a-bouts?"

"Sure do, pretty lady. You ought to come on over."

"I've seen you in the store more often lately. Is your place close by?"

"Nowhere near here. We park it out deep in the woods."

The younger one in the group added, "To get ther,' ya take the Golden Road and then go right towards the Deadwater."

Red snapped. "Pipe down, Junior. I'm sure the lady doesn't have time for your stories."

She told Henry that once they all left the store, she watched them outside standing around the trucks. Red was yelling at Junior something fierce.

"Thanks, Bonnie. That sure is useful information. It narrows down where I need to start looking for that crew."

"Don't you go chasing them all around the Allagash, Henry! Tomorrow's Thanksgiving and I'm sure Alice will want you home early tonight."

"Thank you, Ma. And that location ain't nowhere near the Allagash anyway." Henry winked, knowing Bonnie knew that.

Bonnie refilled his thermos and put another blueberry muffin in a brown paper bag for him. She knew it didn't matter what she said, Henry was going to do what Henry was going to do, but she tried anyway.

"Henry, I'm serious. My knee is acting up and that can only mean bad weather's on the way."

"Bonnie, you sell papers here right?"

"You know we do!"

Henry opened one of the two-day old papers on the counter to the weather forecast. (By the time papers were delivered up this way it was already old news.)

"I'm certain you can read as good as I can, Bonnie. The forecast is showing no precipitation." He pointed at the page with the weather map. "We'll see you and Wilson for turkey tomorrow afternoon at our place. Alice said the turkey will be cooked by noon." He tipped his hat and was out the door.

Bonnie watched Henry pull out and head north towards Lazy Tom Bog. She looked out at the horizon over Sugar Island. The sky was a bright blue with not a cloud in sight. She stated to herself, "Hmm, maybe Henry's right about the weather."

* * *

Henry's cruiser bounced down the Golden Road, squeaking all the way. He knew even with the nugget of information from Bonnie, he was still looking for a needle in a haystack. Last summer he chased the Bandits all the way to Graveyard Point. He was only able to locate them because one of the old timers in Chesuncook Village remembered seeing Red and his crew. The man, known to all the locals as Raven, had lived in the area all his life. They say he was born in 1865. He sat in the same rocking chair, on the porch of the general store, almost every day from April until the cold weather of November.

Raven told Henry he was dead sure the men had passed through the village. "See here, Warden, I've been sitting here all summah long, an there was only one different truck the entire time. A red Ford."

Thanks to Raven, Henry had found the Bandits up at the Point. They were three times over their fishing limit. He wanted to fine them all, but one of the gang took the rap and said all the excess fish were his. Henry revoked the man's license, but knew it wouldn't do much good.

This year Henry's warden intuition told him that gang was up to more than pulling out a few extra fish. With the new information from Bonnie, he tore off for the Deadwater. He already knew Alice was going to be mad if he wasn't home before dark, he'd have to deal with that later. This might be his last chance of the year to get those guys. He was also sure that by now Bonnie had called Alice and told her about his plans to head north. He could only hope his sister-in-law wasn't telling his plans to anyone else.

As Henry's sedan creaked and groaned over the ripped-up road, he wished he had one of those Ford trucks right now. He thought with his name, the Ford Motor Company ought to give him one to prove out on the tough roads of Maine.

* * *

From up on the ridge, Joe saw his dad sitting on a log in the blind. Joe moved his field of view to where his dad was spotting, and saw four deer entering the meadow on the south end. They strolled slowly, nibbling at the weeds and searching the ground for acorns.

When he looked back towards the blind, he saw his dad sneaking around the side. Joe couldn't believe his eyes as he watched his dad slowly roll an apple, out into the meadow. The apple came to a stop directly in the deer's path. He'd never in a million years think his dad would do something like that. Joe watched, barely able to blink or take a breath.

It seemed to take forever for the deer to make their way to the apple. They sniffed the air. The deer approached the apple, and without any sense of danger, the smallest deer took a bite.

Joe thought at any moment he'd hear the shot. He panned from the deer back to his dad. He expected to see the barrel of a rifle sticking out of the front opening. He watched as Stan raised his camera. Joe was relieved to see Dad wasn't baiting the deer, except to capture some memories.

Deer in the meadow.

The deer took their time crossing through the meadow and walked off into the woods. Joe saw his dad pack up his bag and head down the path. Not seeing any signs of the man in the cap, he sat for a few more minutes and collected his thoughts. He thought about the fake bird calls and the vehicles he heard. He wondered about the man today and if it was the same person he saw yesterday behind the tree.

Not being able to make any sense of it at all, Joe headed down the trail to meet his dad. At first, he started off at a brisk pace. Then he realized he had no idea where the man in the cap had gone. He might at any moment run right into him. Joe slowed his pace, not wanting to make any sound by snapping a twig, or crunching leaves. He tuned his ears for someone else's movement. His eyes moved side to side, and every forty paces he'd stop, turn, and listen. He had spooked himself into believing he was being followed.

* * *

Stan hiked the Lost Swamp Trail, glad to be out in the woods on such a beautiful fall day. Up ahead he heard an odd noise. He listened carefully. The sounds of the rustling indicated something big. He took his rifle off his shoulder, and standing still, tried to guess the size of the beast. He certainly didn't want to surprise a bear, but he hoped it might be a buck.

Stan crept along the trail, then leaned against a tree. He could hear the crunching of the dried maple and birch leaves clearly, but he couldn't see any animal. He moved closer and stepped on a dried branch. The snap echoed on the quiet trail. Immediately, the shuffling stopped. Stan stood still, barely breathing.

* * *

Joe was half way down Rum Ridge Trail, when he heard two shots ring out. He froze, dead in his tracks. He remembered the signal he and his dad had worked out if either of them shot a deer. He waited for one shot, pause, three shots, pause, one shot. No more shots rang out. He raced down to the bottom of the trail unconcerned about being quiet or watching for strangers.

At the bottom, he wasn't sure what to do. His first instinct was to head towards Lost Swamp and the direction of the shots. He decided he'd stay put for ten minutes, before heading down the trail to find his dad. He was worried and looked over his shoulder every few seconds. The feeling that he was being watched returned. He wished his mom was around – at least she'd know what to do.

At about the time Joe was going to start walking towards the sound of the shots, his dad came around the bend in the trail. Joe was relieved to see him, and jumped right into telling him about the man he saw earlier in the meadow. He completely forgot to ask if his dad heard the gun shots.

Stan considered the description Joe gave of the man. "Sure doesn't meet the description of Red or any of his crew. None of them dress in anything but flannel and suspenders. This is getting stranger and stranger. In all my years around these woods, this has to be the biggest mystery since Grandpa's story about the apple pie that disappeared. Until Grandpa finally put a latch on that kitchen window, those racoons were having a field day stealing from us."

Joe laughed, remembering Grandpa's story. "And the man didn't look like he was a hunter at all. I've never seen anyone dressed the way he was."

"Do you think it was the same man you saw behind the blind yesterday?"

"I'm not sure. It was hard to see a face yesterday. But that man was not wearing a strange cap. If I saw the man from today up close, I'd recognize him. I got a good look through my binoculars."

There was silence as they began to walk down the trail towards the camp. Both of them were deep in thought about who this strange person in their woods might be.

Joe tried to forget worrying about it and asked, "Dad, why don't we skip the fishing and continue hunting? It's our last day here and we don't have our deer. Besides, I am all fished out."

"That's fine with me, son. Either way, we don't need to have fish tonight."

Stan pulled two grouse from his pack. "I was able to snag these two on the swamp trail. They had wing injuries and could no longer fly. I'm not sure if they inflicted the injury on one another or were in a scramble with a fox or bobcat. They were making one heck of a ruckus on the trail."

"Those are some nice birds, Dad. Grouse with potatoes and apples like Mom used to make sure will hit the spot on a cold night. That also explains the two shots I heard earlier." Joe was relieved this was the reason for the gunfire.

"What do you say we head back, grab Sparky, and then take the truck to hunt over on the west side of Lobster Lake? That's always a good bet this time of year for deer. You can drive."

"Sure, Dad. We can let Sparky hang in the truck as we hunt, and then I'll run him around a bit before we head back."

"Great idea, he could use the exercise."

As they walked along Bug Bog trail, Stan wondered if they were in any danger. He hoped that Henry might stop back at the camp if he discovered anything suspicious on his investigation.

The Deadwater

Driving the dirt roads, at a speed too high for the twists, turns, and bumps, Henry's mind raced with clues about Red and his gang. Last summer, every time Henry came across them, they were over the daily catch limit. This time of year, most of the freshwater fisheries had already closed, at least for the legal season. So, if Henry caught them fishing, most likely they'd be fishing on closed waters. Henry suspected if they weren't fishing, they might be doing their share of game poaching. No matter what the circumstances, he had a good hunch these guys were up to no good. The next story he wanted passed around at the diner was how Ford caught the poachers. Before he could catch them, he had to figure out how he was going to find them.

When he made the turn toward the Deadwater area, Henry realized he didn't know if he should head towards Cassidy Deadwater or Caribou Deadwater. To contemplate his dilemma, he pulled off the road to think about which would be the best hideout for the gang.

Thanks to all of Bonnie's coffee he had gulped down, he had to step out of the car to visit Aunt Abby. As he walked to the side of the road, a black pickup truck came rumbling over the hill. The truck looked new, but sounded worse than one that was old and worn down. It wasn't a truck Henry recognized, and he knew just about everyone that would be driving out here. It definitely wasn't one of the Lobster Lake Bandits. By the sound of it, the truck was missing its muffler.

Henry took a step toward the road to get a better look. The truck slowed down but did not stop. A man wearing a green cap gave Henry a two-finger salute and drove on. Henry acknowledged the man with a raise of his own hand. He had never seen the person before. Henry continued on his way, but couldn't get his mind off who the man in the black truck may have been.

At the Hannibal Brook crossing, Henry noticed the ground to the right of the bridge was all torn up. He pulled over to take a closer look. It appeared that someone had decided to make their own crossing through the shallow water. Based on the ruts through the mud, it was obvious the driver became stuck when trying to drive up the bank on the other side. Henry drove over the wooden bridge and parked to investigate.

He noticed there were two sets of truck tires and four different sets of boot prints in the mud. A coil of rope was discarded, or forgotten on the ground, indicating whoever was stuck had help getting pulled out. Henry suspected immediately it was Red and the Bandits. He leaned against a tree and concluded the two trucks were probably having a road race when one truck decided to make a pass through the stream and got stuck in the mud.

Henry was proud of himself for piecing together the crime scene, north woods style. He made a note of his findings in his warden log – date, location, and description. Fishing for his camera in the clutter of the back seat he discovered he was out of film. He made a mental note to pick up more on his next trip to the Augusta warden supply warehouse.

The tracks through the mud gave Henry the assurance that the information from Bonnie was accurate and he was hot on the gang's trail. Red and his cronies probably drove this way not too long ago. Before getting back in his car, Henry stood by the tire tracks trying to understand why any outdoorsmen would drive through a stream, when there was a perfectly good bridge to use.

He was annoyed, because while it might not seem a big deal to drive through the stream bed, doing so meant mud would be washed into the water from the channels left by the tire ruts when it rained. Henry knew that the cloudier the water, the less the sun could penetrate the surface to generate food in the form of algae the fish needed to live. Aside from that, most of the fresh water fish, such as bass, are sight feeders. The murkier the water, the harder it would be for them to survive.

Henry shook his head, more determined than ever to catch up with Red. The frigid wind blowing down the alley of the stream reminded Henry that he was losing daylight. He hurried back to the warmth of the car to continue his pursuit.

Henry knew he had to hustle if he was to go all the way to the north and still be home at a reasonable hour. It always worried Alice when he was out alone in the woods long after nightfall, especially this time of year. More than once Henry had to sleep in his car due to a breakdown, a double flat tire, or running out of gas. As the November sun went down earlier and earlier each day, the temperature dropped quickly and sleeping inside a car was no fun. The deathly cold was not the only danger of being out in the woods alone. Henry also knew that drunk hunters were an unpredictable bunch. Usually, if a warden felt it necessary, he would travel with backup. But that could take days to arrange, time Henry didn't have this afternoon. He figured Red and his gang were more troublemakers than serious trouble, and he'd be fine going it alone.

Dirt road to the Deadwaters.

It was already past two o'clock when Henry reached Beaver Bog Brook. He slid out of his cruiser to stretch his legs. Standing next to his vehicle he thought he was hearing things. Then he realized that the sounds were men laughing. He walked along the side of the road sticking close to the cover of the tree line. Just around a curve in the road, not more than thirty feet from where he left his vehicle, Red's 46' Ford and his buddy's green truck were idling side by side in the center of the road. The men weren't laughing, they were arguing something fierce.

"If I didn't pull your sorry truck out of that mud back there you'd still be there," Red yelled through his window into his buddy's truck.

"Bull! Junior and I would have been able to get out and still beat you to camp."

"Well why don't you put your money where your mouth is. I'll race you from right here. Five bucks on it."

"You're on. On the count of three."

The two trucks started revving their engines. Henry could barely hear the count. The trucks kicked up dirt and gravel and barreled down the dirt road. Henry hustled back to his cruiser. He couldn't believe his dumb luck. Had he driven a few more feet, and rounded that corner, his surveillance game would have been blown.

When Henry crept his cruiser around the bend in the road, the Bandits were long gone, the dust they kicked up was still settling. To avoid coming up on them and being spotted, Henry drove on at a slower, more cautious pace. If he couldn't find their hideout by dusk, he figured he'd loop around the Deadwater and head for home. With a little luck, Alice would have a few pies done for tomorrow's feast. She'd surely be happy he was home and might let him cut into the apple one. With the vision of pie in his head, Henry was confident that he was at least closer to knowing where the gang was hiding out. In his head, he put a plan together to locate their camp, and then travel back up this way with a partner the day after Thanksgiving.

*　*　*

Stan let Joe drive the truck up Rum Ridge Road and across to the north side of Lobster Lake. Joe loved driving around these old logging roads kicking up gravel and dust. By the time he parked, the afternoon sun was already low in the sky and the temperature was dropping fast. They only had a short time to do some hunting before dusk.

"Sparky, we'll be back in a little bit, boy."

The dog, recognizing the tone of the words, curled up on the seat in his fox position for another nap.

Joe and Stan walked along the road for a hundred yards until they reached a clearing.

"I bet deer travel through here regularly. Let's walk a ways along the wood line," Stan said.

Where a brook ran through the woods, they sat on a fallen tree, and waited for the deer to come to them. Not a creature stirred the entire time they were there. With the sun setting, they both knew they had to call it a night.

On the way back to the truck, Joe said, "Dad, I've been thinking. We'd better leave a little earlier tomorrow to make a stop at Henry's. I want to let him know what I saw back in the meadow, you know, about the man. If someone strange is out here in the woods, I'd rather Henry know in advance and not get surprised."

"That's a good idea. I also want to tell him about the perch we pulled out of Duck Pond. It'll have to be a quick visit so we're not late getting to your Aunt's house."

"I sure am looking forward to that meal."

"Hey, I thought you said you liked my cooking?"

"I do. But Thanksgiving only comes once a year, and Aunt Shirley makes the best stuffing and gravy. Next to Mom, that is."

"They both had the same recipe from your Grandma."

"Oh, that explains…ahhh" said Joe, trying to catch his balance as he fell to the ground.

"You okay?"

"Yeah, I think so. I tripped on this." He pulled out a heavy-duty canvas bag that was stuck under the pine needles and some sticks.

Joe opened the cowhide lacing. "It's empty."

"Strange. I've never seen a bag like that before. May as well keep it, could be useful for something."

Taking his dad's suggestion, Joe stuffed the bag in his pack.

Back at the truck, Joe let Sparky jump out. The dog ran up and down the side of the road sniffing every tree and weed.

"Here, boy, fetch." After chasing the stick twice, Sparky bolted back to the truck, and barked at the door.

"It must be even too cold out here for Sparky," Stan said.

"More likely he knows it's close to dinner time and he wants to get back to camp."

"I'm pretty hungry myself. Let's go cook up those birds and the last of the vegetables. We can then get a start on packing up for the morning."

As Joe drove the truck down the dusty dirt road, his dad asked, "Are you disappointed you didn't get a deer this trip, Joe?"

"It's a little disappointing, but it's been fun anyway. The mystery of what's going on out here is exciting. I can't wait to tell Don about it." Joe pulled the truck down the camp drive and put it in park.

"Nice driving, Joe. You're getting good shifting the gears in this old truck."

"Thanks. You taught me well."

Walking up the porch steps, Joe came to an abrupt stop. "Dad, you'd better look at this."

Stan came over and looked down to see three cigarette butts crushed into the ground. Stan had never smoked. The only person that would have been around might have been Henry and neither of them knew him to smoke.

"The man I saw in the field was smoking. Could it have been him?"

"If he had time to smoke three cigarettes, he must've been here for more than a few minutes," Stan said.

"Why would he sit on our porch and smoke?"

"I have no idea. But he certainly wasn't stalking around hiding. Let's get inside. You load up the woodstove and I'll get dinner started. The sky is clear as glass tonight. It's gonna be a cold one."

Red and the Bandits

Red peeled down the camp's grassy rutted path, sliding to a stop inches before ramming into Al's rear bumper. He jumped down from his truck, all two-hundred and fifty pounds of him, his boots pounding the frozen ground with a thud.

"You're a cheat. I am not paying you a dime," he bellowed.

"Now, Red, I won fair and square." Al tried to hide his smirk.

"You cut through that woods trail. You know I ain't gonna take my new truck through there an get it all scratched up!"

"Well, next time ya better spell out the rules. This time you owe me five bucks and I don't want any deer antlers. I want it in cash."

The others laughed, knowing Red was one to take things to the literal extreme, especially if he had lost a bet.

"We'll see about that," mumbled Red.

Red then turned his fury on Junior. "Junior, go and break up any ice that has formed on those barrels and then bring in some firewood."

With darkness fast approaching, the gang stumbled into their crude camp, a single room building with a dirt floor. Inside four army cots topped with sleeping bags were lined along the sides. An old wooden picnic table with knife marks in the surface sat at the center of the room. Two ten-inch hunting knives were stabbed deep into the wood. The table was compliments of the State of Maine, seeing it was left alone at the interstate rest stop last winter. A couple of non-functioning old gas lamps hung on the walls, thanks to a seasonal restaurant that left them unattended after closing in the fall. The wicks in the lamps had long ago burnt down and Red was too cheap to replace them. Instead, Red lit a kerosene lantern that sat on the table. He had acquired their newest lighting from a tent site along Allagash Stream a few days earlier. They waited for a hunting party to leave, and then made off with their lantern, bacon, coffee, and even the sleeping bags that now made the cots much more comfortable.

In the corner was an ancient iron cook stove that they had saved from an abandoned camp on Maple Ridge, west of Allagash Pond. At least the camp was unoccupied and abandoned for the season when they happened by. The stove, being poorly vented, always filled the one room camp with black smoke when lit each morning and night. Red, not taking any ownership for the poor installation, would cuss the former owners, "I bet they're glad this thing is gone from their camp. I should bring it back to them."

Two wooden chairs with wicker webbing were placed near the stove. Upturned wooden milk crates with, "Property of the Maine Dairy" painted in white on the sides, served as foot rests. Along the back wall the gang had stacked a collection of items they found in other 'abandoned' camps. They had an assortment of fishing poles, oars, tackle boxes, buckets, cookware, saws, gas cans, three or four axes, and even a boat motor. A bookcase, all the books dumped and left in the reading room of the Pemadumcook Lake Summer Camp for Girls, displayed six tube radios Red had acquired. When Al asked what the point was of having radios at a camp with no power, Red hit him with a tennis racket, also stolen from the girl's camp, that Red had no use for until that moment.

A clothes line, which was actually some poor soul's boat anchor line, stretched from one end of the camp to the other. Each night the gang hung their sweaty long johns and undershirts to dry across the rope. An old pickle barrel, never washed out, was turned upside down for the kitchen counter. A few fish parts were left on the top from the breakfast preparations earlier this morning. The fish guts, sweaty clothes, wet dirt floor, and general mildew and filth smell, gave the camp a stench so strong that even the local bear population kept their distance. The thick black smoke from the stove Red started, took over the other smells, at least temporarily.

Al opened the camp's only door to let in some air. That was some relief from the smoke, until Red yelled, "Al close the darn door. I'm not slaving here to start the fire to heat the outdoors!" Al took one more whiff of the biting cold fresh air before closing the door.

* * *

Henry pulled into a logging clearing along the Deadwater Pond Road and parked his car deep in the bushes, out of eyesight from anyone who might happen by. Over his field coat he put on his heavy green hooded parka. He grabbed his flashlight, hung his rifle over his shoulder, and set out on foot. He knew of a camp that was up-a-ways on the road and didn't want to risk losing the element of surprise. As he hadn't been up this way in months, he wasn't sure how far he was going to be walking. It might be a quarter of a mile or it might be closer to a mile. He hoped for the shorter.

After walking for a half mile, he came to a pond, where he heard someone talking. Henry took slow, cautious steps, avoiding twigs and crispy frozen leaves. Twenty feet from the person, he hid behind a tree and listened.

"Junior do this. Junior do that. I'm not even a junior and I don't want to be 'Red Junior,' ever! Why did he name me Michael if he doesn't use my name?"

In the moonlight, Henry watched the young boy, who was not more than seventeen, swish a thick stick around inside fifty-five-gallon drums that were lined up in rows. Henry recognized the boy as the youngest of the Bandits, but only now knew that Junior was Red's son. Each time he swooshed the stick around a new barrel, the sound of thin panes of glass cracking echoed across the pond. As he stirred, the boy continued to complain out loud about Red and the others. It was obvious he didn't enjoy their company, or how they treated him. When he finished breaking up the ice in the last barrel, Junior flung the stick into the bog and headed back up the trail.

Henry waited a few minutes and then crept over to the nearest drum. His face became flush and his anger boiled once he saw what was in the barrels. Forgetting he had walked a half mile from his car, he turned in a rush to get to his vehicle and grab his camera. "Doggone it." He stopped short when he remembered where he was and that the camera had no film anyway.

Without picture evidence those darn defense lawyers would make sure Red was never charged for this. And if he was lucky enough to get a charge against them, the liberal judges in Augusta would just as soon throw the case right out on some technicality, like not having a search warrant. Henry thought, "Who the heck could get a search warrant way out here in the woods?"

Walking along the trees, Henry tried to find the path the boy had taken. Darkness had settled in, making it difficult to see more than a few feet ahead. More than once Henry ended up getting a branch in his eye. He surprised a couple of deer that were out strolling for their evening dinner. The closer one let out a bark that was a cross between a hiss, a throat clearing, and a scream. He motioned to the deer with a finger over his lips to be quiet. The doe cocked her head and walked off.

Henry continued on. He didn't want to chance using his flashlight. A branch caught his hat and flipped it to the ground. Startled he grabbed his sidearm. Only then he realized he had not been marking his trail through the thick brush. A thought ran through his mind that it could be a long night if he couldn't find his vehicle again.

It wasn't until he came to a dead tree blocking his way, that Henry realized he must have passed the path. He was considering having to use his light, when he heard a door slam off to his left. He couldn't believe his luck. He walked in the direction of the slam and ended up right in the camp's grass driveway. The two pickup trucks were parked right at the door.

Henry approached with caution to get a better look. His heart started beating faster. He didn't want to surprise a member of the gang since he wasn't sure how they'd react to seeing him out here, especially alone.

Creeping along the side of the trucks, he spotted empty fifty-five-gallon drums lying down in each truck bed. Henry started to put the pieces together. Getting angrier by the second, he told himself to keep calm. Standing next to Red's truck, he noticed a dim light was shining through the camps only window. He stayed low and crept up to the building. The window was covered in so much dirt and grime, that someone had intentionally smeared on the inside, he could only see the silhouettes of three people sitting at a table.

He walked around to the back of the cabin. There he found more barrels. Turning, he saw a deer hanging on a tree. Henry checked it over. By the state of the aging, he figured it must have been shot early this morning or late yesterday. With no tag on it, he reached for his camera. "Son of a poacher!" he whispered, remembering he didn't have it, or any film anyway.

Someone coughed, catching Henry off guard. Henry figured he was spotted. As he slowly turned, the outhouse door opened. Henry crouched behind the nearest blue drum. Red emerged, his frame filling the entire door frame, his head almost touching the moose antlers hanging over the door. Pulling his wide red suspenders up over his shoulders, Red gazed over in Henry's direction, looking directly over the drum Henry was hiding behind. Henry peaked around the side of the barrel to see Red in a trance looking up at the deer.

Red stood admiring the deer he had shot earlier that morning before sunrise. He had used his typical technique. He woke up while it was still dark, grabbed a flashlight, and his rifle. Quietly opening the cabin door, he surprised a deer eating the apples he had left in a pile the night before. He never even had to leave the cabin doorway. Shining the flashlight in the eyes of the deer, the animal never had a chance. The shot rang out, startling Al, Moose, and Junior out of their sleep.

Henry watched as Red lit a cigarette and walked slowly to the cabin taking gulps from his can of beer. On the way, Red stopped and examined the pile of apples on the ground. He slammed the door behind him. Henry could hear him yelling something at the others inside. The door opened, Junior came out and threw another dozen apples on the pile, and then ran back inside.

Without a camera, a search warrant, or backup, Henry knew there was only one thing to do – he had to head back to town. By the looks of things here, he could tell these boys were planning a night of drinking. He figured he could be back at first light with his supervisor, and maybe another warden. The three of them could easily get the jump on the gang before they even opened their eyes. For a bust this big, even Alice would understand the need to delay Thanksgiving dinner.

Feeling confident he wasn't going to be spotted, Henry headed back out the easy way, following the driveway to the road. Once in the clear, he flipped on his flashlight and hustled back to where he left his cruiser. Sitting behind the wheel, with the heater blasting, he was glad to be on his way home.

* * *

Alice had been so busy preparing for tomorrow's meal, she had forgotten to worry about Henry for the past hour. Just then, from the kitchen sink where she was standing peeling potatoes, she noticed the headlights swing across the grass driveway. Instantly she was relieved that Henry was home at somewhat a reasonable hour.

Instead of hearing Henry's greeting, "I'm home," a knock on the door startled Alice. She wondered who could be calling on Thanksgiving Eve and what type of animal they might be dropping off. The last thing she needed tonight was a delivery of raccoons to deal with. She wiped her hands on her apron and turned the door knob. In the shadowy darkness on the porch was a man Alice had never seen before.

"Hello."

"Yes, may I help you?"

The man was dressed in green army pants, a matching jacket, and a weird style cap. It was an outfit she was not accustomed to seeing here in the north woods.

"Good evening, Mrs. Ford. I'm Special Agent Jim Smith, from the Brink's Security Company. I wonder if you might know when you expect Warden Ford this evening?" He flashed Alice his badge and identification for her to inspect.

"Come on in out of the cold, Mr. Smith. What brings you out our way? Don't tell me you have an interest in poachers or those that break the fishing laws out here in the woods."

He laughed. "No, Mrs. Ford. It's none of that. I'm sure Warden Ford keeps those activities under control in his district."

"Excuse me a moment," said Alice. She turned, pulled a pie from the oven, and turned off the wind-up timer that was ringing.

"Sure does smell good in here."

"Would you care for a piece of apple pie?"

"I couldn't be having you cut a Thanksgiving pie early on my behalf, Mrs. Ford."

"No trouble at all. I suspect Henry will come home with some story about his chasing poachers in the woods and how much he sure deserves a piece. So, I baked an extra. I already have the coffee ready, I'm expecting him home soon. Have a seat there at the table." She poured the agent a cup of coffee.

Alice carried the potatoes she had been peeling over to the table and continued her work while she asked questions. "So why is a Brink's investigator all the way up here in the woods on Thanksgiving Eve?"

"I really can't say too much about the specific purpose, but I'm following up on some leads."

"What kind of leads and how can we help you out?" pried Alice, who had learned well from Henry in asking multiple questions and not letting go without an answer.

Jim Smith answered vaguely, "The agency has been informed that there may be evidence we have been searching for at a camp near here. I thought maybe Warden Ford might have seen or heard something."

"I'll tell you one thing, Agent Smith, if there's any suspicious activity around here, Henry knows about it. There might be a lot of woods out here, but not much gets by those who live out this way." Alice was particularly thinking of her sister Bonnie, but she decided not to say so.

"I can imagine. Do you happen to know the father and son that have the camp over by Lobster Lake?" the agent asked.

"You must mean Stan Parker and his son Joe. Sure do. They're like family to us. There's no way they could have anything to do with what you are looking for," Alice snapped, getting defensive.

"No. Not at all. I came upon them out hunting today while I was searching around." He paused and lowered his voice. "I think I may have spooked the boy when he spotted me. I went by their cabin late this afternoon and waited to introduce myself. Nobody was around. Do you mind if I have a cigarette, Mrs. Ford?"

"Unfortunately, I can't stop you from inhaling that poison if you want to. However, I don't let anyone smoke, or drink alcohol, in my house. You are welcome to smoke outside. Maybe the cold will help you stop that nasty habit."

Agent Smith nodded and placed the pack back into the square pocket of his field coat. "Mrs. Ford, you remind me of my own mom. I thank you for that. It's a bad habit for sure."

"If Henry's out chasing poachers he might be late getting home. You're welcome to wait and have supper with us when he gets in. But if you do, you're expected to work for your keep," Alice said.

"I really appreciate that. I'll wait a little longer if that's all right with you. I'd be happy to help you out. What can I do?"

"It would be great if you could bring in some firewood for the stove and oven. Then get washed up so you can peel these here carrots." Alice was glad for the company, and that the agent was willing to help. She still had a lot of preparations to get through before she could get to bed tonight.

The agent found it refreshing making himself useful helping Mrs. Ford. He'd been out searching the woods alone for three weeks and these chores made him feel at home. If he was in Massachusetts right now, he'd be doing the same for his mom. While outside getting the firewood, Jim lit up a cigarette. The warm smoke heated his lungs at the same time the cold air burned his nostrils. He stumped out the cigarette, only half smoked, when he looked up and noticed Alice watching him from the window. He loaded up his arms with firewood and headed back inside. He removed his field coat and hung it on the peg near the door. After washing his hands in the basin, he sat at the table peeling the carrots.

Alice was determined to find out more about what the agent was searching for. She told him how Henry typically dealt with expired fishing licenses, night hunting, and people being over their catch limit. She tried to get the agent to tell her about the crimes he usually solved, but no matter how she asked, Agent Smith swiftly changed the subject back to Henry. They both looked up from their vegetable prep when they heard a vehicle in the driveway. Before Alice could even wipe her hands, Henry had flung the door open.

"Whose truck is that in the drive, Alice?" Henry's voice trailed off once he noticed a strange man sitting in his chair at the table peeling carrots. He was taken back by the scene and was speechless.

"This is Jim Smith. He's here working on an investigation."

Agent Smith headed over to shake Henry's hand. Henry immediately caught sight of the gun in the man's shoulder harness.

"I'm a special agent with the Brink's Security Company. We manage large sums of money and valuables."

"I'm aware of what that company does." Henry eyed the man, wondering what he was doing up in Greenville. In all the times he had seen Brink's employees, they were always wearing gray uniforms. This man was wearing green pants and strange looking combat boots.

"Would you mind showing me your identification, sir?" The agent already had his credentials out, expecting Henry to ask. Holding the badge in his hand, Henry noticed it was a much heavier weight than his warden badge, making him a bit envious.

"So, what brings you all the way up to our neck of the country, Agent Smith?"

"As I explained to Mrs. Ford, I'm investigating a crime related to the Brink's company. We have reason to believe some evidence has been stored up in this area."

Henry, getting over the surprise of seeing a strange man in his house peeling vegetables with his wife, was back to his old self. "What kind of evidence? Where might it be located? Who's involved from around these parts?"

"I apologize, Warden Ford, I really am not at liberty to discuss those details at this time. I hope you understand."

Thinking about his next question, Henry went to hang his coat, only to find the man's green coat hanging on his hook. He draped his own coat over a chair, calmly walked over to the wash bin, poured in some hot water, and washed up. Taking a seat at the table he noticed an empty plate with a fork and some crumbs on it. Alice, seeing Henry's face, brought him a dish.

Henry dug in. "This is great pie, dear."

"I'm glad you like it." Alice placed a mug of coffee down for Henry and refilled the agent's cup.

"I hope you enjoyed the pie. The apples were picked right here in our orchard out back." Henry motioned out the window, into the darkness.

"It was delicious. Mrs. Ford is a wonderful cook."

Alice watched and listened to how the two men were trying to get a feel for each other's demeanor. She knew Henry would be suspicious of any stranger, investigator or not.

"That she is. I believe it was you earlier today that passed me out on the Golden Road."

"Yes, that was me. Sorry about not stopping, I was in a hurry to check on something, and then I had to get back to the garage in town to get my muffler fixed. The shops around here close mighty early – don't they?"

"This certainly isn't a big city. How can I help you then?"

"Headquarters told me to head to Caribou Deadwater. The day before they told me someplace by Caribou Lake. I think the guy with the desk job is sending me around up here, while he sips coffee with his feet up."

Henry wanted to say he knew exactly what the agent meant, but he figured dispatch in Augusta wasn't even close to the bureaucracy at a company the size of Brink's. Instead, he took another big forkful of pie.

The agent continued to describe the place he was searching for. "The information I was given, was to find a place near McGinnus Pond – a camp with moose antlers over the outhouse door."

Crumbs flew from Henry's mouth.

"Do you know this camp, Warden Ford?"

"Are you kidding me? Every camp up here has an outhouse. And ninety percent of them have moose antlers over the outhouse door. Sometimes these proud princes of the woods will hang antlers not only outside, but also inside that they can admire as they sit on their throne."

"Oh. How about around McGinnus Pond? Do you know it?"

"Have you been there?" Henry asked the agent.

"I cannot locate it. It's not on any map and I've driven around these bumpy dirt roads for days."

"Driving around is only going to get you lost," Henry stated.

"Do you know where this pond is, Warden Ford?" the agent pressed.

Henry rubbed his forehead. "Can't say as I do. Never heard of such a pond." Henry didn't let on what he was thinking.

Alice refilled their cups and asked, "Henry, do you think he might mean McGooseley Pond?"

Staring into his mug, Henry thought his wife always had a way of knowing what he was thinking, but had yet to learn not to say it out loud.

"McGooseley and McGinnus, don't sound the same to me," Henry said, trying to divert the conversation as he sipped his coffee.

"Now, Warden, let's not dismiss that suggestion. Mrs. Ford, where is this McGooseley Pond?" Agent Smith stared at

Alice. He was interested in what she had to say and was hoping Henry would let her say it.

"Henry would know better, I just remember a pond by that name."

"I actually was within a few miles of that pond today and..." Henry started to say something when he abruptly stopped, wondering if this agent was chasing Red and his gang. He wasn't about to let some Boston security guard take the credit for his bust. It could very well be the biggest crime operation ever discovered by a single warden. Without pictures of those blue drums at Red's camp, Henry had little proof that he had found the crime scene on his own. Then he realized the agent must have no clue about where the Bandits were, otherwise why would he be here. He figured a bust between the investigator and the Maine Warden Service might make for some spectacular news. He might even get to meet the governor.

"And what, Warden? You were up that way and what?" The agent tried to get Henry to continue.

"I was up that way doing some surveillance on a group of poachers that keep me busy. What type of crime did you say you were investigating?"

"I didn't. That would be against my orders to disclose the nature of an investigation, unless it was directly necessary. Did you locate the group you were looking for?"

"Sure did. They are at a camp right now along the Cassidy Deadwater."

"Another Deadwater? What is it about naming these places around here?"

"Actually, Cassidy and Caribou Deadwaters are connected by Deadwater Stream. So when you drove by me earlier, I ended up right where you wanted to get to." Henry was more and more suspecting that Smith was chasing Red and the Bandits for their activity.

"What did you find up that way, Warden?"

"As I said, I located this gang, the Lobster Lake Bandits, as I call them, at a rundown shack of a camp. Outside their cabin there was a hanging deer that they may have shot illegally."

"And that was it? That's all you saw?"

"That's it." Henry decided it wasn't yet necessary to tell the agent about the drums.

"Might I convince you to drive up there with me now and investigate?" the agent asked.

Alice, who was standing at the counter kneading bread dough, stopped what she was doing, and gave Henry a concerned look.

Henry thought about how to respond. He sure wanted to nab Red and his buddies. They'd be surprised to see Henry show up tonight, and having Jim Smith along as backup would certainly help. He also knew there was a chance he wouldn't be able to convince his boss to send someone tomorrow, not on Thanksgiving.

He answered the agent after thinking it over. "It's awfully late and cold tonight. Those guys are busy getting drunk and aren't going anywhere. I say we head out before first light. We can show up before they're even out of bed. They surely won't be expecting any company. And in the morning, they won't be three sheets to the wind with rifles in their hands."

"But, Henry, tomorrow is Thanksgiving and my sister Bonnie and Wilson are coming," pleaded Alice.

"Mrs. Ford, I promise we'll be back by afternoon."

The agent stood to leave. "Warden, I'll be back here by four-thirty. I'll follow you up to that camp. If there are four of them, we'll need both vehicles if an arrest needs to be made." He turned to Alice. "Mrs. Ford, thank you for the pie and coffee. It reminded me of home." And with that the agent was out the door, not staying for supper.

Henry walked over to the wall where the phone was hanging. He was thinking he should arrange for a backup warden to go along with him and the agent. He picked up the handle. He dialed the first three numbers of his superior officer, District Warden Guilford H. Bingham. Warden Bingham was so named by his mother, a teacher from Guilford, who married a man named Bingham, who settled the family in Hermon. Mrs. Bingham always said she had enough to think about with a baby on the way, and it was the best she could do for a name at the time. Aside from a four-year deployment with the Marines, Bingham had spent his entire life in northern Maine and did everything by the book, all the time.

Henry stopped dialing and hung up the handset. First, he realized it was 9:02 p.m. Unless there was a murder, and deer or moose didn't count, Bingham had made it plenty clear to Henry to never call past nine. Since there never had been a murder, Henry had never called his supervisor in the late evening before, and he wasn't going to start now. Second, he already had backup. He figured the special agent would certainly provide the kind of cover needed to deal with Red and his gang, why bother Bingham at all, especially on Thanksgiving Eve.

Henry was writing in his warden log, when Alice sat down and waited for him to look up. She always did that when she had something on her mind.

"What is it?"

"Are you sure you have to go all the way up to the Deadwater again tomorrow? It's a holiday."

"We'll be fine. Those men are up to no good, I know it. They won't expect us on Thanksgiving. I have a feeling they'll be pulling out tomorrow to get home. We need to get there before they do."

He shuffled through the papers on the end table. "Did you happen to pick up today's paper? I wanted to read the sports section and check the weather forecast."

"They didn't have it. Susy at the Trading Post said the delivery never made it from Bangor today."

"That figures."

Henry read from his Dickens novel until his eyes were too heavy to keep open, and then went to bed hoping to get six hours of sleep before the morning road trip. Instead, he tossed and turned all night thinking through a game plan to nab Red and the Bandits this time.

Thanksgiving Surprise

"Henry! Henry!" Alice poked Henry in his side.

"What is it?"

"Your alarm clock, it's going off. Can't you hear it?"

In that place between sleep and being awake, Henry couldn't believe that 4 a.m. had rolled around already. He tried to shake himself awake. The fog of his dream, the one where he was the Chief of Wardens on a Caribbean island, came floating back to him. In the dream, he was wearing shorts, a holster belt, loafers, and a Hawaiian style shirt. He hated Hawaiian shirts and didn't even own a pair of shorts. It was his worst recurring nightmare. He pulled himself from under the warm covers and was jolted awake once his feet hit the icy cold pine floor boards. No tropical weather in sight.

Dressing in record time, he went to the living room and added logs to the coals in the stove. He threw on a pair of boots, his hunting jacket, and headed out to the outhouse. When he opened the front door, his mouth dropped. It was still dark out, but the yard was looking very different this morning.

"Alice, you'd better come see this."

Still in her flannel nightgown and slippers, Alice walked up behind Henry. "Oh my. We haven't had a white Thanksgiving in years."

Four inches of fresh snow was covering the ground, and it was coming down fast and heavy. Henry knew there was no way he'd be making a trip up to the Deadwater in this weather.

Even though he was looking forward to nabbing the Bandits, he felt more relaxed, and went about his morning routine at a much slower pace. For a fleeting moment, he thought about going back to bed, but he didn't want to have a repeat of that dream. Rather, he sat down and read his *Fish and Fowl* magazine, while waiting for the coffee to brew.

Watching the snow fall, Henry was certain that Agent Smith would hunker down for the day. He decided he'd give a call to the inn, where the agent was staying, after his breakfast. It was too early to start calling anyone at this hour anyway.

Henry was pouring his second cup of coffee when he heard a vehicle in the driveway. He glanced up at the clock on the wall. It was 4:25. A horn honked. Henry stepped out onto the covered porch. With a slow sip of his coffee he shook his head. He couldn't believe this agent.

"What's he thinking driving in this storm in that little truck?" Henry said out loud.

Smith yelled from his open window, "We'd better hurry, Warden, if we are going to beat this snow."

"Agent Smith, you don't beat snow. This is Maine. Snow beats you every time. Now that you're here, come on in and have coffee?"

Alice, standing next to Henry on the porch, was a little shocked at the determination of the agent. Agent Smith turned off his truck, ran through the snow, and strode up the porch steps.

"Good morning, Mrs. Ford."

"Good morning to you as well, Agent Smith. We're surprised to see you driving around in this weather."

"I had a heck of a time getting up that hill right outside of town. My truck doesn't seem to be equipped to handle the snow."

"You should realize you're in the north woods, not the maintained roads of Boston. You could get yourself stranded."

"Why don't we all go inside. Standing out here in the cold isn't going to make the snow stop any sooner," Alice said, in her wisdom to avoid a showdown.

Inside, Henry immediately went to the phone. "I'd better call down to dispatch for a weather update." He held his index finger next to the number for the central office and dialed.

"Good morning, this is Warden Henry Ford, up in Greenville. Could you tell me what the weather forecast is for today?"

"Yes, sir. Snow is expected all day in that area," came the reply from the on-duty dispatch officer.

"Can you give me any more details than that?"

"Not really, Warden Ford. A brief came over the teletype a few minutes ago, but there weren't many more details."

"May I ask what the teletype printout said?" asked Henry, a bit impatient.

The dispatcher let out a deep sigh, as if Henry was keeping him from something important. "Please hold. I already filed it."

The dispatcher came back on the line and said, "Hello? Are you there?"

"Yes, I'm here."

"The report reads,

'A surprise winter storm has developed off the east coast of Maine in the past several hours. It has characteristics of a Nor'easter. Downeast should expect sleet and freezing rain. Northern Maine should expect snow on the order of eight to twenty inches between 3 a.m. and 9 p.m., depending on the elevation. Happy Thanksgiving. stop'

That's it, Warden. I'm not sure if that last part was a true wish or a sarcastic remark."

"Okay, thank you. Happy Thanksgiving," Henry added, before hanging up.

Alice was staring at Henry with an expectant look. When he didn't say anything, she asked, "What did the dispatcher say, Henry?"

"It's going to be a tough storm. Up to twenty inches." He stood with his hand against the window frame staring at the pines painted white. He knew this much snow, on a day a lot of people would want to travel, was going to cause a lot of problems.

The agent had none of the warden's concerns. He had one thing on his mind, and that was his investigation. "We'd better shove off, Warden Ford, if we are to get you back in time for your turkey dinner."

Henry turned to look at Jim Smith. He realized Smith was not all that familiar with the north woods, but the man must have some common sense to know going out in weather like this wasn't a smart idea.

"Did you happen to see that sedan parked out in the driveway, Agent Smith? It drives about as well in five inches of snow as it does in quick sand. And once eight inches piles up, your truck ain't gonna fare much better. And that's if there are no hills along the way, which isn't the case at all. Right now I don't see us going anywhere. If we did, we'd get about an hour out of town and we'd end up completely stranded with no way to get help. Even the town plow will not go north of the Lily Bay store."

"Why don't the two of you sit down. I'll make you some eggs and bacon while you decide on a plan," Alice said, trying to keep the peace.

As the two men tried to get a better idea on how to approach their predicament, the snow came down even harder. Sitting at the kitchen table, they stared out the window, not saying a word. The rising sun struggled to shed some light on the darkness. They sat in silence eating the eggs, bacon, and home-fries Alice served them. After Henry had seconds of the bacon, he took down his snow stick, an old yardstick broken at the twenty-five-inch mark, from over the front door. The agent followed him outside.

Henry pushed the stick down into the snow a few feet from the porch. The snow was already over six inches. Even though he knew it should already be daylight, the sky wasn't much brighter than when he first woke up, thanks to the thick storm clouds blocking out the sun. He trudged back inside and sat down in his chair.

A little before six, the phone rang. Alice picked it up. "Good morning, Bonnie. Yes, we've seen it. No, we certainly don't want you attempting to drive down here. We can have Thanksgiving dinner tomorrow, after the weather clears. Knowing Nate, I'm sure he has the town plow already out and about. We'll talk later, bye."

Jim Smith went to the window. "Are we going to sit here all day, Warden?"

"Right now, I can't think of any other place I'd rather be." Henry watched as Alice slid the turkey into the oven.

* * *

Joe's alarm clock rang and bounced off his shelf onto the floor. "I really have to make that shelf wider," he said picking it up.

Sparky slowly lifted himself off his crumpled-up blanket on the floor next to the bed, stretched, and let out his morning groan. He walked to the front door and gave a whine.

Joe threw on his boots and the camp hat his mom had knitted for him. When he opened the cabin door, the wind howled and a stream of flakes came floating into the room. His mouth dropped as he looked out at the sea of white that covered the entire yard. Sparky barked.

"Hey, Dad, you'd better come see this."

Stan looked over Joe's shoulder. "Uh oh, the paper never said anything about snow."

"Can we drive through it?"

"We'd better try. It's going to take us twenty minutes to pack up and close down the camp, so we'd better get a move on it – and quick."

Without a fire burning, they had to wear their winter coats and hats as they packed. Stan drained all the water pipes, and put up the winter shutters preparing for a full season shutdown. Once they had stuffed their gear in the bed of the truck, they struggled trying to tie down the tarp in the wind. By the time they were done, their fingers and toes were numb.

"My toes are about frozen," Joe said.

"The truck will warm up quick once we get going. You obviously didn't put on the good wool socks your aunt made you to wear with those hunting boots."

Ignoring the well-deserved lecture, Joe asked, "Do you think the truck can get through this much snow, Dad?"

"We're about to find out."

As Stan put the truck in gear it slid sideways. He rocked the truck back and forth and gave it some gas. The tires spun and the truck lurched forward. Stan struggled to keep the truck in the center of the road. A thin layer of ice coated the dirt under the snow, making for slippery conditions. As he rounded a bend, Stan noticed that the grade up the hill toward Rum Ridge looked a lot steeper in the snow. Joe swallowed hard as his dad gave the truck some gas to build up speed to get over the hill.

Halfway up the incline, Joe screamed, "Dad, look out!"

A doe and a fawn shot out from the side of the road and ran in front of the truck. Stan hit the brakes to avoid a collision and the truck went into a skid. He tried to keep the wheels straight but the ice under the snow took over. The rear tire dropped into the ditch along the side of the road. A large bang indicated the bottom of the truck had hit the hard ground.

Stan contemplated the two deer, who had stopped on the other side of the road and were looking back towards the truck. "Do you think they are sorry about that, or glad to have disabled the two mighty hunters?"

"I don't know, but right now, I wish my hunting rifle wasn't back at the cabin," exclaimed Joe.

They both laughed at the irony of the situation, not yet comprehending the predicament they were in.

* * *

Al opened the camp door, on his way to the outhouse, and stopped short. "Hey, Red, you better have a look out here."

"What is it? A warden?" Red let out a big laugh, not yet moving from his cot. "What time is it?"

"It's seven. And it's worse than a warden."

Hearing the commotion, Moose rolled off his cot, held his head, and walked over to the door behind Red. The three men had all slept late from their boozing most of the night.

Junior, was glad they passed out, since it gave him more time to sleep and less time getting yelled at. He also went over to see what was going on.

At first, they were speechless seeing the snow, which by this time was getting close to the top of their truck tires.

"Yikes. The paper I swiped from the lady at the Lily Bay store had no mention of snow! What the heck are they trying to do, strand people out here?" Red groaned. He pulled on his boots and sloshed to the outhouse, jumping ahead of Al's turn.

"Do you think we're gonna be able to drive out of here, Uncle Al?" Junior asked.

"I doubt it. This here's gonna be a big problem. A light snow we could drive over. A few inches would melt in a day or two. But this? There's already more than seven inches and it's coming down heavy. When it snows this much, this early in the season, there's usually snow all the way until May."

"What about getting home for Thanksgiving turkey?" Junior whined.

"Turkey? Are you kidding me? We won't miss that. We have that whole deer hanging out back, best eating you can imagine. Do you think the Pilgrims ate turkey? They had grouse and deer for sure. And we have plenty of fish."

While Al and Moose talked about living off the land, like the settlers did, Junior didn't want to think about eating any more fish, he was sick of it already.

"But how are we going to get out of here?" Junior persisted.

The seriousness of the situation was starting to sink into his uncle's aching head. Shoveling miles and miles of back roads was not an option he wanted to consider.

By this time Red had returned from the outhouse. Pulling up his suspenders, he barked, "Stop your whining, Junior. You can walk, can't you. Maybe I'll make you push me in my truck." He let out a deep bellowing laugh. None of the others saw any humor in the situation.

"Junior, go break up the ice on those barrels while I figure how to get us all outta here," Red said, while opening his morning cans of beer and Spam.

Stranded

The two lawmen sat at the table staring out the window. Agent Smith's truck was barely visible behind a snow drift the wind had driven against it. Henry would have been content to sit and listen to the roar of the fire all day, watching the snow pile up, with the smell of the roasting turkey filling the room. The investigator had other ideas.

"Warden, how about the town's plow? Couldn't they escort us up to the Deadwater?"

Alice looked over at Henry, hoping he wasn't going to consider such a suggestion.

"That's one heck of a long way to plow outside of the town jurisdiction. They certainly aren't going to be doing it on Thanksgiving."

"The Brink's Company would reimburse the town for gas and salary for the employee."

Henry gazed down into his coffee mug, obviously thinking about it. "It's unlikely the town manager would approve such an expedition for a few poachers."

Alice was in the kitchen, rinsing cranberries. "Henry, did Stan say when he and Joe were leaving? Do you think they might be snowed in?"

Henry turned toward Alice, hand on his chin. It was one thing to leave Red and his poacher crew stranded for a few days, but leaving Stan and Joe up there, that was a different situation.

Alice and the agent stared at Henry, waiting for him to say something.

Henry walked over to the woodstove. Opening the iron door, the fire crackled and sucked in air from the room. Flames reflected off Henry's spectacles. He placed another large maple log into the firebox. "Getting reimbursed for time and gas might make the plowing acceptable to the town selectmen. I would have to check with them."

Henry caught Alice's thin smile. She turned and went back to her cranberry sauce preparation. While she wasn't thrilled to have Henry going out in the storm, she was worried about the Parkers.

Henry picked up the phone. His eyes searched the yellowing sheet of paper taped to the knotty-pine wall, for the home phone number of the town manager, Mike Muzzy. He dialed.

"Happy Thanksgiving to you too, Paula. Is Mike available? Oh, I see. Can you see if you can catch him? Yes, this is an emergency."

While he was waiting, Henry turned to Alice and Agent Smith. "He's outside putting on his snowshoes to go hunting. That's what I should be doing this morning, it's the one thing this snow is good for, tracking deer."

Agent Smith reached into his pocket for his pack of cigarettes. Alice gave him a look with a raised eyebrow. Realizing his mistake, he put the pack back in his pocket.

"Hi, Mike, yes, yes, Happy Thanksgiving. Yes, Paula told me. I'm sorry to interrupt. Look, Mike, I have a situation and I need your assistance." Henry explained the need for a plow, without giving away too many details on his poaching sting or the Brink's investigation. Convincing Mike there was a legitimate reason to plow so far out of town wasn't going to be easy.

"Mike, how can I possibly get the Brink's Company to give you a written contract for the amount today? It's Thanksgiving. Not every place is like Greenville. Do you have any idea how many signatures and approvals this might take in a big company? And besides all that, there are people stranded right now up in the Deadwater. You can't possibly be serious about needing to wait for approvals and the receipt of a check."

Alice and Agent Smith could hear Mike's voice getting louder on the other end of the line.

"Look, I'll vouch for Smith. Anything goes wrong, it's on me and the Warden Service."

Henry knew Guilford H. Bingham would never approve of such a risk. He just had to plan on being back without any problems, and hope Brink's would settle the payment with the town quickly. Mike, wanting to get out hunting, agreed to have the plow driver alerted at his next gas and sand fill up at the town garage. There was nothing more Henry and Agent Smith could do now but wait. So, wait they did.

An hour later the town's plow truck rumbled into Henry's driveway. The truck was an ancient dump truck painted partially orange, the rest covered in a crust of rust. It was second hand, bought at auction from the town of Waterville. The bed of the truck was piled high with a sand and salt mix. The driver, Nate Philbrick, leaned his head out the window. "Good morning, Warden Ford. Happy Thanksgiving. It's been a while since we had a white one of these – huh?"

"Hello, Nate. A good morning is a matter of perspective, but thanks for coming along to give us a hand."

"The boss says I'm to give you folks a plow escort."

"We'd sure appreciate it. We need to first get over to Lobster Lake to check on the Parkers, and then up to Cassidy Deadwater to plow out some other folks."

Nate busted out laughing. "Henry, you're one funny guy. Now really, where do you need to get to here in town?"

"I'm serious, Nate. I'll ride with you. This here, is Special Agent Jim Smith from Boston, he'll be following behind us in his truck."

"Are you trying to pull a joke here on me, Warden?"

Smith was growing impatient. He walked over to the plow truck and showed Nate his badge and his sidearm. Nate dropped his smile, realizing this day just became worse than it was.

Henry piled all his gear into the cab of the plow truck, along with the supply of food Alice had packed to feed him, the agent, Nate, and the Parkers.

Once Henry was in the truck, Alice waved her index finger and shouted, "Henry, you be careful!"

Henry yelled, as loud as he could over the sound of the plows idling engine, "Alice, this is going to be slow going. If we're not back by quarter to nine, call Guilford. Tell him not to start out until tomorrow morning. We have enough supplies to get us through the night."

Nate turned to Henry, "What do you mean if we're <u>not</u> back? And what is this about getting through the night? Why wouldn't we be back?"

Henry ignored Nate's questions, figuring it best not to worry the man. He leaned out the truck's window, "Alice, please also give Nate's wife, Corinna, a call. Fill her in on when to expect Nate back home. That will be enough, Alice." He stressed this last sentence, trusting Alice understood his message. The last thing he needed was Corinna to start calling all the ladies in town about what was going on. Henry wasn't sure himself what actually was going on anyway.

Nate pulled the truck out of the drive and headed north. He was a bit uneasy about the entire situation and watched in his side mirror as the agent followed close behind.

When they reached Lily Bay, they made a stop at the store. Bonnie and Wilson, came out to greet them. "Happy Thanksgiving. We've been watching for the convoy," Wilson yelled.

Bonnie, seeing the opportunity for a good story chimed in. "Alice called and told us to keep an eye out to let her know when you passed by. She said you were going up to rescue the Parkers. Has the town approved this, Henry?"

Henry, hoping Alice hadn't said anything further to Bonnie, walked up the porch steps and said, "Happy Thanksgiving to the two of you as well. We've been on the road for over an hour already. It's slow going. Any chance you have a pot of coffee brewed?"

"Knowing you'd be passing by I have one ready. Why don't you have everyone come on in and warm up?" Bonnie offered.

"We can only stay a few minutes. Daylight is going to be gone fast today."

After their quick coffee break, Wilson helped the men gas up the trucks and he gave them four extra tanks of gas to take along.

The plow truck was idling hard, vibrating the porch where Bonnie was standing. She cupped her hands around her mouth and shouted, "Stop back in on your way home for a rest break."

Henry waved, not saying anything more, he knew her first motivation was to be the first to hear about their expedition.

Nate gave a long blast of his horn, and the two-truck convoy pulled out and headed towards Lazy Tom Bog.

* * *

Red had decided they weren't going to travel while the snow was still coming down. He knew his family up in The County wouldn't care if he was there for the Thanksgiving meal, but they'd be mad to not have any venison. Red's dad was going to be the sorest of all. The old man was grumpier than Red, and meaner than a wounded coyote.

After two hours playing cards, Al was bored and started practicing his bird calls.

Red, still nursing his hangover, threw his empty beer can at Al. "What the heck are you doing?"

The can landed near Al's foot and he kicked it away. "Don't I sound authentic? You should have seen how Moose and I fooled that kid the other day. He never knew we were there."

"No. It sounds like a bird is being tortured and you're giving me a headache," grumped Red.

The four men were getting on one another's nerves being held up in a sixteen by twenty-foot room, not much bigger than a jail cell.

The Agent's Secret

"We better see how bad this is," Stan said.

Stan and Joe stepped out of the warm truck and into the knee-deep snow. Seeing the rear end was pitched down low and the passenger side front tire was in the air, Stan knew immediately they'd be needing a tow to pull them out of the ditch.

Not wanting to alarm Joe of their predicament, he tried to remain calm. "The best thing for us to do is to head back to camp. The stove will keep us warm and we still have enough oatmeal and pasta to eat. Worst case, we can hike out in the morning. Let's get some supplies to take with us before it gets even deeper out here."

They selectively picked items they could carry from the back of the truck. Joe dug through his pack for his wool socks, climbed back in the passenger seat, and put them on before starting out. Stan made sure he had his camera and what was left of his film.

Sparky did fine jumping in the snow for the first hundred yards, and then he started to lag behind. Stan wasn't feeling so great about this walk either. He was weighed down carrying a box of supplies along with his knapsack on his back. The wind was blowing drifts every which way making it a tough trek.

"Too bad the snowshoes are in the shed at camp huh, Dad?"

Walking back to the cabin

"Yeah, I guess we didn't think that through. We should have packed them. Make a mental note of that for future winter travel."

Two more deer crossed the road up ahead of them, or maybe it was the same two that ran them into the ditch.

"It's a deer convention out here all of a sudden," Stan said.

The wind blew snow directly into their faces, no matter the curve in the road. Trees along the road were bent over from the heavy precipitation. Every few minutes, the crack of a branch would interrupt the quiet. By the time they reached the camp drive, their earlier tire tracks were covered over in a fluffy white layer.

Stan motioned for Joe to stand still a second. "Wait a minute, Joe." He pulled the camera from his backpack and snapped a couple of pictures of the cabin all snowed-in. He then snapped a couple of Joe and Sparky.

Before he could put the camera away, Joe said, "Wait, Dad, let me get one of you and Sparky too. It'll be a good addition to the camp wall once developed. This is a day to remember for sure."

Stan grabbed a load of wood from the porch and fired up the woodstove. Joe tied on his snowshoes and walked over to Duck Pond to get some water. Next to the shore, he picked up a large rock and dropped it through the ice. The cymbal crash echoed across the pond. Liking the sound, he dropped two more rocks before filling the buckets. He hustled back to the cabin trying not to spill too much of the water as he walked.

Joe dumped the buckets of wash water into the cast iron pots on the stove. "Do you think Henry will worry about us being here?"

Stan thought about the question before answering. "I'm sure he'd expect we would've called him, if we got out before the snow. Since we haven't, he's probably either figuring a way in or thinking we hunkered down. I hope he doesn't try to drive in here with the green turtle. He could be off the side of the road right now if he did." Stan wondered if that might be the case. He didn't want to think about Henry trying to get his car out of a ditch by himself, or walking for miles in the snow and ice. Stan now started to worry about one more thing.

For lunch, Stan dropped slices of their last apple into the bowls of oatmeal. The two of them ate in silence. Everything outside was white. The wind driven snow had even coated the bark on the sides of the tree trunks. Neither wanted to say what they were thinking, but they were both worried.

When they finished eating, Stan lay down on the couch, closed his eyes, and within minutes was asleep. Sparky was on his blue flannel blanket chasing something in his dreams. The trek through the snow had worn them out.

Joe sat down at the desk and decided to write in the camp journal. He reached for the one with the binding labeled, "1954, 1955, 1956." The shelf by the writing desk held the journals of years past. Joe's grandfather had started the tradition more than fifty years ago. He said it was important to keep memories alive. He felt so strongly about this, he hand-carved a sign on a piece of drift wood, and he hung it over the writing desk. His message declared:

> "Whoever shall sleep under this roof, shall preserve in these journals, the memories of Parker Camp for those not fortunate to be here, or not yet with us."

Joe titled a blank page, "Stranded in the Snow – Thanksgiving 1956." While thinking about how to start his entry, he flipped through the older journals. The oldest notebooks included chronicles on how the camp came to be, the weather, the number of fish caught, or who came to visit. Sometimes world events were combined into the stories. Grandpa George had written memories of World War I, the family's first automobile, the great depression, and World War II.

Over the years, the stories in the journal became more and more detailed. Joe's mom would describe the types of flowers she came across, and his dad would sketch pictures of the animals they would spot along the way. And of course, the highlights of each Red Sox season were captured on the pages. However, with little to no communication on the actual details of the games, the accuracy was always suspect, but fun to read anyway.

Growing up, Joe had spent many rainy days and late evenings reading the pages in the books. Each time he opened one, he discovered a new story about the history of the camp and his family.

Sitting there in the chair, thinking about the past few days, Joe started to worry about how long it was going to snow, if they could get their truck out, and if not, would Henry rescue them. When his stomach growled, he wondered about what they were going to eat.

This was the first time in all the years going to camp that Joe felt cut off from the rest of civilization. He was in a trance when Sparky jumped up and headed for the window. The dog balanced his front paws on the window sill and let out a series of low barks.

"What is it, boy?" Joe asked.

Sparky's barking woke Stan. He lifted his head off the pillow and swung his legs, which felt as heavy as tree trunks, to the floor and walked over to the window.

The ground started vibrating. For a few seconds, Stan thought a train was going to roll through their yard and knock the camp right off the stone supports. Then the unmistakable cab of the town's orange dump truck appeared in the sea of white. Snow, and everything in its path, was being thrown to the side by the large iron plow. Nate sounded six successive blasts of his horn. The noise was music to Stan and Joe's ears. Sparky was not as appreciative of Nate's way of announcing their arrival. He howled and then hid behind the sofa.

Seeing Henry saluting from the passenger window of the plow, Stan said, "Looks like Henry brought the cavalry."

Behind the plow truck, Nate was pulling Stan's truck. They had rescued it from the ditch, which relieved Stan a great deal.

"It's good to see you, Henry. And you too, Nate," Stan said, shaking their hands.

"Thought you might want your truck back," Henry said with a pat on Stan's shoulder.

"Thanks for that. A couple of deer ran us off the road this morning."

"You probably wouldn't have made it much farther anyway. It was tough even following behind the plow truck," stated the man who had walked up next to Henry.

Henry made the introductions. "This here is Special Agent Jim Smith. Agent, this is Stan Parker and his son Joe."

"An agent?" both Joe and Stan blurted out at the same time.

"He's with the Brink's Security Company, out of Boston," Henry explained.

Joe and Stan looked at one another. The agent held out his hand and shook Stan's, and then Joe's hand.

"Nice to meet the two of you. I hope I didn't startle you yesterday, Joe, when I was in the meadow. I was investigating some tips I had about a case over that way." The agent lit a cigarette and adjusted his cap.

"So, it was you making those bad bird calls out behind Joe's blind?" Stan jumped in.

"Bird calls? No, I don't know any of those. I was standing at the end of the meadow while you were watching the bears from a tree on the other end. I could see you with my binoculars. I looked up on that rocky ridge and saw your son looking down at me. Isn't that so, Joe?"

Joe nodded, but wondered who made the bird calls, if not Agent Smith.

Stan smiled at Joe, realizing his son had done the same spying on him from Rum Ridge, that he had done the days before.

The agent continued, "I didn't want to disturb your dad's hunting, or startle those bears, so I thought it best to keep quiet, slip away, and meet the two of you back at your cabin later in the day. I waited here, for about half an hour, but then had to go. Tell me about these bird calls you heard?"

"Why don't we go inside and talk about birds. I'm freezing out here," Nate complained.

"For a snow plow driver, you sure freeze easily."

Nate took offense at Henry's light-hearted jab. "Usually, I stay in my nice warm rig."

"Joe, please bring in some firewood, while I get some supplies from the back of the truck."

Jim Smith lit a cigarette. "Henry, should we really be stopping here for long? Let's get a move on."

"We'll stop here for lunch and then be on our way."

Once everyone was inside, Stan brewed up the last of the coffee, and Henry unpacked the food sack Alice had prepared. Inside it were large portions of fresh bread, bacon, homemade pickles, coleslaw, three-bean salad, pickled beets, hardboiled eggs, apples, cookies, and even hot cocoa mix for Joe.

Nate filled his plate twice and listened to all the talk about Red's gang and what Joe had seen in the meadow. He thought it was more exciting than when some teenage boys 'borrowed' Doc Pritham's row boat for joy riding on the lake last Fourth of July. They were going to surprise the town by setting off fireworks from out in the center of East Cove. Before they could get one rocket to go off, the wooden boat caught fire, and they all had to swim to shore. While none of them were hurt, they did, however, spend the rest of the summer doing chores for the Doc for sinking his fishing boat.

"I bet it was Red making those bird calls," Henry said. "Those Lobster Lake Bandits are up to no good." He gave them a debrief on what he saw, starting with their truck races through the brook, their camp with the dirt smeared window, and the deer he saw hanging out back. After he finished, he realized it didn't sound like much of a crime spree to be investigating. For the time being he left out what he found in the large drums.

They all turned to Agent Smith, wondering if he would now tell them what he was investigating. Henry figured that whatever the agent was looking for, it surely must be connected to the drums out behind Red's camp. Stan wasn't sure what to think, but he couldn't imagine why the agent would be interested in poachers. Nate, who ate more than usual when he was excited, reached for a piece of cranberry bread.

Joe realized he now had pages of exciting material to add to his camp journal entry beyond the snowstorm and being run off the road by deer. He sipped from his warm mug of hot chocolate, trying to figure out what was going on.

Jim Smith spoke in a serious tone. "Since all of you are now assisting with this investigation, I can fill you in with some information that is not classified. This will help to explain why I'm here."

Henry put down his coffee mug and took out his pad.

"Please, no notes, Warden," stated Agent Smith, who then started his story. "Six years ago, on January 17, 1950, eleven men robbed the Brink's Company money depot in Boston of more than two and a half million dollars."

"Whoa," said Nate not able to maintain his quiet, even though he had just placed an entire hard-boiled egg in his mouth.

"That was big news. It took the FBI years to catch some of those men," Stan said.

Henry jumped in with, "What's the connection up here? Do you think Red's gang is connected with the Brink's Robbery?"

"No, not them. They couldn't plan their way out of a cardboard box," said the agent.

"I agree with you there," Henry said. Although in truth, he thought the Bandits were a slick bunch, always staying one step ahead of him. He reconciled this with the fact that there were millions of acres of forest up in these parts, giving the gang plenty of places to hide from him.

"I watched that crew for a couple of days. They did a lot of fishing. I saw them at one pond dragging a net between two row boats to haul out their catch."

Henry was listening intently. Now he had an independent eyewitness to Red's crimes. He could see a promotion in his future, probably including a brand-new green warden pickup truck.

"Don't you know that fishing with nets is illegal around here, Agent Smith?" asked Henry.

"Is it? I had no idea. I don't think I have the jurisdiction to do anything about that anyway, Warden Ford."

"Hmmm. Well, now you know, and you can call in the Warden Service for assistance," Henry replied proudly.

Ignoring the hint of sarcasm, Agent Smith continued his story about the gang. "I also overheard them talking down at the diner. They told some large stories, especially how they enjoy messing with the local warden."

"You can't believe anything you hear that crew saying," interrupted Henry. Nate and Stan laughed at Henry's thin skin.

Agent Smith changed the subject back to the robbery. "The Brink's thieves planned their crime for two years. They made keys to the locks, stole plans for the alarms, and even made practice runs when the staff had gone home for the day." He paused his story, and poured himself a refill of coffee.

The story was making Nate hungrier than usual and he took the opportunity to shake some salt on another hard-boiled egg and popped it in his mouth. Joe watched as a lump traveled down the front of Nate's neck.

Putting his cup down and standing up, Agent Smith began again. "Over their faces, they wore rubber Halloween masks, with exaggerated facial features. They dressed like Brink's employees, and wore Navy peacoats and chauffeur's caps."

Joe had goose bumps hearing the story the way the agent was telling it in a whisper. Then, realizing something, he asked, "Like the cap you wear?"

"Yes, Joe, maybe so. Although, today I wish I had a coon hat, like Nate's."

Nate beamed and fiddled with his hat that was on the couch beside him.

"How did they pull off such a crime?" asked Stan.

"They may have had inside help, although, we've never been able to prove it. More likely, they cased the building and were meticulous in their planning. They almost got away with it. It wasn't until this past January, when the gang members started talking and turning on one another."

"I remember reading the news about that when the trial began over the summer," Henry added.

"That's right. The FBI and Brink's have tried to find the money that was taken, and so far, only a small portion has been recovered. The men are not saying what they did with the loot."

Henry's eyes narrowed. "And you think the money is hidden somewhere around here?"

"I didn't say that, Warden," the agent was quick to correct. "But we have a few leads that the suspects may have spent time at a camp in this area. I have a responsibility to follow up on all potential leads."

The room was quiet except for the crackling coming from the woodstove. Stan, suddenly feeling cold, put two more logs on the fire.

Nate removed his heavy red flannel shirt, and piled more of Alice's coleslaw and pickled beets on his plate.

"If you don't think Red and his gang have anything to do with the Brink's robbery, why are you out searching today, in this storm?" asked Stan.

"Our informant told us of a McGinnus Pond location."

"I don't know any pond by that name," said Stan.

"Stan, remember the McGinnuses who had a camp up on McGooseley Pond?" Henry asked.

"Sure. They were a rough bunch of poachers. We haven't seen them in at least six years…"

Henry nodded.

"And you're thinking of going up there today to have a look? In the middle of this storm?" Stan asked, looking at Agent Smith.

"Yes, that's the plan."

Henry stood and walked next to the agent. "And Stan, Red and the Bandits are held up in a camp by the Deadwaters. We'll be checking in on them as well, they're up to no good."

Nate raised his head from his third helping of food. Chewing on a piece of bacon, he realized that his journey for the day had not come to an end. "I don't know, that road is rough going without snow. I can't risk getting the town plow stuck way up there until spring for some craziness. No offense, Agent Smith."

"Mr. Philbrick, there are four men out there who could be stranded. The warden needs to go check on them. I'm only tagging along for the ride."

Nate jumped up. "Those men are backwoods boys. They could last there all winter without us risking our necks for them. It's Thanksgiving for pete's sake! We don't even know if they're still there."

Henry attempted to ease Nate's concerns. "Nate, it's a forty-five-minute drive when the roads are clear. Given our progress to here, I estimate it'll take us less than two hours to plow the road and arrive at their camp. The snow looks to be slowing down, so coming back should be much quicker. You'll be home to have turkey and all the trimmings, just not as early as your wife had planned."

Nate studied Henry's face, considering what he had said. He stuck his hands in his pockets, and looked out the window at his plow truck.

While waiting for Nate's reply, Henry realized as a warden, his days were unpredictable. There were plenty of events he and Alice had missed, or she had to attend alone because he was called out. Nate's job was more predictable and he was never more than several miles from home. Even when plowing on a winter's night, he would stop home for a meal Corinna would have waiting for him at precisely the same time every day. This was a new experience for Nate, and Henry understood this did not fall into the realm of normal responsibility for a town employee.

"Nate, I'll take full responsibility for the plow. I've told Mike Muzzy as much. If anything happens we'll get resources up here to rescue your plow. Besides, you're getting double time for your efforts."

Nate, who hadn't realized he was getting that much overtime pay, said, "So when do we leave?"

Stan and Joe laughed.

Agent Smith wasn't in a laughing mood, he wanted to get moving. "Good. Here's the plan then." He outlined what each person was to do when they arrived at Red's. He stressed they were not to deviate from the plan.

When he finished, they went outside to the vehicles. The four men were talking next to the plow truck, making last minute preparations, when Joe came running out of the cabin with his snowshoes and rifle.

Stan, Henry, Nate, and Agent Smith looked at the teen.

"Son, I think it's best you stay here," Agent Smith said, and turned to Stan to reinforce the call.

Stan could see the pleading in his son's eyes, but he knew he had to tell Joe to stay at the cabin. First, he had no way of knowing if they would end up stranded on the road and be stuck out in the cold. In fact, Stan was not too pleased to be going himself and leaving Joe alone, but he knew the men might need help. Second, he didn't want his son mixed up with the Bandits, the situation could become unpredictable.

"Agent Smith is right, Joe. I need you to stay here."

"But, Dad, I'm sixteen and I can help out."

"I know you can. But I don't want to leave Sparky here alone and taking a dog with us is probably not such a good idea." Stan wasn't worried about Sparky but figured that was a good way to make the case for Joe to remain behind.

Joe looked over at Sparky, who had not left the porch. It was obvious he was still worn out from the hike back to camp earlier, and he had no interest in getting back down into the deep snow. Joe agreed to stay behind, although he did so reluctantly.

Stan grabbed his snowshoes, a pair for Nate that had belonged to his dad, and Joe's for agent Smith. Carrying the snowshoes across the yard, he recalled how his dad showed him how to steam the wood for the framing and helped him prepare a deer hide for the webbing. The snowshoes had been re-webbed a few times since, but had served the Parkers for more than two decades. Handing a pair to each man, Stan was proud to have the shoes when they needed them most.

Henry said, "I don't think my state issued snowshoes are built anywhere close to the quality of those. You and your dad did a great job on these."

Stan nodded, appreciating Henry saying so.

Henry then reached into the cab of the truck and pulled out another sack. He handed Joe some rations and placed the sack back in the plow cab. Nate was glad to see there was still plenty of food, and that it would be riding along in the truck with him.

Leaning his head out the window, Henry called out the location of trees to Nate. A few birch saplings had to be sacrificed in order to get the truck pointed in the right direction.

Agent Smith, with Stan riding shotgun, followed, literally with a shotgun alongside him.

Sparky barked twice and then ran to the door, eager to get back inside. Within a minute, the snow muffled all the noise and Joe could no longer hear the trucks. A lone chickadee, called out from the hemlock trees. Joe was relieved to know the call was from a real bird.

He let Sparky back in the cabin, and made a trip over to the outhouse. On the way back, there were fresh deer tracks through the side yard that weren't there two minutes earlier. Joe noticed that the deer took the easy path, and followed the route of the plow out to the road. Back inside, Sparky had already fallen asleep, but his paws were kicking the air. Joe shook his head and laughed, thinking that the dog must have been dreaming of summer and swimming after a duck.

Joe sat down and started again reading entries in the older journals. He read one written by his grandfather.

> *"October 1934. Took Stan out hunting at 5:30 this morning. Hiked up Black Cap Mountain tracking the deer herd. Twenty does and three bucks stood in the old logging clearing down the other side. Too far from us. By the time we made our way down, they had gone. Ma had Boston baked beans, brown bread, and ham ready for us when we returned to camp. Stan fell asleep as soon as he was done eating."*

Joe read entry after entry that painted a vivid picture of the fall deer hunts of his dad's youth. Between his reading, Joe rummaged through the food Alice had sent along, not because he was hungry, but because he was worried about his dad, Henry, Nate, and Agent Smith. He worried they might get stuck, or would have to spend the night somewhere on the road. He worried what might happen once they reached the gang up at the Deadwater. He ate three chocolate chip cookies, and followed that with a bowl of three bean salad.

With darkness approaching, the cabin started to get chilly. Joe added a couple of big logs to the fire, and soon after he was fast asleep in the chair.

Catching Poachers

The two-truck convoy turned off the Golden Road heading towards Beaver Bog. A mile down the road, Nate pulled over and put his rig in park. They had not seen another track, vehicle or animal, since they left the Parker's camp. He jumped down from the cab, and followed Henry back to Agent Smith's pickup truck. When they reached the open driver's side window, cigarette smoke was escaping into the cold air.

Nate coughed. "A slight change of plans. I'll make a turnaround before we get to Beaver Bog bridge. That log structure is certainly not built for my plow truck to go over. Leave plenty of room behind me, I'm not sure when I'll come to a wide enough spot to turn around."

"That'll also give us the element of surprise. It's an easy snowshoe walk in from there," added Henry.

Agent Smith dragged on his cigarette and nodded in agreement. "That's a good plan. Tap your brakes when you've found a turning spot, so I can keep back. My tires aren't gripping so good."

When the vehicles were in motion again, Stan asked Agent Smith, "Do you think the four of us can restrain those four men?"

"There are three of them and one boy. Warden Ford and I are trained professionals. Those men are hunters, not dangerous criminals. I don't suspect there will be any need for violence."

"Sure, but hunters that are accused or caught in the act of poaching can become downright unpredictable." Stan decided to use the opportunity of riding along to explain that Henry's job wasn't only about counting how many fish someone was over their limit. Stan was well aware of Maine Game Warden history from Henry, who made it a point to keep the memories of the fallen heroes alive and marked every anniversary with a tribute. He told the agent that since being founded in the 1880s, three Maine Game Wardens had been shot and killed in the line of duty tracking illegal hunting activity.

"My dad told me the story of the scare they all had in 1927. Warden Lee Parker was shot at close range when he stopped a vehicle for night hunting. We were all here at camp at the time – my grandparents, my parents, and me. I was only eight. Even though it happened up near the Canadian border, my grandfather made me stay close to the cabin until the criminals were found. I remember it well. As a boy, I was used to running wild around the camp trails and I wasn't too happy with the restrictions."

Stan continued, "And back in 1922, around this time of year – hunting season, Wardens David Brown and Mertley Johnson died investigating illegal beaver trappings. Their bodies were not located until the following spring. How they died has been the cause of much speculation."

The agent listened intently to the stories about game wardens and hunters. "When we get there, you hold your ground and keep eye contact with one of the men. I'll take care of the one they call Red," Smith said.

"How will I know which one to watch?" Stan asked with a tremble in his voice.

"I'll be talking to Red. I'll tell Warden Ford to watch his partner, the big one with the white beard. That leaves the third man for you, and the boy for Nate."

Stan was impressed that the agent had already played out the scene and who would cover what gang member.

Out in front, Nate was doing a great job of plowing the road ahead of them. The chains on the plow truck's tires cut ridges for added traction and the sand helped Smith not slide off the road. During the remaining drive to the bog, the snow continued to fall and at one point it was so heavy Nate couldn't see more than five feet in front of the windshield. The two trucks had to stop for twenty minutes and wait.

Watching Nate rummage through the food bag, Henry said, "Ya know, Nate, if you keep eating like you are, you're not gonna have any room for turkey later."

"The way I see it, we're not getting back in time to have any turkey. I'm sure my father-in-law had Corinna serve up the meal without me. He probably ate the drumsticks, knowing those are my favorite."

Henry laughed. "You might be right. I'll make sure Alice gives you a drumstick off our bird if that'll make you feel any better."

Once the squall passed, the four men stretched their legs, and enjoyed the last of the semi-warm coffee that was left in the thermos. They went over their plan one more time.

Henry concluded with, "We're not far from their camp now. Let's get moving so we can wrap this up and get home."

When they were close to the bog bridge, Nate tapped his breaks four times, and then expertly maneuvered the plow in a three-point turn, not an easy feat in a large truck, on a snow-covered narrow road, with rock ledge on one side and a drop-off on the other.

They tied on their snowshoes and had one last discussion on their approach. Henry took charge and gave directions.

"Seeing as I was here yesterday, I'll lead the way in. There's a path through the trees that will lead us around the side of the cabin. When we get there, we'll have to take them by surprise. The one window is filthy and impossible to see through. There's only one door. I'll engage with Red. Each of you focus on one of the others. As long as they don't have their rifles in their hands, we should be able to arrest them without incident."

Both Stan and Nate's eyes went wide when Henry mentioned rifles. Neither of them was counting on violence.

Jim Smith knew he'd need time to find what he was looking for, and he might need the cooperation of the Bandits to do so. He didn't see any reason to charge in and anger those men. "Warden Ford, that sounds like a fine plan. However, we don't have a search warrant and besides that we have no reason to bust in and arrest them."

He dragged on his cigarette. "Red will be suspicious as to why four men are outside his camp in the middle of a snowstorm. It's important then that we stick to plan "A" which we agreed on back at the Parker cabin. They don't know me, so I'll knock on the door. I'll tell them we're out searching for a hunting party who may be stranded due to the storm. That should get us at least an open door into the camp without violating search and seizure. Once inside we'll be able to see if anything suspicious is out in the open. Remember, not a word about the McGinnus camp, or the Brink's robbery, to any of them. Henry, you stay behind Nate since they'll recognize you immediately. You'll be mostly hidden behind him for sure."

Nate interrupted, "What are ya trying to say there, Agent Smith?"

Smith smiled at the big man and went on, "Nate, you stay behind Stan. Stan, you stay behind me. Once we are in, or I have to push past Red, follow close behind."

Getting anxious, Henry wanted to jump in and explain about the drums. He reasoned that was evidence enough to bust in and arrest the Bandits. But he wasn't sure the drums were still there. What if Red had already disposed of any evidence? What if they escaped before the snow hit this morning and were already gone? Then he came to his senses. He really had no evidence of wrong doing. Yet.

Henry agreed to stick to the plan, and besides, he still felt in charge as he was the one leading the team through the woods. Wearing snowshoes, the trek was fairly easy, except for Nate, who kept asking, "How much farther?" Other than that, it was quiet except for a few words about probably missing Thanksgiving dinner, but those came again from Nate.

Once they were close to the 'camp, Henry motioned for everyone to be completely silent and they walked single file behind the row of snow-covered fir trees. The gang's two trucks were still parked right where they were yesterday. The only tracks were a beaten path to the outhouse. Henry led them to where the blue drums were, figuring he'd show them what he had found.

He was about to say something, when the camp's door opened and Red stepped out. They all ducked behind the drums

"Don't any of you look at my cards," Red said, and slammed the door.

Stan thought Red resembled an oversized mean elf, wearing the same outfit whether it was the heat of summer, or a snow storm – green work pants, red flannel shirt, checkered hat, and suspenders.

Red stumbled into the outhouse with a beer in one hand, and a lit cigarette in the other. Henry peaked into the barrel he was crouched behind. He could see more than a dozen perch swimming under a thin ice layer forming on the top. The others took Henry's lead and also looked into the barrels they were behind.

Stan said, almost too loudly, "Henry, these are full of perch."

Nate whispered, "What are they doing, having a fish fry out here in the middle of a storm?"

"I'm fairly certain they're stocking with these perch," Henry said.

Nate, catching on, said, "I'll kill'em!" way too loud.

Smith, having no clue about illegal fish stocking, said, "Nobody is killing anyone. We stick to the plan."

When the outhouse door opened, Henry forgot all about there being a plan. He jumped from behind the barrel and surprised Red, who had yet to pull up his suspenders.

McGooseley Pond

"What's with all these perch here, Red?" Henry yelled in a commanding voice, as he jumped up from his position behind the blue barrel.

Surprised at seeing the warden, Red raised his hands, as if he was being arrested, causing his pants to drop down around his ankles. When he tried to pull up his suspenders, he dropped his beer can. He then lost his balance, partly due to the ice under the snow, and his pants twisted around his legs, but mostly on account of his drinking last night, and again all of today. Reaching down to grab his pants, he fell, face first, into the snow. Nate and Stan could not help but bust out laughing.

Red, getting over the shock of these men being out here during a storm, was madder than heck. He was yelling and hollering as he slipped around on the ground trying to get a hold of his pants, and save the rest of his beer.

The other three Bandits came running out of the camp. When they noticed Warden Ford walking towards Red, their first instinct was to get back in the cabin. As they turned around, Agent Smith, who had calmly walked around as the commotion was going on, was already between the three of them and the cabin door. Once Henry had blown using plan A, Smith had improvised and decided to cut the gang off from heading back inside where their guns were stored.

Surprised by the tall man in the doorway, Al shouted, "Who the heck are you?"

Smith quickly flashed his badge so that they couldn't make out the issuing department. Placing it back in his pocket he swiped his jacket aside to give them a good look at his sidearm.

"Everyone remain calm. I'm Jim Smith and I am here assisting Warden Ford on a search for a missing hunting party."

Red doubled over laughing. "What's this, Ford? You now need help out here finding hunters? Who would have guessed that!"

Henry wasn't sure how to respond, or who he was more upset with, Red for his comment, or Agent Smith for his. How was he ever going to live this down? What was Smith trying to do to him? The next time this crew was at the diner they'd be bragging all about how he needed assistance. He was about to say something when Stan tapped him on the shoulder.

Stan whispered, "Henry, the other day Joe and I caught six or seven perch in Duck Pond. There have never been perch in those waters before." This was circumstantial, but enough for Henry to run with.

"Red, we have evidence that you dumped perch into Duck Pond. These here barrels full of perch, out in the open, are enough to charge you. Maybe even get you some time at the local county hotel," Henry said.

Red, finally getting his suspenders on again, said, "You ain't got nothin' on us, Ford. Those fish in those barrels aren't even ours. They were here when we got here."

"You can tell that to the judge," said Henry, forgetting for the moment that Agent Smith had witnessed the gang netting fish.

"You all are trespassin' on my property without a warrant. No matter what you tell any judge, there won't be any fine I'll be paying." Red eyed Stan and Nate, and looked around. Not seeing any vehicles, he demanded, "And how in the heck did you get in here today? Did ya snowshoe all the way from town?"

Agent Smith, wanting to defuse the situation, said, "Mister, we are not here trespassing. As I already told you, we are on a call for a missing hunting party. We came across your cabin here and thought you might be in need of assistance as well."

"Assistance? Assistance! Us? From the Warden Service? Out here in **our** woods?" Red laughed, assuming that Smith was another warden.

Smith wasn't about to blow his cover, and thought it was best Red had no idea who he was.

The rest of the Bandits looked on and wondered if the wardens might actually help them get out of here. Junior, for one, wanted to get home.

"We have a plow truck and can get you out of these woods and back to town. Unless you'd rather shovel all the way out of here?" Smith wasn't fazed at all by Red's roaring laughter.

Red thought about it. He didn't want to walk all the way out, and he certainly didn't want to shovel his way out. He knew he had to get his truck out of here or he'd be out of a job for sure.

"Well, Mr. Warden, seeing as I pay taxes, I don't mind you plowing us out."

Agent Smith was not yet ready to tell Red he had no intention of plowing their trucks out, exactly. "Here's how this is going to go. Mr. Parker and I are going to scout the area for the missing hunters who were last staying close to here. You four will remain here, unarmed, with Warden Ford and Mr. Philbrick, both of whom, will be armed. When Mr. Parker and I return, we'll all leave together. Any problems with that?"

Red was red in the face, but he was getting cold standing out in the snow holding up his pants. He thought about the offer. He was tired of being in a dirt floor shack with three other men who had not showered in a week. Even in his hung-over state, he considered his options. He was curious what the wardens might really be doing all the way out here on Thanksgiving during a snowstorm. He didn't believe for a second they were searching for a hunting party.

Red knew all the camps in the area. In his line of side work, it was important to know who was where and when. He tried to think quickly about where a hunting party might be staying within walking distance of his cabin. His head was hurting too much from his night of drinking, and his face plant into the snow to piece any of this together at the moment, so he said, "Al'right, Mr. Warden, that's a deal."

They all went into the cabin to ensure all weapons were confiscated from Red and the men. Henry and Nate sat on one side of the room, rifles at their sides, Red and his men on the other.

Agent Smith and Stan strapped on their snowshoes and set out on the hike to McGooseley Pond. If it had been the dead of winter, the Deadwater swamp area would have been frozen over and they could have walked straight across. As it was, it was a good two miles around to get to the pond. To make matters worse, Stan could not totally recall where on McGooseley the McGinnuses had their camp. He knew that could add two-miles to their walk if they had to go completely around the pond. He suspected it would take them about two hours to get there and back tracking through the deep snow.

Finally, the heavy snow had stopped coming down and the sun, although low in the sky, was breaking through the clouds in the west. They followed an old logging road, saving them from having to bushwhack through the woods. This allowed them to make good progress given the conditions.

Stan thought he should see if Agent Smith understood the seriousness of the perch situation. "Agent Smith, do you do much fishing?"

"No. Never had the time to fish."

"That's a shame. But you see, Henry Ford, aside from being sworn to uphold the game laws, is a big fisherman, as are we Parkers, and just about everyone else around here. If Red is stocking perch in lakes and ponds in this area, that's a big problem."

"Why's that? The federal and state governments spend millions of tax payer dollars a year stocking fish in lakes and ponds across this entire country. If those men are doing it for free, you should thank them."

Stan realized the agent wasn't aware of the implications of what might be going on.

At this point, Agent Smith, not interested in the fish problem said, "How many cabins are on this pond we are headed to?"

"As far as I recall, only the one. But it's been ten years since I've been up this way. My dad and I used to go on overnight hiking trips in the area. When the McGinnus clan moved in they didn't welcome people being here. Even though the pond's official name is McGooseley, I recall now that it became known as McGinnus. This was mostly propaganda by the McGinnus crew to give the illusion that they owned the land around the entire pond, which they didn't. With all the terrific places to hunt, fish, and explore around here, we just went elsewhere to stay away from them."

They rounded a turn in the road and came upon the south end of the pond. There was a skim coat of ice on the surface. When the wind blew it moved like cellophane over a bowl of jello. Through the bare trees, Stan spotted a cabin a few hundred yards up the opposite shore. He sure was hoping it would be the only camp they needed to check, since he didn't want to be searching long after dark.

The narrow road that curved around the pond was wide enough for a car or small truck, or it would have been if it hadn't been totally blocked off. At points along the road, the boughs of the hemlocks were so weighed down from snow they had no choice but to clear the branches in order to pass. The snow would fly off in the wind and the branches would spring back to height.

At a few places they had to climb over trees that were down across the road. Stan began to question why the agent was so intent on getting to this cabin. There couldn't possibly be anyone here. The road hadn't been used in years.

The only tracks they saw were from a rabbit. The hare appeared to be confused by the snow; his tracks went in three concentric circles before heading into the trees.

Their progress was slowed when they came to what at one time must have been the driveway. Now, large tree limbs and branches that had fallen to the ground, were blocking the path. The interlocking limbs formed a battle field blockade. Their snowshoes kept getting caught up in branches protruding through the snow. Stan knew that if there were so many of these limbs on the ground it could only mean one thing. He looked up and took notice of the stately pine trees.

"Agent Smith, be on the lookout," Stan pointed up. "See those large dead branches swaying up there? We call those widow makers. If they break free they can kill a man or beast."

"I see. But by the way Mr. Parker, I'm not married."

Stan thought, either way, he didn't want the agent to become victim to bad timing. With every creak of a branch he readied himself to dive clear of a falling limb. Joe was already without a mom, he intended to be around for a long time.

For as quick as he had answered Stan, Agent Smith thought about his widowed mother, and if things were to work out the way he was hoping, the payoff for hiking in a storm would be worth it.

Once they were through the mine field, they stopped and assessed the camp. The tiny a-frame construction was the size of a shed. The clapboard shingles were painted white or were white at one time. Now the paint was peeled in places and dirty in others. Amidst the blanket of pure white snow, with green evergreens in the background, the cabin stood out like a dirty gray sock. On one side, trees had grown so close they were angled pushing against the building trying to knock it off its blocks. On the other side, trees were pushing to keep it from sliding off.

An old wagon sat near a fenced corral, a reminder that horses had once pulled it here. The snow was up to the bed of the wagon indicating the spoke wheels were probably sunk in the dirt almost to the axel. There were a few other corrals with wooden fences in all states of disarray around the property. Stan had the feeling that some homesteaders had tried to make a go of sustenance farming way up here in the woods, but had given up a long time ago. They walked closer to the building. Slatted shutters were nailed on all of the windows making it impossible to see inside. Stan was ready to suggest turning around.

What Smith didn't tell Stan is that he didn't expect anyone to be there, this was more of an investigative trip. From the look of it, this cabin didn't match the description that he was given either. He was told the cabin to search for was an old trapper cabin. It was described as something that was handmade from rough cut logs and was surrounded by swampy beaver bog on three sides. This certainly wasn't that cabin. He decided to look around anyway. He was already figuring on being the first person back here when the snow melted to start his search again in the spring.

Smith took a tiny box from his shoulder bag. At first, Stan thought it was a cigarette case, but was surprised when the agent held it to one eye, and pushed a tiny button.

"That's a camera?" asked Stan.

"Yes, it's a CMC mini spy camera. Made by the Japanese." Smith snapped more pictures.

Stan thought the tiny device was amazing; compared to his large Kodak camera, the agent's neat little camera would fit in his shirt pocket.

When the agent was done taking pictures, he slid the top of the camera open and pulled out an actual match to light a cigarette. "It also holds matches," Smith said.

The men continued across the snowy yard. The drifts on the porch were blown into hip-high piles. Spider webs spread across the entire top half of the door frame from one side to another. Stan tried the doorknob; it was locked.

Agent Smith tapped his shoulder and said, "Give me some room." Stan could see he was positioning himself to kick the door in.

"Now hold on a second, Agent Smith. We can't be breaking and entering. Don't you need a warrant? There's obviously been nobody here for ages."

"I don't have time to get a warrant, Mr. Parker. With the winter already here, if I don't get inside this cabin now, the investigation may be stalled for months."

"Wait just a minute. This is somebody's property and breaking the door down isn't right."

"What do you suggest then? It's getting later by the second. Don't you want to get back to your boy?"

Stan dropped his head, about to give in, when he noticed a ceramic planter the size of a large pickle jar. He walked over and picked it up.

Smith said, "So what are you going do with that? Pound the doorknob?"

Stan didn't say a word. Under the planter there was a platter. On the platter there was a key. Stan picked up the key and walked back to the door. He slipped the key into the lock and the door swung open. He gestured to the agent to go first.

As Smith walked by him, Stan said, "Now wasn't that easier than breaking down the door?" The agent ignored the rhetorical question and stepped inside.

The air in the camp was colder than outside. The two men stood in the entry. Thin strips of light filtered in through the shutters. There was nothing that could be hidden from view. All the walls were bare down to the studs. The furniture, including an old couch, was made completely from wood that was either second hand, or recycled from some other purpose. All the cabinets were door-less. The shelves displayed plates, glasses, fishing tackle, and jars of screws and bolts.

The agent looked quickly around the cabin and snapped pictures. He flipped over the mattress on the only bed. He rummaged through the dresser draws and the closet. Stan went around behind him putting things back in place. He didn't feel right about snooping through someone's cabin, even if maybe it still belonged to the unfriendly McGinnus family.

Agent Smith opened the tops to a few large pots on the highest shelves and looked inside. He was not sure what he might find, but figured he'd come all this way he may as well check. His informant told him that if there was something, it was not in a cabin or structure of any kind but would be buried outside. Since he had dragged Stan Parker all the way out here, he figured he may as well put on some sort of investigative show to keep the suspicions to a minimum.

Before leaving they strapped back on their snowshoes and walked down to the shoreline. Standing next to an old rotting wood dock, Stan pointed across the pond. Sticking out of the white snow were two blue fifty-five-gallon drums matching the ones seen back at Red's place.

Stan crossed his arms. "I guess this means this pond has been stocked with perch as well."

"Sure would have been better if that water was frozen. We could have cut right across." Smith stepped back, and took a few pictures of the pond.

"You need pictures of the pond for evidence too?"

"No. I was thinking to make a blow up for my apartment. I enjoy taking pictures. It's a bit of a hobby of mine. Maybe someday I'll open up a small shop to sell photos and such."

Stan was starting to see a human side to the agent, even if he still was indifferent to the fish stocking.

The two men hit the same trail they had come in on, making going back a bit easier. Stan said as they walked, "This McGooseley Pond is a great brook trout fishery. At least it was when I fished it with my dad."

"Well, if Red and those men put more of those fish from the barrels in here, I'm sure it still is."

"That really isn't such a good thing. You see the fish in the barrels are not brook trout. Red and his crew have been stocking perch. A female brook trout might only lay eight hundred eggs in a season," Stan stated.

"Holy cow! You people should have plenty of fish if they lay that many eggs each. Why do they need to stock more?"

Stan would have laughed at the agent's ignorance, but the situation was too serious. "It doesn't work like that. While a brook trout may lay several hundred eggs, only a small portion will hatch. With typical fishing by man, bird, and other natural predators the numbers work just fine. The bigger issue is that a perch can lay about a hundred thousand eggs in a season."

"Holy moose! I had no idea. Talk about a multitude of fishes," the agent exclaimed.

"That's one way to look at it. The other is wildlife vandalism."

"Vandalism? How so?"

"When people illegally stock fish that are not native to a waterway, this threatens the native species. A lake or pond can only sustain so many fish. When a perch lays a hundred thousand eggs, even if only a fraction hatch, that fraction is thousands more than the small fraction of brook trout that hatch. The perch need to eat. Fish eat fish. Not only will the bigger perch eat smaller perch, they of course eat the hatchling trout. With fewer trout in the waters, it doesn't take long for the perch to outnumber the trout, eventually extinguishing the native fish population."

"I see. But isn't catching one fish the same as catching another?" the agent asked.

The sun was going down behind the trees. The sky was still scattered with thin high clouds, but it promised to be a clear night. The moon was rising over the pond. The agent slowed and took several more pictures.

"Is catching one criminal the same as catching another?" Stan asked right back.

"No. Not at all. Some are dangerous. Some are smart. Others are easy to catch. Others take years and years of patience."

"That sounds a lot like fishing," Stan said with a laugh. "You see, different fish require different types of fishing techniques. And beyond that, the fish react differently when caught. This gives fishermen the bite for the sport as we say. While perch can be good for eating from unpolluted waters, they are not all that fun to catch. Some days, a fisherman may enjoy catching perch to have a fish fry. Other days we enjoy the challenge of catching a trout or a salmon."

"I'm starting to understand why Warden Ford was getting so red under the collar."

"Henry's a great man and he loves the woods. This adventure today will be something he'll talk about for years to come."

The two men picked up their pace back to Red's. The full moon provided light for the hike back. Stan was looking forward to getting someplace to warm his feet, even if it was inside that smelly shack.

The Jig Is Up

Due to the unexpected snowfall, Alice spent most of the morning getting as many of the smaller foster animals into the garage as possible. To make room, she moved out a contraption that Henry had been working on. He told her it was some sort of motorized sled. Ever since he saw Doc Pritham riding one across East Cove last winter, he had been determined to have his own. Since it was for driving in the snow, she saw no harm in leaving it outside, especially since it didn't work.

After the injured and orphaned deer, rabbits, and ducks had been taken care of, she went inside to check on the turkey. As she bent down to open the oven door, the phone rang. Alice slid across the pine floor in her wool socks.

"Hello?"

"Hello, Alice. It's Mike Muzzy. Is Henry there?"

"No, Mike. He's still out with Nate I assume."

"Where the heck are they? We need the plow back here in town. The roads are all blocked. The selectmen and grandmothers are calling me every five minutes. They are complaining people can't get to their Thanksgiving meals."

"There isn't much either of us can do. Doesn't the town have a spare plow?"

"The other truck is smaller and can't keep up. When do you expect Henry back?"

"I'll make sure you're the first person he calls when he gets in."

"You tell him he's going to have to pay overtime for Roger, our other plow driver. He's fixing to quit if he doesn't get to go home for turkey soon." And with that, he hung up.

"Happy Thanksgiving to you too, Mike," she said, into the already buzzing receiver.

Remembering what she was about to do before the phone rang, Alice checked on the turkey. The skin was bronzed and crispy, just the way Henry loved it. She pulled the big roasting pan from the oven and set it on the counter. Standing at the kitchen window, she sure hoped all the men would be back soon. She walked over and picked up the phone.

"Hello, Bonnie. Any chance the boys have been by on their way back to town?"

"Not yet, Alice. Wilson and I have been sitting by the window all afternoon. Wilson's so anxious, he ate an entire pie." Wilson frowned at Bonnie. Sure, he was worried about his friends, but he was also hungry, it was Thanksgiving and there was no turkey to eat.

"I sure hope they're headed back by now. Mike Muzzy called a few minutes ago. He says the town is in dire straits and needs their plow driver back. Please give me a call as soon as you see them pass. Bye, Bonnie."

Alice picked off a piece of the turkey skin and took a bite, the exact thing she would have yelled at Henry for doing. He did it because he loved the crunch of the crispy skin; she did it because she was nervous. Looking at the clock she realized how late it was getting. She hoped the men weren't stranded somewhere between Lily Bay and the Deadwaters.

Tapping her fingers on the counter she again picked up the phone and held it in her hand. Even though Henry had told her to wait until later to inform District Warden Bingham, she was thinking she ought to call now. She ran her finger down the phone list.

"Yes, this is Alice Ford, wife of Warden Henry Ford here in Greenville. I'm wondering if you could help me get in touch with a Mrs. Shirley Rockwood in Bangor."

Reconsidering calling the district warden, she instead decided to call Stan's sister-in-law. Alice had met Shirley several times over the years during picnics and get-togethers. Waiting for the dispatcher to look up the number, she thought this was one of the few advantages of being a warden's wife, she had connections. A couple of minutes later, the dispatcher came back on.

"Yes, I have a pen. Go ahead. Got it. Thank you. Yes, that will be all. Happy Thanksgiving to you, as well. Bye."

Alice dialed, and without giving away any details, told Shirley that Henry had gone to plow out Stan and Joe. Alice reassured her she'd have Stan call when they returned to the house. She placed the receiver back on the hook, and picked off another piece of Turkey skin. Taking a bite, she knew her nerves were getting the best of her.

* * *

After their hike in the cold, even Red's cabin looked appealing to both Stan and Agent Smith. Opening the door and getting a whiff of the stench, Stan realized he had the better assignment, even if his toes were numb. In a loud enough voice, so that the gang could overhear at the other side of the shack, Agent Smith advised Henry and Nate that they had located a cabin, and there was nobody stranded. Henry and Nate, knowing this was just a ploy, were interested if any evidence was discovered about the robbery, but they knew enough not to ask right then.

"Okay, we've waited long enough, now plow us outta here so I can get my truck home to my dry garage." Red was more ornery than usual on account Henry had cut off his beer supply.

Agent Smith, switching tactics, improvised. "We might be persuaded to plow out your camp if you were to tell us more about those barrels of perch."

Nate's head snapped around. He had told the agent earlier that plowing over the rickety bridge was not an option. The heavy truck would crash into the stream and they'd be stranded.

Henry perked up as well, wondering why all of a sudden the agent was interested in the fish. It didn't take him long to jump to the conclusion that since the agent didn't find anything at the cabin, he must be interested in getting credit for the illegal fish stocking operation. Before he could say anything, Red spoke up.

"Like I told Ford earlier, these barrels were here when we arrived. Someone must have dumped 'em here." Red took a step toward the agent.

"Then why were you telling Junior to break up the ice in them?" shouted Henry.

Agent Smith glared in Henry's direction, indicating for him to take it slow.

"No sense in wasting the fish, they make good eatin," stated Red calmly.

Agent Smith walked towards the door to leave. "If you don't want to tell us, your trucks should be good and rusty by the time you can get them out in the spring."

Red flung a chair to the corner of the cabin.

His buddy piped up. "Listen, Red, I need my truck. Without it I can't get to work at the mill. If I lose that job, Clara will leave me for good this time, and the bank will take the trailer from me. We need to make a deal."

"Shut up, Moose!" yelled Red.

Smith, his hand on the doorknob, turned and faced Red. "It's interesting, Mr. Parker and I spotted drums, the same as the ones you have here, near another pond when we were out searching. Would you know anything about that, Red?"

"Why would I know anything about that? Lots of people have those barrels," Red said. He glared at Al, who looked down at the floor trying to remember all the places he may have forgotten barrels.

"Mr. Moose, why don't you come outside with me for a few minutes?" asked Smith.

"My name is Maynard, Maynard Randolph. Red just calls me Moose."

"Don't you say anything, Moose." Red pounded the table with his fist as Maynard walked outside with Smith.

A few minutes later, Smith came back and announced, "Everybody get ready to pull out. Moose here, I mean Mr. Randolph, was extremely helpful in filling me in with the details of your operation, right down to this map showing all the ponds that have been stocked." He held up a map that was full of X's, which Moose had given him from Red's truck.

"Moose, you idiot. What'd you tell 'em?"

"Calm down Red, you all brought this on yourselves. Now let's get going," said the agent, on his way back out the door.

Pulling Agent Smith to the side, Henry asked, "What about all the perch, we need them for evidence,"

"Warden, I don't think anybody is going to bother those tonight, we certainly can't transport twenty barrels of fish. It'll all be here tomorrow."

"Those barrels will be solid blocks of ice by morning," complained Henry.

"Nah, nothing to worry about, Henry"

"How's that, Nate?"

"The temperature is expected to rise overnight," replied Nate confidently.

"Now how do you know that?"

"That was the forecast earlier today. Us plow guys need to know this kind of stuff. And look, the snow is already slushy, it's above freezing and getting warmer already."

"He's right, it's thirty-four now," said Stan, pointing at the thermometer hanging on the camp's doorframe.

"Let's hope you're right, Nate."

Agent Smith turned to the Bandits, "We're all hiking out together. You men will ride in the back of the plow truck, up on the sand."

Red glared with his meanest grizzly impression. "You lying cheat. You said you'd plow us out of here tonight."

Henry glared right back and said calmly, "Once you post bail, you can come back and shovel, or hire a plow, to get to your driveway."

Red hurled foul language at Henry. "We didn't sit here all day to shovel. We never agreed to anything of the sort. Or riding all the way to town in the back of a plow truck."

Henry went on. "We never said we'd plow all the way to your driveway. You assumed that, Red. That bridge can't support that dump truck and you know it. Now let's move out."

Red, Al, and Moose were out of shape and it wasn't easy for them to walk through the snow, especially without snowshoes. Junior didn't seem to be having too much of a problem and was smiling seeing Red struggling. It was double difficult for Red, since Henry made him drag the cooler of venison from the deer he had shot; the meat would be donated to the town's food pantry.

Once the Bandits were uncomfortably settled in the bed of the plow truck, Henry pulled Agent Smith out of earshot and asked, "What made you get interested in wildlife vandalism?"

"Mr. Parker helped me understand a few things," said Smith, giving Stan a nod.

Nate gave Stan a pat on the back and then turned to Smith. "Where are we taking these men?"

"When we get back to town, the police chief and Henry can charge them with illegal perch stocking."

"I'm not the game warden, but are some fish in barrels going to be good enough to arrest and hold these men?" asked Stan.

"Not to worry there, we've nailed them on more than that. On a supervised trip to the outhouse, Junior let it slip that all the stuff in the cabin were things they'd stolen. While you were out on your hike, I took inventory of every item they have back there. Chief Bartlett will have plenty of reasons to hold these men for the night," added Henry proudly.

"Good thinking, Warden," said Smith.

"But, we do need to go plow out my truck and pick up Joe," Stan said, making sure everything was getting planned out.

"Not a problem. I'll swing in there on the way out and re-plow."

Red yelled down from on top of the hard, cold sand, "Can we get a move on? It's freezing up here."

Nate and Henry climbed up in the rig and Agent Smith and Stan followed behind. The moon was now high in the cloudless sky lighting the way.

In the plow truck, Nate was driving Henry crazy talking about how he couldn't wait to get home to the turkey.

"Nate, can we talk about something other than food?"

"Sure, Warden. Do situations like the one we had today, ever make you think about retiring?"

"Why would I do that? This is a great job. And besides, with what they pay me, I'll never be able to retire. Ahh, it wouldn't matter, I'd probably do this job for free."

"Doesn't Alice get worried with you being out alone on the back roads and in the woods all the time? Corinna sure worries about me, and I'm usually close to town."

"Sure, she does. I tell her she has a responsibility keeping me safe."

"How's that?"

"If I'm not home when I say I'm going to be there, she's going to be the first to know. I've told her, I'm counting on her to call me some help."

"And that makes her feel better about it?"

"Not really. At least she knows she'll have something to do though," Henry said, only somewhat joking. "Although today I'm hoping she didn't make any rash decisions and call my supervisor."

"What's going to become of all those perch in the barrels, Henry?"

"I've been thinking about that. We can't dump them in the waters around here. It's going to be enough to deal with the damage Red already caused. Let's just hope the perch they stocked don't get a chance to reproduce."

"What about transporting them up to Mud Pond? It has no outlet and is already full of perch."

"That's a lot of barrels to move and the roads up there aren't going to clear themselves any time soon. The best we can do is take pictures of the evidence, pack it on ice, and have Father Paul announce a big fish fry for Sunday afternoon."

"Now you got me thinking about food again. But that sure sounds like the best plan yet."

"I knew you'd like that idea."

* * *

Sparky heard the rumble of the plow truck, jumped up on the window sill, and sounded a warning. Joe was startled awake to see headlights swing across the front yard. He pulled on his boots, threw open the door, and ran over to the truck with Sparky following right behind. When he noticed Red, whose beard was caked in ice, scowling over the side of the dump truck, he took a step back. He was relieved to see his dad step out of Agent Smith's truck.

"Dad, why are those men in the back of the plow?"

"I'll tell you all about it as we drive to Henry's. Right now, we need to quickly pack up and follow Nate back to town."

Joe carried the last box of supplies to the truck and turned to see his dad locking the cabin door.

"Wait, Dad, I need to get something." He ran back inside and came back out with a journal. "I want to finish up the story of this week. I don't want to forget any details."

"I can't wait to read that." Stan gave a honk, signaling they were ready to go. When Nate reached the Lily Bay store, he blasted his horn and plowed up to the door. Wilson and Bonnie came running out to the porch.

Henry shouted, "Bonnie, no time to stop. Please call Alice and tell her we're coming home. Oh, also, ring up Chief Bartlett, we need him to meet us at the station. Thanks." Without getting into more about it, he gave a wave and told Nate to get going.

* * *

All evening, Alice tried to occupy herself with a crossword puzzle, but she couldn't get her mind to concentrate. When a truck pulled up outside, she was out of her chair in a flash. Stan and Joe were climbing the steps when the front door flung open.

Only seeing Agent Smith stepping from his truck, Alice's head shot back and forth looking for the others. "Stan, where's Henry? And Nate?"

"He's fine, Alice. They're transporting the Lobster Lake Bandits down to the station."

"Oh, those guys. He's been chasing them a long time. Come on in, get warmed up, and tell me about it."

Drinking a coffee, Stan filled her in on their drive up to the Deadwater in the storm, but he was careful not to say anything about the gang or the investigation, he'd leave that to Henry.

While they waited for Henry, Stan called his sister-in-law to let her know they'd be staying at the Ford's overnight, and they would visit with her over the weekend.

* * *

The Chief of Police was standing next to his cruiser when Nate and Henry pulled up. He wasn't at all happy about being pulled off his couch after a big holiday meal to go out in the snow. He started ranting before Henry could even get his feet on the ground.

"Henry, you know we only have a temporary holding cell, it's for one person, and it's to be used for daytime transfers only. Where do you expect me to put these men overnight?"

After letting Henry explain, and after much debate, it was decided they had to place the four men at the local motel until morning. Given the Bandits had no trucks, money, or any other means to skip town, neither Henry nor the chief were worried about them going anywhere. Junior thought the hotel was the fanciest place on earth, it was the first place he ever stayed where there was a toilet inside.

Nate drove Henry back to his house, plowing the town roads as they went.

"I really appreciate all your help today, Nate, and sorry for making you miss out on your turkey dinner."

"Ah, it's okay, Henry. I'll never forget this adventure."

Hearing the approaching plow, Sparky barked and ran to the door; Alice followed.

"Did you boys have a grand time playing out in the snow today?"

"It was…," Henry stopped and instead asked, "Alice, why's my snow machine out in the yard?"

"I needed the room for the animals."

"It still needs to be covered." Henry walked towards the shed to get a tarp.

Alice shrugged at Nate and said, "Nate, please tell Corinna we're sorry about your missing the holiday."

"It's all in a day's work around Greenville, Mrs. Ford." He honked the air horn and drove off.

With the road from Lily Bay to town plowed, Bonnie convinced Wilson to drive her to Alice's to hear the full story. Her sister wasn't surprised when Bonnie came strolling in, she expected the queen of gossip wasn't going to miss this gathering.

The men were all tired, but extremely hungry, so Alice and Bonnie served a late-night Thanksgiving dinner. It didn't take long until they had finished most of the turkey, along with all the yams, potatoes, and stuffing.

Before the table was even cleared, Bonnie couldn't help herself, she had to have the details. "Henry, are you going to fill us in on what's really going on here?"

Agent Smith shot Henry a quick look. Henry answered, "How about we go sit in the living room by the fire and enjoy some pie."

The Mystery Deepens

The friends, new and old, gathered around the Ford's hearth. Raising their mugs of warm apple cider, they gave a special toast of thanks to Alice for the wonderful meal.

Agent Smith turned to Henry. "Good work out there today, Warden Ford. It was an honor to work beside you."

"Please, call me Henry. And you did great on your first poacher case, Agent Smith."

"Thank you, and it's Jim. I think we've been through enough together to use first names by now."

Stan, happy to see the two on friendly terms, led a "Here, Here, to both of you for a job well done." Everyone toasted in agreement.

Alice presented Joe with a small box of chocolate fudge she had made especially for him. He ate piece after scrumptious piece, listening to stories about past law enforcement adventures, until he eventually fell asleep on the couch.

"Looks like Joe has turned in for the night," said Alice.

"I'm exhausted myself, it's been a long day," said Henry.

Jim rose to leave. "Henry, Mrs. Ford, thank you so much for a wonderful evening and all the hospitality. I had better be getting back to the inn."

"My legs could use a stretch, let me walk you out," Henry said.

On the porch, Jim lit a cigarette.

"Will you be leaving town tomorrow?"

"You bet, the weather up here is too unpredictable for me," Jim said with a grin. He added, "Who knows, Henry, maybe I'll be back up this way again in the spring, after the snow melts."

Henry nodded, knowing the agent hadn't found what he was looking for, and there was a good chance he'd be back to continue the search.

"Drive careful now, you city slickers aren't used to our roads up here." Henry winked, and shook Jim's hand.

No sooner had Henry closed the front door, Bonnie blurted out, "Okay, Henry, now that he's gone, tell us what this was all really about." Henry wasn't budging to give her any more details, he knew from experience, she was prying for news to spread around town.

Thankfully, Wilson rescued Henry. "Bonnie, we need to be going too. We have to open the store at five tomorrow for the hunter's breakfast."

While they said their goodbyes, Bonnie whispered to Alice, "I'll call you in the morning so you can fill me in." Alice hugged her sister but knew she'd have to find some excuse to be away from the phone in the morning. That wouldn't be too difficult given the number of animals that would be pacing in their stalls for breakfast.

While they were washing dishes, Alice handed a glass to Henry to dry and asked, "So you went on a wild goose chase in the snow today? Did you ever make it to McGooseley Pond?"

"Jim and Stan found it. And it wasn't exactly a goose chase Alice, more a perch pursuit. We discovered that the Lobster Lake Bandits have been illegally stocking perch."

Alice, being an avid fisherwoman herself, threw down her soapy dish rag, and went on a tirade about such acts of north woods vandalism. By the time she had finished preaching to the choir, Henry decided to not even mention the Brink's robbery investigation, especially without any hard evidence at this point. The last thing he needed was for her to slip during a conversation with Bonnie, who would broadcast it to the entire county.

Later that night, Alice was lying in bed, and although she was exhausted from cooking all day, caring for the animals, and worrying about the men, she couldn't sleep. She kept hearing her sister's voice whispering in her ear, "*Alice, Alice, see if you can find out more information.*"

"Henry, you awake?"

"Mmm," Henry murmured, which could have meant yes or no. Alice took it as a "Yes."

"Do you think Agent Smith may have been looking for the old trapper cabin? That's down on McGooseley Stream, not up on McGooseley Pond."

"Hmmm, I'll think about it." He rolled over, fell right back to sleep, and never remembered the suggestion.

In the morning, Alice was back to her routine feeding and caring for the residents in the Ford zoo, and she also forgot all about it.

Henry was outside with Joe and Stan, helping them pack their truck, when District Warden Guilford H. Bingham came flying down the driveway. Warden Bingham jumped out of his state issued shiny green cruiser, and without even a "Hello," began interrogating Henry.

"Henry, what the heck do you have going on up here? I had the Chief of the Warden Service calling me this morning. He's on his way with six men – told me he was notified by Chief Bartlett about a poaching ring. His call was a complete surprise. How do you expect me to inform the chain of command if you don't keep me informed? I hear there are four dangerous criminals being housed in a motel at the State's expense. What's going on?"

While Bingham was reading Henry the north woods riot act, Stan said to Joe, "Let's get this tarp tied on and get out of here." Stan beeped the horn, waved a goodbye to Henry, and pulled out. Joe was glad to be out of ear range of the district warden, who continued to yell, not letting Henry get a word in.

"Why don't you come on in Guilford and have a piece of pie. I'll tell you all about it over a pot of coffee."

Bingham calmed down at the mention of pie, and by the time Henry finished telling his boss about the perch and stolen goods, he didn't even need to mention the Brink's robbery.

Softening after hearing the facts, Bingham complimented Henry on a great job considering the circumstances. "Henry, I want to say, you did a fine job out here yesterday, dealing with those vandals and the weather. We'll prosecute those crooks to the fullest extent of the law."

"Thanks, boss. We'd better hightail it over to the motel and transport the Bandits to more suitable accommodations. I don't want them causing any more trouble."

At the motel, Red was standing outside smoking a cigarette and coughing up a storm. He wasted no time addressing Henry.

"It's about time you showed up," Red said, and spit into the snow.

"Good morning to you too, Red," said Henry.

"When do we get our call? I need to call my brother-in-law to get his lazy butt up to camp to plow us out."

"We're going to transport you over to the Greenville Police Station, from there the State Police will move you to the county lockup. You'll get your call from there," said Warden Bingham in a serious and firm tone.

"What! I ain't got time for that."

"This isn't about your time, sir. You and your pals are going to be booked for illegal stocking."

"You mean to tell me, you're wasting the taxpayer dollars, my tax dollars, over some phony charge for releasing a few fish?"

"A few fish? A few fish!" Henry was starting to steam up.

Bingham held out his hand and stated, "And possession of stolen property. You boys have done some mean things out here to people. I intend to be sure we spend whatever it takes to have you charged appropriately. You'll have plenty of time to think it over in your cell because there won't be any hearings with a judge until Monday."

"Me too?" asked Junior quietly.

"No, son. We've arranged to have you driven back to your mom's house in Dexter. She's been notified to expect you."

"Ah, that woman don't know nothin' about teaching this boy," griped Red.

"What about getting our trucks?" asked Al.

"You'll be pleased to know that the state will transport your trucks down to Augusta, where…," started Bingham.

"Well that's mighty nice of 'em, they better not get one scratch on mine," interrupted Red.

"Where they'll be impounded until you can post bail and pay your fees," finished Bingham. Henry laughed out loud and received a glare from his boss.

"That's great. You wardens are too much," complained Red.

"Let's go - all of you, out to the cruisers. I don't have all day. You ruined my Thanksgiving yesterday, so today I'm looking forward to a heaping plate of leftovers smothered in gravy, and you're holding me up," said Henry.

"What about food for us? This here hotel manager wouldn't even give us beer this morning."

"There will be old coffee and stale donuts down at the station," Henry said. Bingham shook his head at Henry.

* * *

The Parkers arrived home late Friday afternoon. Taking a break from unloading the truck, Joe was chasing Sparky around the snow-covered yard when the dog pulled the canvas bag from Joe's backpack. Joe grabbed it to play tug of war. Then he suddenly stopped, realizing it was the bag he had tripped on near the trapper cabin.

"Hold it, boy. Drop it." Sparky obediently let go. Joe examined the bag with new eyes. It was dirty with a rawhide string looped through metal eyelets at the top. Looking at it closely, Joe noticed it was turned inside out. Pulling the bottom through the top opening he read the lettering. The first row of letters was **BR** space space **K**, followed by a faded S. The second row had a **C** space **MP** space space and what looked like a small V, that Joe thought was probably the top of a faded Y.

BR KS

C MP Y

Excited, Joe ran to his dad who was piling the gear in the garage. "Dad, what do you make of this? I think it spells, Brinks Company."

Stan felt the heavy-duty canvas. "I completely forgot all about you picking up that bag. That certainly is a possibility."

"What should we do?"

"Why don't you finish unloading the truck and I'll call Henry. This piece of evidence, and knowing where we found it, might be of great interest to Agent Smith. I'm sure Henry can get the news over to him."

"Hello?"

"Hi, Henry, it's Stan."

"Hi there. Made it home okay?

"Yep - no problems at all. Listen though, I have an interesting development here."

"What's that?"

"When Joe and I were out hunting, he found a canvas bag."

"So?"

"You see, we forgot all about that it was in his pack until we were home."

"I'm not following you, Stan."

"Well, let me finish."

"Whose stopping you?

Stan sighed.

"Go ahead, I'll shut up,"

"Thank you. The bag is an old canvas bag. I think a money bag."

"Wait a minute, are you saying?"

"Henry!"

"Sorry, go ahead."

"It's pretty worn. We found it on the ground near that old trapper cabin. It has the Brink's Company name on it." Stan paused and hearing nothing asked, "You still there, Henry?"

"Yeah, I was keeping quiet. Is that it?"

"Is that it? Don't you think this bag is something that Agent Smith might want to have?"

"You're probably right. I'm about to sit down and have a turkey leg for lunch. I'll swing by the inn in a little while."

"Don't you think you ought to go now? He might be figuring to hit the road, if he hasn't already."

"You're starting to sound like my boss, young man."

"I'm just saying, this might be a big clue."

Henry scratched his head, and realizing he never asked for the agent's phone number, said, "I guess you're right. If he's not there, his contact information should be on the guest log. I'll head out. I can eat this turkey leg on the way. You take care and I hope to see you for ice fishing season."

"You too, Henry. We'll see about the winter trip. I'll give you a call. Bye."

* * *

Eddy Walsh slept through his wind-up travel alarm. He would have slept longer, but the sun finally rose high enough to hit his eyes through the thin frilly curtains. He dressed and started to pack for the ride home. Lifting his jacket off the bed, the badge and ID case fell to the wood floor with a thud.

He bent down and held it in his hands. Anticipating it wouldn't be long before someone tracked him down, he thought about how to get rid of it. Having a stolen badge on his possession could be big trouble. The guy Eddy bought it from, down at the Boston docks, told him it was found during a robbery, years earlier. He told Eddy, "Don't go showing it around. Don't be stupid."

Eddy intended to keep it, as a collector's piece. That was until he heard the rumors circulating about the Brink's robbery at Murphy' bar, rumors that the loot was buried someplace in Maine. Then he had a reason for the badge and decided to use it; his mother needed the money. He ran his finger over the silver plating. He wanted to keep it.

A knock on the door scared the hell out of him. He fumbled with the badge and stuffed it back in his jacket.

"Mr. Smith? Mr. Smith? Is everything alright? I heard a loud noise up here."

"Just a moment, please." Eddy grabbed the pile of papers from the bed, and stuffed them in the nightstand drawer. He opened the door to see the frail innkeeper staring at him with a curious look.

"Good morning."

"Good morning, Mr. Smith. Will you be having breakfast before you check out?"

"Maybe just some coffee. I need to be heading out shortly."

"Very well," she said, peeking around him into the room, "Coffee is ready when you are."

"Thank you."

* * *

The bell hanging on the door jingled when Henry entered. His boots on the creaky wooden floor echoed into the parlor where a fire was burning. A woman's voice called out from down a dark hallway towards the rear of the inn.

"I'll be right there."

Henry peeked into the rooms off the main hall. He had never been inside the Junction Inn. It was one of the oldest in town, right next to the defunct train depot, which at the turn of the century delivered passengers from Boston, New York, and Philadelphia for their summer holiday in the country. And to Henry, it seemed the furniture hadn't been updated since then either.

The eyes on a painting over the fireplace gave Henry the creeps. He was assessing the haunting portrait of Cornelius Commodore Harriman, the original owner of the inn, when a voice came from behind him.

"Good morning, Warden Ford,"

He turned to see Florence, a friend he had known since grade school. She was as tiny now, as she was then, her hair still in the same style atop her head in a bun, except now it was gray, just like his.

"Good morning, Florence. How was your Thanksgiving?"

"It was nice, spent it at the neighbors, though. None of my family could make it up from Monson - on account of the snow."

"That sure was a surprise."

"Yes. Very unexpected. What brings you over this way, Henry?"

"I'm checking to see if Jim Smith, the priv..." Henry stopped, he wasn't sure Jim had mentioned his profession to Florence, and probably the fewer people who knew, the better.

"Jim Smith? Yes, he was here, the only guest I had all week, but he's checked out."

"Do you happen to have any contact information for him?"

"No, sorry. He showed up, paid cash in advance, and left every morning to go out hunting. At least that's what he told me. I tell you Henry, I was concerned that he was out in the storm all day yesterday. I had even called Chief Bartlett to see if anyone came across him stranded on the road. Is there a problem?"

"No, not really. I was hoping to ask him some questions, that's all."

Florence thought for a moment. "When I cleaned his room this morning, I found a stack of old newspapers in the nightstand drawer. I put them over here on the fire starter pile." Florence bent down and picked up the papers from the kindling basket. She handed them to Henry.

Henry's eyes went wide seeing the headlines on the stories. The inn's loud ringing phone echoed from the kitchen.

"Excuse me, Henry." Florence turned and headed down the hall.

Henry sat down in a narrow-upholstered chair to look through the articles. He sorted through the stack, reading the headlines, "Brink's Robbery Money Found," "Loot Located Behind Office Wall in Boston," "Rotting Bills, Worth Nothing." Henry read the one titled, "Families and Businesses Devastated by Robbery."

The Walsh Grocery stores, a long-time family run business outside of Boston has had to close. In a case of bad timing, money was being transferred for the business when it was stolen during the robbery. The over one-hundred thousand dollars was not insured for theft. Mrs. Walsh, whose husband passed away last month of a heart attack, spoke to the press. "They stole our life savings, we have nothing. Frank is gone, I've lost the business, I don't know what to do." Her son, Eddy, stood by her side, smoking a cigarette, looking helpless.

The Walsh family business is one of many in a state of disarray since the robbery. With the money and securities stolen still missing, investigators are working new leads every day. Of the stolen guns and Brink's employee badges, only two have been recovered so far.

Henry re-read the article three times. When he heard Florence hang up the phone in the kitchen, he pitched the stack of papers into the roaring fire, and shouted, "Thank you, Florence. I'll be seeing you."

"Bye, Henry."

Henry slunk into the front seat of his cruiser. He could already hear the town manager screaming about not getting reimbursed for the plowing. Feeling confused, and wondering if he was jumping to a conclusion, he headed home to call Stan back.

* * *

"Stan, look, it appears that maybe Jim Smith wasn't who he said he was."

"How's that? What do you mean?"

"He was registered as Jim Smith, but I have my doubts."

"Who was he then?"

"I'm not certain, but he may have been a guy by the name of Eddy Walsh. I'll make some calls on Monday and have the State Police run both names. Maybe we'll get lucky. Hold onto that bag."

"All right, let me know what you find out."

"Will do. Take care of yourself."

"You too, Henry."

Stan hung up the phone and scribbled the name, *Eddy Walsh* on a scrap piece of paper. He held it in his hand and stared at it. When Sparky barked to go out, Stan stuffed the paper inside the canvas Brinks bag and placed it in the cabinet over the kitchen sink.

Maine Clues

The Meadow at Lobster Lake
September 1988

"And here we are at the meadow where it all began," said Joe, as he, Sarah, Don, and Linda emerged into the clearing.

Sarah didn't remember it at all, but it was less intimidating than it was in her imagination. Standing there, close to Joe, among the trees and wildflowers, she began to get over the scare she had experienced as a young girl.

"I could see how you might have gotten turned around out here, Sarah. If you don't know the trails and where you are, it all looks the same," said Linda.

"That's exactly right. I can remember the panicked feeling I had. I don't feel that way now." Sarah gazed into Joe's eyes. She pointed up at a high, rocky point and asked, "Joe, is that where you were when you saw me?"

"Yep, that's Rum Ridge. We're headed there next."

At the top of the ridge, Joe indicated where he first spotted Sarah. "You were right over there, where I built the blind. I could see you were yelling, but I couldn't hear what you were saying and you couldn't hear me."

Sarah took Joe's hand and squeezing it lightly whispered, "Thank you, Joe, for running down to come and rescue me."

For the first time, Joe felt the magnitude of his actions from when he was a teenager. A bunch of questions ran through his head. He wondered what would have happened if he had not seen her that day, or if she had wandered off before he was able to reach her. The worst was thinking that he would have never have met her. He'd rather not think about that.

They walked to the edge where Don and Linda were taking pictures. Joe pointed, and said, "And over that way is the trail where Don and I had the showdown with the moose calf when we were kids."

"I remember that. You were scared stiff. At least that one didn't leave you with a scar." Don touched his own chin and pointed at Joe.

"You two have been friends a long time. How about you, Linda? Did you grow up with these two?"

"Me? No. I ended up here for a job assignment and you might say that Don 'flew' me off my feet."

"Ahh, that's cute," said Sarah.

Joe rolled his eyes. "Yeah, he's a regular romantic."

After taking a few pictures at the summit, R.C. led them down Bug Bog Trail. Back at the cabin, they sat on the porch drinking lemonade.

"Joe," Linda asked, "whatever happened to the canvas bag you found?"

Joe went inside and when he came back, he placed the bag on the picnic table. "And this was all I had left of that year as a reminder. That is until now." He shared a long look with Sarah.

Don picked up the bag and examined the logo.

"But, Joe, what happened?" Linda asked, interrupting the tender moment between Joe and Sarah.

"Red and his crew were fully charged for illegal stocking and burglary, the town manager was furious for not getting reimbursed for the plowing up to the Deadwater, the next spring the Warden Service issued Henry a new cruiser, and Sarah hasn't been back to Maine, until now. The End," Joe said with a wink at Sarah.

"No. You know what I mean. With the investigation and Jim Smith, or was it Eddy Walsh?"

"That's an interesting turn of events. The agent, or whoever he was, disappeared as if he never existed. Henry, as I recall from Dad's stories, was never able to get any more information about him. The bureaucracy between the Maine authorities, Boston Police, and the Feds was impossible to navigate from way up here in the late 50s. I have some newspaper clippings about the robbery though. I'll get them." He returned with a journal.

Carefully turning the pages, he said, "Dad always loved telling guests about the possible connection to the Brink's robbery. I wouldn't be surprised if he hadn't gone out treasure hunting himself. Ah, here it is." Joe passed the book to Sarah.

The page was yellow and faded. Sarah, read the headline out loud, "June 1956, *Stolen Loot Found Behind Wall*."

"Go on, Sarah, read it," asked Linda.

"The small print of the story is too faded. It's hard to make it out."

"So, they found all the stolen cash?" asked Linda.

"Not nearly. They found a picnic cooler of bills hidden behind a wall in a Boston building in 1956. The FBI concluded that prior to being hidden there, it was stored someplace damp and wet, probably buried, sometime between the robbery in 1950 and when they discovered it. A good portion of the money was decomposed and they couldn't even identify it. I recall the amount they linked definitively to the robbery was about fifty-thousand dollars, which back then was a boat load of money."

"You mean cooler load, ha ha," Don injected.

"Funny," said Joe, "But it was nowhere near the one point two million in cash that was stolen."

"It was worthless?" asked Sarah.

"Yep, even if the criminals had wanted to use it, most of it was crumbling to pieces, only six-years after the heist."

"What happened to the rest of the money?" asked Sarah, still staring at the article, trying to make out the words.

The Boston News

June 6, 1956

Stolen Loot Found Behind Wall

H. Molloy

According to a source, the FBI today discovered a portion of the money from the big heist. The wrapped bills were located behind a boarded-up wall in an office building in Boston's South End. The source of the information hasn't been able to determine the amount of the money found or the exact location of the discovery.

This could be a significant break for the investigation and for those who have been hoping to get back the money that was stolen from them. Up to this point all leads have turned up empty.

The trials for those so far charged with the crime continue. See section B2 for coverage.

"Nobody knows. It was never found." said Joe.

"Seems as if the Lobster Lake Bandits weren't the only criminals hanging around here that year," added Don. He continued, "I hate to break up the fun, but it's getting late, the wind's picking up, and we have a plane moored over on the lake we need to go catch."

"Oh, it's so nice here, I hate to leave," said Sarah. Everyone looked over and stared at her.

"What?"

"Seems you've had a change of heart about the woods," stated Joe.

"A girl can change her mind, can't she?"

Encouraged by Sarah's words, and wanting to see more of her and Joe together, Don had an idea. "Sarah, as the president of the local snowmobile club, I'd like to invite you to visit this winter, so we can give you a tour on a sled." Linda nudged him for making such a suggestion without asking Joe.

Joe looked at Sarah. When he didn't look away, Sarah answered, "I don't see why not. I like snow."

Don nudged Linda, proud he was such a matchmaker. "Come on, honey, help me get the plane ready."

"We'll catch right up, I need to lock up, and grab a couple of things," said Joe. When he was ready to go, he saw Sarah was still holding the journal.

"Anything wrong, Sarah?"

"Um, Joe. I think my dad wrote this article."

"What? Are you sure?"

"Fairly certain. This article is by H. Molloy. My dad's name is Henry and he was a journalist for The Boston News."

"Sarah, do you know what this means?"

"No, but it's a weird connection."

"Your dad was writing articles about the Brink's robbery, your family just happened to take a vacation here during the summer of 1956, and you get lost in the woods, not two miles from the trapper cabin where I found that bag. It's too much of a coincidence. Don't you think?"

"It's giving me the chills."

"Can you call your dad when we get back to town and ask him if he was here on a lead?"

"Can't"

"Why not?"

"He passed away years ago."

"Oh. I'm sorry about that. How about your mom? Would she know anything?"

"She might. But Dad was always closed lip about his work. I'm sure she read his news articles. She might have even saved some."

"Sarah, this is an amazing discovery."

"I know."

"We'd better head over to the lake to catch our flight before it leaves without us. I wouldn't say anything to Don and Linda about this, yet."

"I think you're right."

As Joe helped Sarah step up into the plane, a pair of loons bid them farewell with their cries. Don did a fly-over of the Parker camp for Joe to take some aerial photos and then banked the plane to head back to Greenville.

"This is the most beautiful place I've ever seen," Sarah said into her headset.

Everyone else agreed with a collective, "It sure is."

Don brought the plane down for a perfect landing in East Cove. After saying their goodbyes, Joe drove Sarah back to the lodge.

"Joe, why don't you come in and have dinner with me?"

"Sounds good to me. We can talk about plans for the next couple of days." He was anticipating showing her his secret spots around Moosehead Lake.

Inside they sat by the window watching the yellow moon rise behind Little Moose Mountain. As they were looking over the dinner menu, Perry approached their table. "Sarah, these faxes came for you today. I would've waited, but they seem urgent."

"Thank you, Perry."

Sarah looked over the pages. The first couple were some questions from the editing department on the article she had faxed in the night before. The last page was written in all capital letters. Joe watched as her eyes became narrow and the smile slipped from her face.

MOLLOY – WHY HAVEN'T YOU CALLED TO CHECK IN? DON'T TELL ME THEY DON'T HAVE PHONES IN MAINE! NEED YOU BACK BY WEDNESDAY. NOVEMBER ISSUE ARTICLE NEEDS TOTAL REWRITE. BARONE

"Great." Sarah sighed.

"What is it?"

"My boss. He's tracked me down. I knew this was too good to last. I have to leave tomorrow."

Joe was visibly disappointed.

"Joe, why don't you come visit me in the city?"

"Me, in New York? I don't know, Sarah. I wouldn't know how to get around."

"I'll make sure you don't get lost," Sarah said, and then added, "Who knows, you might have fun. We'll go see a Yankee game."

Joe laughed. "If we did that, just so you know, I'll be rooting for whomever they are playing against. That's a guarantee."

"Besides the game, there's so much I want to show you. Think it over, okay?"

"Sure. I will."

"Either way, we'll have to talk by phone to discuss the articles in the Moosehead series."

"I'm looking forward to that assignment for sure," Joe said.

They enjoyed dinner discussing Joe's possible visit to the big city, and Sarah returning to Lobster Lake to snowmobile in the winter.

The next morning, Perry wasn't too surprised to see the couple having breakfast together. After checking out, to delay saying goodbye, Joe and Sarah took a walk around the inn's garden.

"Joe, I'm not one for believing in fate, but I've been thinking about the synchronicity of being selected for this assignment, ending up in Greenville, and meeting you again."

He nodded. "Me too. It's been terrific getting to know the real you."

"Oh, there's lots more you still need to find out, Mr. Parker." She squeezed his hand.

Joe walked Sarah to her rental car, gave her a long hug, and then watched her drive away down Moosehead Trail. As soon as her car rounded the bend in the road, he had a sinking feeling in his stomach. It felt the same as when he watched her drive away with Henry, all those years ago.

Luckily, Joe had lots to do at the camp before the winter to keep his mind somewhat occupied. He spent the next month getting the winter preparations done, fishing with the guys, and corresponding to Sarah by mail. Sarah would send him an article to read about Moosehead, Joe would send her back an illustration to go along with the theme of her story.

Back in the city, Sarah corresponded with the owner of the "*From Here to There*" travel magazine, who loved each installment by the new duo. She loved them so much, she requested Sarah write more pieces on Maine. When Barone found out Sarah was researching lodges, he knew his budget was going to be blown. Sarah reveled in the fact that there was nothing he could do about it.

In each package for the articles, Sarah and Joe included a personal letter. Joe wrote about camp, R.C., and the happenings around Lobster Lake. Sarah filled Joe in on the crazy things she'd seen in New York City.

Joe felt like a teenager all over again. Every week, he'd call Sarah from the payphone at the diner, always at an odd hour so Buddy, Don, or Buster weren't there listening to his conversation. He loved hearing Sarah's voice, yet, something wasn't right. He couldn't help but get the feeling she didn't sound happy.

During their last conversation he asked, "Is everything all right? You sound a little down."

"I'm sorry, Joe. I don't mean to sound that way. The city this time of year always does that to me. Winter is coming . . . and the holidays."

"You're always welcome to come up to Maine you know. It's beautiful here once the snow flies."

"That sounds wonderful. I'd like to visit then."

He promised he'd get the latest illustration in the mail by the end of the week and said goodbye. In his next letter, he told her he'd be closing the camp and it would be his last mailing for the season from Greenville. He ended his letter telling her he'd call once he was back in Bangor.

Sarah's Invite

October 1988 – Bangor Maine

Joe pulled into the driveway and said to R.C., "We made good time, boy." He figured the Red Sox pre-game was probably about to start. If the A's won tonight they would go to the World Series and Boston would continue to be under the "Curse of the Bambino," for yet another year.

R.C. was glad to be home and circled the house in an all-out sprint. The same celebration he would do when getting to camp. He was just glad to be somewhere.

Joe was unpacking the truck when his neighbor walked across the front yard.

"Got your mail, Joe."

"Thanks, Charlie."

"Is the camp all squared away for the winter?"

"Sure is. I suspect you and Diane will be heading to Florida soon?"

"Another few weeks. We'll have our mail forwarded as usual, but sure would appreciate if you could keep an eye out for the other junk people leave in the box."

"Of course. Calm down, boy, calm down." R.C. was running between Charlie's legs like he found a long-lost friend.

"Ah, that's all right. I missed you too, boy." He scratched R.C. behind the ears, and said to Joe, "Diane is putting burgers on, and we're going to watch the game. Why don't you join us – there's plenty of food. And beer."

"Sounds great. Let me finish unloading and I'll be over in a few."

"I didn't mean to look, but there's a postcard you might want to glance at in that stack. Sounds as if a certain someone is missing you. I saw that piece she wrote about the Fly-In. Nice article," Charlie said, with a big grin as he turned back for home.

As soon as Joe put his bags down, he sorted through the mail. The postcard was an aerial view of New York City, looking south towards the Empire State building. The shot included Central Park framed by tall buildings. He noted that the biggest pond in the park could fit six times inside Duck Pond. He turned over the card.

Dear Joe,

It was great spending time with you in your piece of the woods. I can't wait to come back in the summer and hike Katahdin with you. My neck of the woods is shown on this postcard. As you can see, we have three ponds and no possible way to get lost. I was thinking, why don't you fly down to the city for the Thanksgiving holiday? (she added a smiley face) I can show you the sites here in my city.

Call me when you are back from camp. I
suspect by then the Red Sox will be done for
another year. (another smiley face)

Warm regards, Sarah.

Joe sat down at the kitchen table. He thought about what
such an invite might mean. Spending a holiday together?
Would he miss being in Maine for Thanksgiving? To be in New
York City, of all places. His stomach suddenly felt a bit
unsettled.

He walked over to the phone, opened his wallet, and took
out Sarah's business card. He flipped it over and stared at her
home number. He lifted the receiver and looked off into space.
He thought, "What am I going to say? Would I go? What if
Sarah had changed her mind? What would I do with R.C.?"

A rap at the kitchen window startled him. It was Charlie.
He yelled through the glass, "Burgers are ready and the game's
starting. Let's go, my boy. Call that nice girl back later."
Sporting a grin, Charlie hustled back across the lawn, thrilled
for Joe.

Joe placed the receiver back on the hook. He'd call later, or
tomorrow. Thanksgiving was more than five weeks away.

Afterword

While this book is fictional and the names of the characters are not real, most of the locations and some of the events are.

The area for the book's setting is known as the Maine Highlands – which extends from Bangor in the south to beyond Baxter State Park in the north. It includes the state's highest peak, Mt. Katahdin; longest river, the Penobscot; and the largest lake, Moosehead. It's a region almost as large as the state of Massachusetts.

The Boston Brinks robbery occurred in 1950. There have been books and movies made about that crime. I have no knowledge of any connection to Maine – this is a novel.

In 1985, two men were arrested and pled guilty to illegally stocking perch in the Moosehead Lake Region. Wildlife vandalism and poaching is real and everyone needs to remain vigilant to keep the natural beauty of the woods protected for generations to come.

Some of the ponds, lakes, and bogs in the story are real, others have been fictitiously added and will not be found on any map. No matter, Maine has over 6,000 lakes and ponds and more than 30,000 miles of rivers and streams. Get out and explore.

The Annual Seaplane Fly-In takes place in Greenville each September. I would highly recommend a trip for that yearly tradition. Go for a hike, or a ride in a seaplane while visiting.

People do get lost, hurt, and some die on the trails and waters of Maine. The State of Maine Game Wardens, State

Police, and all first responders are first rate. I am thankful for their presence and service. However, always be sure you are prepared and leave word with someone on where you plan to be.

As for Joe and Sarah, their adventures together have only just begun. Watch for future books in the Moosehead Mystery series.

The second book

in the

Moosehead Lake Mystery Series:

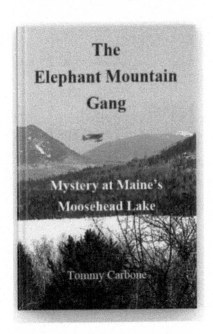

Dear Reader:

Thank you for reading. I hope you enjoyed this novel.

Please keep in touch. You can find me on my social media pages.

Lastly, I'd love to hear what you thought about, "The Lobster Lake Bandits – Mystery at Moosehead," with a review or by sending me a message.

See you on the trail,

Tommy

For books and links visit:

www.tommycarbone.com

About Tommy Carbone

Tommy Carbone lives in Maine with his wife and two daughters. He studied electrical engineering and earned a Ph.D. in engineering management.

He writes from a one room cabin, on the shores of a lake, that is frozen for almost six months out of the year, and moose outnumber people three to one.

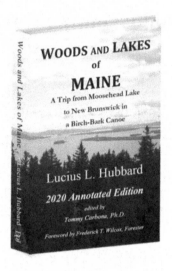

A memoir of a wilderness excursion in Maine.

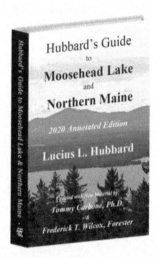

A guidebook with history of the Moosehead Lake Region.

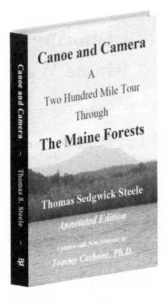

Canoe and Camera

Annotated Edition

of

Steele's first memoir
from Moosehead Lake
to Medway.

Paddle and Portage

Annotated Edition

of

Steele's second canoe
trip memoir from

Moosehead Lake to
Caribou.

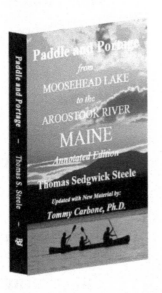

Also available in a **Two-book Hardcover Collector Edition**:

Thomas S. Steele's Maine Adventures (978-1954048089)

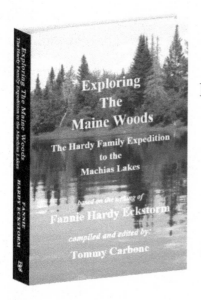

Exploring The Maine Woods

Based on the writing of **Fannie Hardy Eckstorm** this memoir is a wonderful tale of an expedition through the **Maine woods.**

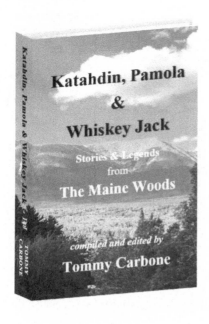

Katahdin, Pamola & Whiskey Jack

Stories & Legends from

The Maine Woods